*Theater critic Artemus Bancroft
isn't sure what to expect
when his aunt summons him home
to California with vague but urgent
pleas about being unable to cope with
"the situation."*

*The situation turns out to be
the apparent haunting of
Green Lanterns Inn—
along with alarming rumors
that long-suffering Auntie Halcyone
may have murdered
her philandering husband.*

*In fact, the rumors seem
to have been started
by the late Mr. Hyde himself—
from beyond the grave.*

SÉANCE ON A SUMMER'S NIGHT

JOSH LANYON

VELLICHOR BOOKS

An imprint of JustJoshin Publishing, Inc.

Séance on a Summer's Night

November 2018

Copyright (c) 2018 by Josh Lanyon

Cover by Kevin Smith

Edited by Keren Reed

ISBN: 978-1-945802-99-7

Published in the United States of America

JustJoshin Publishing, Inc.

3053 Rancho Vista Blvd.

Suite 116

Palmdale, CA 93551

www.joshlanyon.com

This is a work of fiction. Any resemblance to persons living, dead, or UNdead is entirely coincidental.

To my Patreon subscribers, past and present. Thank you for being part of my story.

CHAPTER ONE

Insanity runs in my family.

That should go without saying. What the hell else could explain what I was doing sitting in a cab outside the Green Lanterns Inn at that time of night.

"This is it," the driver said when I showed no sign of moving. And when I still made no sign, he said helpfully, "Green Lanterns Inn."

Summer rain beat down, fat silver drops blistering against the windshield. The wipers squeaked out each second, dashing the rain away, illuminating the ivy-covered building before us for an instant before the scene melted away again. The seven eponymous brass lanterns were dark in the yellow glare of the car's high beams. Not a light shone in the entire house.

But then at two o'clock in the morning, I'd have been surprised—even alarmed—to find a light on.

I felt ridiculous. I should have asked Aunt Halcyone for clarification. Insisted on a little more information. It wasn't like me. But I'd felt her unease, her uncertainty in that last letter, and that was what had sent me jetting across the country. I couldn't ever remember my aunt admitting she was in over her head, let alone asking for my help.

Come as soon as you can, Artie, Aunt Halcyone had written. *The situation has spiraled out of control. I need your cool head and strong shoulders.*

I guess my shoulders are strong enough and my head is relatively cool, but she'd never required them before, not even when Ogden, her second husband, had died the year before. As for the situation spiraling out of control, I'd had no idea there *was* a situation.

Anyway, at the time Ogden had died, I'd been dealing with my own situation. Aunt H. had been as unenthusiastic about Greg as I'd been about Ogden, and refraining from saying *I told you so* had been about the best we could offer each other.

"Are you sure you don't want me to stay for a while?" I'd said after the funeral.

"No, no. I'm all right. I just need a little time," she had returned.

She had seemed all right. Sad, of course; weary but not broken. It would take more than one dead, philandering husband to break my dear old Auntie H. When two months later she'd phoned to say she had decided to turn Green Lanterns into an inn, she had sounded enthusiastic and upbeat—almost like her old self.

"You sure they're open for business?" the cab driver asked.

"Uh…yes." I sounded as doubtful as he did.

"Okay. Well."

My words exactly. I opened the door. The driver jumped out and grabbed my bags from the trunk. Shoulders hunched against the rain, he followed me as I ran up the flight of shallow stone stairs to the shelter of an overhanging portico. Ivy draped over the roof, crystal drops falling from the dark, glistening leaves. The brass gargoyle door knocker eyed us balefully.

The driver dropped my bags at my feet.

"Funny they don't have a night window or something." He surveyed the darkened house dubiously.

"Yeah, it's not really that kind of a hotel." I pulled a couple of bills out of my pocket, and he whistled.

He was still whistling—a cheery, ghostly little tune—as he trotted down the steps and jumped into his cab. As the red taillights disappeared through the gates, humid darkness closed in. I pressed the doorbell, listening to it ring through the silent, sleeping house.

Once this had been my home. But that was a long time ago. I'd moved to New York over five years ago—when Aunt H. announced she was marrying Ogden Hyde. It had been a shock at the time, but really, Ogden had turned out to be the best thing that ever happened to me. Without the spur of his arrival in my aunt's life, I'd probably still be living at home, venting my frustrations in my column for the *New Fillmore*, and spending too many nights with snarky old college theater pals who were equally afraid to test their wings in the big, wide world beyond Russian Bay. As it was, I had taken the leap and moved to the Big Apple, where I'd met Greg. I was now the theater critic for *New York Magazine*. Even removing Greg from the equation, it really didn't get a lot better than that.

Or if it did, I didn't want to know.

I had been back twice. For Aunt Halcyone's wedding, and for Ogden's funeral. Aunt H. came to New York for a couple of weeks every spring, so it wasn't as though we hadn't seen each other. I called her every few weeks. Well, perhaps not as often as I imagined, given that the summons home came out of the blue.

Rain, surprisingly cold for August, was dripping on my head and trickling down the back of my neck. Somewhere out in the wet, wind-whipped darkness, a dog began to howl, and I felt like howling with him. I leaned into the doorbell.

Where the hell was—

A white crescent appeared behind the fanlight. I stopped pressing the doorbell. The door creaked open, and a pale, suspicious eye peered out at me.

"Yes?"

I recognized the voice, if not the lack of welcome. "Hello? Tarrant? It's me. Artemus. Artemus Bancroft."

"Mr. Artemus?" His colorless eyes widened. "Mrs. Bancroft say you are not coming until tomorrow."

"Well, I'm here now. I decided to catch an earlier flight."

Tarrant didn't open the door. "House has all gone to bed."

"So I see." What the…? Was I supposed to leave and come back tomorrow because I'd arrived before check-in? With twenty-five rooms, I was pretty sure they could squeeze me in somewhere. I said impatiently, "Would you mind letting me in? I'm getting soaked out here."

He widened the door but made no attempt to assist as I carried my bags over the threshold. I dropped them with a landslide of *thumps* on the gold-and-black Aubusson carpet.

We stood in the grand central hall with its sweeping white staircase and eight-arm macaroni bead crystal chandelier. A giant gilt-framed portrait of my aunt, painted right before her marriage to Edwin Bancroft, gazed bemusedly down at me from the first landing. She had been twenty-one at the time, and I had grown up thinking she was quite a mature lady in that portrait. Now that I was thirty, she looked like a kid to me.

"You should have called," Tarrant said.

I didn't think I imagined the hint of accusation in his voice. I took a good look at him. The absence of his dentures gave his face a caved-in look. He was wrapped in what looked like one of those original gray-and-white plaid Beacon bathrobes from the 1930s. It grazed his bony, bare ankles. Not that I expected him to be dressed at two in the morning, but I'd never seen him anything but immaculate in his severe black and snowy white butler's garb. It was like sneaking a peek behind the stage curtain. It sort of took away the magic.

"Aunt H. sounded like the situation might be urgent."

"Situation? Urgent?" He seemed more confused—and affronted—than ever.

"Right. Anyway, sorry to drag you up at this hour. If you want to tell me which room I'm staying in?"

"Your old room, of course. Is made ready for you." He stooped to lift one of my suitcases, and nearly dropped it. "What is it that is in there?" His pale gaze was reproachful.

"I'll carry them up."

I reached for the suitcase, and he turned away, swinging the suitcase away from me.

"I have got it!"

"Really, Tarrant. There's no reason I can't—"

I was talking to his back as he lumbered unsteadily toward the staircase. Short of tackling him and wresting the suitcase away, there wasn't much I could do. I picked up my other bags and followed him, swallowing my exasperation. He was an old man now. Nearly eighty. Time to retire, really, but it would have to be his choice. Aunt H. would never put him out to pasture against his wishes.

"How's Betty?" I asked when we had safely reached the first landing.

Tarrant's daughter was named Ulyanna. For some reason, in my younger days, I'd thought it was funny to rename her Betty. Fortunately, Betty had thought it was funny too.

Betty had replaced the late Mrs. Tarrant (née Amy Bent) as cook and housekeeper. There had been Bents at Green Lanterns nearly as long as there had been Bancrofts.

"Poorly," Tarrant said grimly. "Very poorly."

"I'm sorry to hear that."

"She is not young woman! House is too big for her," he burst out.

"Oh? Well…" I wasn't sure what to say. The outburst was as out-of-character as all the rest of this.

"We cannot get any help now. Twenty-five rooms and girl is only coming twice per week."

"What girl? What happened to Mabel and Cora?"

"Gone."

"Gone where?"

"Left. Packed their things, like rest of them. They run off like scared rabbits."

"But why?" I couldn't understand it. Aunt H. had her faults, but she paid well and treated her staff with affectionate respect. "Mabel must have been with Aunt H. ten years at least. And Cora must have been nearly that long. Didn't her mother work here before her?"

"Superstitious nonsense," muttered Tarrant. He dropped my suitcase on the pale blue and ivory runner and mopped his forehead.

I shifted the bags. "Here. Let me—"

His look of outrage stopped me mid-reach.

I pretended we had simply paused for a bit of sightseeing, gazing around the landing as though I'd never seen it before. In fact, I never *had* seen it before. Not like this. The carpet smelled musty, and a film of dust coated the railing and edges of the bannister. There was even a cobweb—granted, a tiny one—on one of the brass wall sconces. The very lamplight seemed faded and tired.

"How many guests are staying here?" I asked.

Tarrant picked up the suitcase again. "None."

"*None?* But I thought—"

"People say house is haunted." His gaze was bleak.

"Haunted," I repeated. And then, when it was clear he was not joking—not that he had ever been one for joking, "*Haunted?*"

"That is right. Yes. Haunted."

"Who's supposed to be…" I stopped. My heart sank. "Oh no. Is *Ogden* supposed to be haunting the place?"

Dour satisfaction gleamed in Tarrant's eyes. "That is one opinion. Is not only one."

"Why the hell would Ogden haunt this house? He barely lived in it. If anyone ought to haunt Green Lanterns, it's Edwin. He loved the place."

Green Lanterns had been in my family for generations. Edwin Bancroft had been a distant cousin of my aunt's, so he'd spent a lot of his youth in the house even though it had not been his official home until he and Aunt H. had tied the knot.

"Is not for me to say."

"It's bull—nonsense. The girls got tired of having to maintain such a big house or didn't like the place being turned into a hotel. That's all. They felt guilty about taking jobs that suited them better, so they cooked up some ridiculous story." Even as I said it, I felt the wrongness of it. Mabel had been blunt and forthright. I couldn't imagine her lying about her reasons for leaving. Neither woman had been the fanciful type.

Tarrant turned away. "That may be, Mr. Artemus. We hire two new maids last month. They stay for one night. Both leave next morning, with same story. Only new help we can keep is gardener. And he do not sleep in this house."

I stared at his retreating back.

"Why would Ogden haunt this house?" I demanded. "What are people saying?"

Tarrant stopped, giving me a funny sideways look. "People talk foolishness."

"I know people talk foolishness. What foolishness are they saying about my aunt?"

His struggle seemed genuine. He said at last, "Only that Mr. Hyde's accident is maybe not accident."

"*What?*"

"It is gossip. That is all. People say maybe police hurry their investigation because Chief Kingsland is such great friend of Mrs. Bancroft."

"They suspect Aunt H.?"

He shook his head quickly. "No. Not that so much. More they say there was not real investigation."

I had no response to that. We went up the next flight of stairs in silence.

The family suites were on this level. Aunt H.'s rooms at the far end. Liana, Ogden's sister, near the staircase. My old room sat between them.

Tarrant stopped in front of a heavy oak door and threw it open. "Everything is as it was," he announced as he switched on the light.

He was right about that, although hopefully the sheets had been changed. A giant bed with a brown velvet canopy and draperies fringed with gold dominated the long room. At the far end was a marble fireplace. The tables and dressers were all marble-topped. Bronze and gold Persian carpets. Brown velvet draperies looped back with gold tassels. Ridiculous accommodations for a seven-year-old boy, but this had been my father's room, and Aunt H. had decreed that I would grow into it. And I did, sort of, although my apartment in New York was furnished a lot more simply and cozily.

Everything was familiar—except the cold. The house had always felt warm, alive, welcoming.

I shivered. "It feels chilly for August."

"Furnace, it is out," Tarrant replied with gloomy satisfaction. "Man is supposed to come yesterday. He did not. Fire is laid." He nodded at the fireplace, where a couple of logs and twists of kindling had been stacked on the grate, but made no move to light it.

In fact, he stood eyeing me, purple-veined hands at his sides nervously plucking at the nap of his robe. Was he trying to decide whether to speak or not? I couldn't tell, but under his somber stare, I felt uncomfortable, unwelcome.

"Was there something else?" I asked.

An unreadable emotion flickered across his face, but his features smoothed into blankness. "Good night, Mr. Artemus." He turned away.

After he had gone, I touched a match to the kindling and watched as a tiny blue flame licked through the twigs and newspaper, catching at the larger log with a comfortable crackling sound. I put my hands out toward the heat.

It was late, that was all. Tarrant had been half-asleep and grouchy at being hauled out of bed at this ungodly hour. He was always a little on the eccentric side. They all were in this house.

I was no exception, according to Greg.

Even so, and despite my exhaustion, I was too uneasy to sleep. I rose and began to unpack, quietly sliding open drawers and cupboard doors. The closets and bureau smelled of moth-balls. I glanced at the clock on the fireplace mantel. Two-thirty. Maybe I'd slip downstairs and get a drink from the liquor cab-inet. Assuming the liquor cabinet was where I remembered it. Nothing else had really changed, at least not as far as location. In other ways…everything had changed.

There was a soft tap on the door.

I knew that diplomatic knock. Smiling, I went to answer it.

Aunt Halcyone stood in the hall. She wore a pink silk bro-cade dressing gown and a sleepy smile. "Welcome home, dear Artie!"

We hugged tightly, and I kissed my aunt's cheek, which was soft and warm—as if she was the only living thing in this house. She smelled like Chanel No°5 and apple-blossom soap—scents straight out of my childhood. When she rested her head briefly on my shoulder, I felt a sudden onrush of pro-tective tenderness that closed my throat. I hadn't realized how much I missed her—or how worried I'd been.

She held me hard for a moment, then pushed back. To my alarm, I thought I saw a glitter of tears in her eyes. I could only remember her crying once before, and that was at the funeral of my father and mother.

"Let me look at you!" Auntie H. said. "Still handsome as ever! I suppose you've been breaking hearts up and down Broadway now that Gregory is out of the picture."

I laughed. "Hardly. I'm too busy dashing the dreams and desires of starstruck kids and hacks old enough to know better. How are *you*, me old darling?"

"Wonderful, now that you're here. I've missed you so, Artie."

She was still smiling, but the smile couldn't hide the worrying change in her appearance. Aunt H. had always looked much younger than her years, and after all, fifty-five wasn't *that* old, but in the months since Ogden had passed, she seemed to have aged a decade. There were grooves in her cheeks and forehead, lines around her blue eyes, and deep creases running from her nose to mouth. That wasn't age, though; it was worry and tension. I could see the strain in her eyes. Even her slim, sturdy body had grown small and frail, as if she'd been buffeted by too many hard winds.

"What the hell has been happening?" I asked, and I couldn't hide my consternation.

"Oh!" Her gaze evaded mine. "Now that you're here, I wonder if I've…"

"If you've what?"

"Let things…get me down. So much has happened. I can't blame it all on Liana." Abruptly, she turned away, clearing a space on the bed and sitting.

"Liana. What's Liana got to do with it?"

"You know how close she and Ogden were."

Yep, and I'd always thought it was a little peculiar, but then I'd been an only child. "I realize Ogden's death must have been hard on her. It was hard on you too."

"Yes. Of course. But Liana is…older."

What the hell did that mean?

"You were his wife. How could it possibly be harder for Liana?"

She was avoiding my gaze again. "She's always been very sensitive."

I snorted.

"But she has, Artie. Anyway, she was in shock at first. We both were. But a few months after the funeral, I think it all hit her. Very hard. That's when everything began to change."

"What everything?"

"Liana locked herself in her room and refuses to see anyone except me and the Tarrants. And Roma, of course. She's become a-a literal recluse."

"*Liana?*" I wasn't sure who Roma was, but this picture of Liana as a hermit was hard to believe. Liana Hyde-Kent put the word *social* in socialite. Okay, it was to be expected she might take a break from the endless rounds of luncheons and cocktail parties and charity balls while she was in deep mourning, but Ogden had been gone for a year. Or close enough.

"She just sits up there, day after day, with the drapes drawn, dealing out tarot cards."

"Tarot cards. Seriously?"

Aunt H. nodded. "That's not the worst of it."

"What's the worst of it?"

"Roma Loveridge."

"And she is—"

"A medium."

"A…"

"Yes. A medium. A very interesting person."

"As in odd? Well, yeah. I would say so."

Aunt H. threw me a quick, chiding look. "Not because she's a medium. I know you're a skeptic, but there are more things in heaven and earth."

"That's right, Hamlet. There's fire and water."

She laughed and caught my hand, gripping it tight. "I *have* missed you so much, dear."

"I'm not surprised, with Liana locked in the attic and the very interesting Roma Lovebridge for company."

"Loveridge, dear. The thing is, Liana seems to live for those séances. For the chance to speak to Ogden once more."

I recalled Tarrant's comments about the maids claiming to have seen ghosts. No wonder, with this kind of bullshit going on. I said, "Isn't it time Liana was thinking of getting a place of her own again?"

Aunt H.'s eyes widened. "Throw her out?"

"I'm sure there's a tactful way to dislodge her."

Aunt H. looked pained. "Oh, Artie. I couldn't do that to her. Especially now."

"Especially now is when a change of venue might be good. For everyone involved."

As mentioned, I always thought Liana's attachment to Ogden was the stuff of bad seventies' horror flicks.

"But this is where she's…comfortable. This has been her home for so many years. And I know what you're going to say, but this is where she's been able to make contact."

Under my scrutiny, Aunt H. lifted her chin with self-conscious stubbornness.

"My darling Auntie," I said. "It's one thing to be open-minded about the possibility of the supernatural. It's another to bundle the Psychic Hotline with other phone and Internet services. Don't tell me you believe Liana is up there chatting with Ogden over a friendly hand of tarot cards?"

"Well, no. That is, Roma uses a Ouija board to speak to Ogden when she requires the use of a divining tool." She clutched my hand more tightly. "Artemus, please don't look at me like that. The thing is, Roma might be an oddball, but I'm absolutely convinced she is *not* faking."

A log settled, shooting a shower of sparks upward.

"No?" I said. "All right, then. What do I know? I guess I'd like to believe there was life after death."

Aunt H. said eagerly, "After all, the greatest religions in the world are founded on the idea of life after death."

"True enough." I was still neutral, still doing my best not to show my increasing dismay.

Aunt H.'s eyes searched my face as though trying to determine if I was sincere or not.

In the ensuing silence, a gust of wind outside rattled the windows. Somewhere overhead a floorboard creaked. My aunt's hand seemed to go ice-cold, and her face had suddenly gone very white.

"What's wrong?" I asked.

"*Shhh!*" Aunt Halcyone put a finger to her lips. "Don't you hear it?" she whispered.

"Hear what?" I tried not to show how freaked out I was by this, but I was pretty sure a photo would show my hair standing up in porcupine quills.

"Someone walking…"

I listened. "It's the wind. A couple of floorboards settling. That's all. That's what you used to tell me," I reminded her gently.

Her eyes flashed to my face. "We can't keep servants anymore. Only the Tarrants. The others have all left."

"Tarrant told me. Superstitious nonsense."

"I don't know, Artie. There are so many strange things happening here."

I wrapped an arm around my aunt's slender shoulders. "Of course it's nonsense. Don't tell me you're starting to get caught up in Liana's fantasies?"

"It might not be fantasy. If she and Roma have truly managed to contact Ogden—"

Once again I had to hope my expression didn't give me away.

I said firmly, "Now look, darling. You're tired. It's late. We're starting to go in circles with this. We'll talk in the morning. How about that?"

"But the thing is…" Halcyone lifted stricken eyes to mine. "Oh, Artie. If it's true—"

"It's not true. How can it be?"

"If it *is* true, Ogden says…"

I sighed. "What? What does Ogden say?"

"Ogden says he was murdered!"

CHAPTER TWO

After ushering Aunt H. back to bed, I retreated to my own room and undressed, frowning over my thoughts.

I shoved the suitcases off the bed and crawled between the sheets. The soft brushed cotton smelled freshly aired, which I was grateful for. I settled my head on the firm pillow and listened to the rain on the roof. For once I did not find the sound soothing or restful. I kept thinking over the last hour: Tarrant's mutterings about ghosts, the unkempt state of the house, Aunt H.'s uncharacteristic strain and nervousness.

The last thing I remembered was the soft, distant chime of the downstairs clock counting out the hour in four solemn knells.

I woke just after six and pulled open the drapes to look out at dazzling blue skies and a morning as fresh as the first day of summer. In the daylight, I felt convinced I'd let exhaustion from the flight and Aunt H.'s unease get to me.

I showered, finished unpacking, and looked in on Aunt H., who was snoring gently in the soft gloom. I eased the door shut and headed down to breakfast.

As I passed Liana's room, I thought I heard her voice. Making an early morning phone call? Wishing Ogden good morning?

Aunt H.'s nervous condition was understandable, really. Regardless of the state of her marriage when Ogden had died, his death had to have been a shock. She had cared enough for him to stay married, so maybe more of a shock than I'd realized. Add to that the morbid direction Liana's grieving for her brother had taken, the new business venture not turning out to be the hoped-for success, the complaints of her longtime staff, and the simple reality of living out in the middle of nowhere in this oversize and isolated white elephant of a house... Yes, maybe I should have anticipated something like this.

When I reached the first floor, the velvety layer of dust on the small tables was more noticeable in the daylight. The house felt unnaturally still. Usually there was a busy, cheerful hum of activity behind the carefully cultured peace. Today it almost felt like I was walking through an empty house.

I needed coffee. Hot, black coffee and plenty of it.

On my way to the kitchen, I paused at the double doors of the drawing room and pushed them open. For a crazy instant I thought I'd walked in on... Well, I'm not sure. Ghosts holding a séance to try to contact the living? White-shrouded forms sat around the long room. Taller draped figures stood in the corners.

I reached for the wall switch, flicked on the overhead light, and recognized the ghosts for dustcovers. The elegantly carved chairs, the velour sofas, the graceful, polished tables, the beaded lamps I remembered so well were all in winding sheets, silent as a cemetery.

It was another unpleasant shock. Like finding Tarrant and my aunt suddenly grown old. This elegant room had always been the heart of the house. Warm and bright, lively with laughter and conversation whether my aunt had company or not—and most of the time there had been company. So many parties and social gatherings. Chic, bare-armed women, their ears and fingers sparkling with jewels; smiling men—all handsome, it seemed to me then—in formal tuxedos; and the maids—their stark black uniforms offset by frilly white aprons—passing among the guests, balancing trays clinking with crystal goblets.

Now this was more like a room in a house closed up and forgotten. The silver brocade drapes were drawn against the shuttered windows. The room smelled of dust, decay. Only the gilt-framed mirrors were still uncovered—and Ogden's portrait, which hung over the Italian-marble fireplace.

I went to stand beneath the painting, gazing up at the smiling face, the soulful eyes under thick, raven brows, the chiseled jaw and perfect nose. Ogden had been the most handsome man I had ever met.

Even now, I couldn't stand him. He'd always been cordial enough, but it irked me that he had treated me like a guest—a welcome guest, but still a guest—in the house I had grown up in. But then he had treated Aunt H. much the same.

That wasn't why I had detested Ogden.

At first, I think he amused Aunt H. Ogden was younger than her, though in some ways he seemed older. That probably had to do with his more conservative and stuffy outlook. He had been courtly, even chivalrous in his treatment of her—well, on the surface. It was seeing him in private with Andi Althorpe, in that very alcove, that changed my initial attitude of resigned tolerance to active dislike.

Aunt H. was nobody's fool, and I think she figured out the truth for herself not long afterward.

"Mr. Artemus?"

I jumped at the sound of that rather shrill voice. Turning, I saw Betty—Ulyanna Tarrant—in the doorway leading to the kitchen.

"Betty!"

"Mr. Artemus," Betty repeated in a different tone. She came forward to take my hand in her work-roughened ones. I don't think I imagined the look of relief on her face. Who had she feared was in here? "I didn't realize… We don't use this room anymore."

"No, I can see that."

Betty hadn't changed much. A bit thinner and a lot grayer. Her father's daughter, she was tall and spindly in her severe black dress, the feminine version of his funeralesque attire, and with a suggestion of wicked witch in her profile. Her iron-gray hair was habitually worn scraped back from her face in a tight bun. By now it probably fell that way naturally, no hairpins needed.

She offered a shaky smile. "My, but you're looking as handsome as ever. Still not married?"

By "married," Betty meant officially yoked to a nice girl from a good, i.e. wealthy, family. I'd been out since my teens, but Betty seemed to think homosexuality was something I'd eventually grow out of.

"Can't find anyone to make an honest man of me," I said.

She gave another of those weak smiles. "Well, a man can take his time to pick and choose." She nervously tweaked the small pearl earring in her left lobe; a long-ago gift from Aunt H. and Edwin. "Coffee's ready, if you'd like a cup?"

"The magic words."

I followed her across the wide hall. I could hear the radio broadcasting the news from the kitchen. Always local news. Tarrant was not interested in national headlines and did not care for music.

"We don't use the dining room much these days either." Betty said, almost apologetically, as we passed another set of white double doors. "Mrs. Hyde-Kent has her meals in her room. Sometimes your aunt joins her, but most times she eats in her own little sitting room."

"You're kidding."

"It's a lovely, cozy room."

Yes, it was, but the idea of Aunt H. not feeling up to presiding over her dining table as she had for the last thirty years was yet another disturbing bit of news.

We entered the enormous kitchen as Tarrant was seating himself at a long, much-scrubbed wooden table. He had a steaming cup of coffee and a plate of fresh doughnuts set before him, but at the sight of me, he jumped to his feet.

"As you were," I said. It was a lame effort at a joke, but for the first time in my life I felt awkward, out of place in this kitchen.

Tarrant met my gaze bleakly before retaking his seat. *He resents me*, I thought. *He's come to resent us all. Why?*

Tarrant had come to Green Lanterns through his marriage to Amy Bent, and he'd spent his entire adult life in service. He was proud of having achieved the rank of butler—and with good reason. It was hard to imagine the kind of sea change taking place where Tarrant would feel justified in almost open insolence.

"I hope you were able to get back to sleep last night," I said.

He grunted a noncommittal reply and dunked a sugared doughnut into the coffee.

In the old days I wouldn't have thought twice about sitting down at the table with them. Now I hovered, distinctly uneasy.

The radio announcer filled the silence. "*Four hundred and three silver balloons will be released at sunset this Saturday. Mrs. Lenton says she hopes the event will revive media interest in her husband's case. In other news, zoning permits have finally been granted to Rational Christians United...*"

Betty was busy at the stove, moving pans around, scraping at cooking food with a spatula. "It won't take me but a minute to fix a fresh pot. What would you like for breakfast, Mr. Artemus? Bacon? Sausage?" She moved to the long counter, dumped out the dregs from the coffee maker, and added water.

"Just coffee, thanks."

"Oh, but you have to have a real breakfast!"

"Leave man alone, *dóčka*," Tarrant muttered.

Betty pursed her lips in disapproval and glared—at her father, not me.

"It's going to be a beautiful day," I said heartily. "Hard to believe it was raining buckets when I got off the plane."

Raining buckets? Really? I sounded like someone in a community theater production of *The Mousetrap*.

Betty shivered. "I don't like the rain in summer. I don't like the sound of it whispering outside the windows."

Her words were followed by a sharp silence broken only by Tarrant's dunking and slurping. Nice. He was never what you'd call garrulous, but he'd always been pleasant enough. Certainly courteous.

I was trying to think how to tactfully broach some of the recent events at Green Lanterns, when Tarrant abruptly wiped his chin and got to his feet. "I must fix shutter. I hear it knocking all night."

"It didn't sound like any shutter to me," Betty said.

They exchanged odd, almost angry looks, and I knew if I hadn't been standing there, they would have argued.

What the hell?

Tarrant stomped off without another word, and Betty poured the freshly brewed coffee and brought a white-and-gold cup and saucer to the table. Wedgwood Oberon. I'd grown up with that china pattern, but it was discontinued now. Like a lot of other things, it seemed.

"You really don't have to wait on me, Betty. I'm used to doing for myself, you know."

"That's all right, Mr. Artemus. I like having someone here."

I'd been planning to grab my coffee and go, but I changed my mind and sat down at the table.

"Pancakes?" Betty suggested hopefully. "Waffles?" She brightened. "French toast?"

"Really. Coffee is all I need."

She opened her mouth but was forestalled by the distant *bang-bang-bang* of a hammer. We listened for a moment.

Betty sighed. "Father's not much of a handyman."

"No, why should he be? Why in the world is Tarrant out there trying to fix the shutters? That's no job for a butler."

She seemed to avoid my gaze. "We all have to pitch in these days. It's hard to get people to come out this far from town."

"But… It's not *that* far from town."

"Far enough."

I thought this over, frowning. I couldn't see any reason for Betty to lie about finding it hard to get help. Clearly, there was some issue. Better to blame it on geography than ghosts.

I said instead, "Is that what's bothering him? Having to do these menial kinds of jobs? Odd jobs?"

Her cheeks pinked, though I was trying to sound neutral and not critical.

"Perhaps. Father is a…a disappointed man."

A disappointed man? What did *that* mean? Personally? Professionally? Politically?

She did not elucidate, so apparently it was a sensitive subject.

"I haven't seen Liana, er, Mrs. Hyde-Kent yet," I said. "What time does she get up?"

"I bring her coffee and juice at ten. She doesn't come downstairs." She stared at me.

"What, never?"

She shrugged. "Almost never."

"Well, but what about when her friends drop by?"

"None of her friends visit anymore. Nor your aunt's. No one visits. Roma Loveridge is the only one who makes the drive out here. And the chief of police. Not even he comes so often now."

"I don't understand."

She shook her head. "Things changed after the accident."

"Sure. But even so."

She gave me an uncertain look, uncomfortable to be gossiping but clearly needing to tell someone. When she spoke, her voice was so low, it was almost a whisper. "It started with Mrs. Hyde-Kent."

"Why am I not surprised?" I wasn't much fonder of Liana than I had been of Ogden, though in fairness, Liana had never, to my knowledge, betrayed Aunt H.'s trust. Maybe her slavish devotion to Ogden got on my nerves.

"She was so strange after the funeral. Like she was sleep-walking. For weeks. Months. Then suddenly she seemed to snap out of it. But it wasn't a good change. It was her idea to close up the drawing room and the dining room. Her idea to stop taking guests."

"*Her* idea? Technically she's a guest in this house herself. Why would she get a vote?"

"I heard her talking to Mrs. Bancroft. She said, 'We must get out the dustcovers. We must close up the rooms where people gathered. This is a house of mourning.' And Mrs. Bancroft, er, Mrs. Hyde that is, said, 'Liana, we can't hide from the world. Life goes on for the living.' And do you know what Mrs. Hyde-Kent said?"

"No. What did she say?" I asked grimly.

"'You and I are no longer of the living.'"

For a second I was too angry to speak. "She needs to go."

Betty shook her head. "She won't."

"No?" I smiled. Probably not very pleasantly. "We'll see."

"It wouldn't help, Mr. Artemus. This house… Green Lanterns isn't the same. I don't know… It's hard to put into words. It was such a happy place before. Warm. Safe. *Gracious.* Everything the way it should be. It's all gone now."

"It isn't the house, Betty. The house is just…wood and stone. People make a house a home."

Jesus. I'd be sewing samplers in a minute.

In any case, Betty wasn't buying it. "I thought that way once too. It's not true. You'll see, Mr. Artemus. There's something here now." She leaned toward me. "The house smells of death."

I drew back instinctively. "That's ridiculous."

A strange light seemed to glow in her pallid eyes. "It's true. I won't go upstairs anymore. The other girls left! There's something h—"

Tarrant's hammering had grown louder and more ferocious. Now it seemed to shake the wooden cabinet against the wall, and a china cup fell, smashing on the tile floor.

Betty looked at the cup and then stared at me in horror.

"Snap out of it," I said. "The vibrations knocked a cup off the shelf. You don't really think some supernatural presence is having a ghostly temper tantrum?"

Honest to God, I don't think she heard me. Utter terror filled her eyes. She turned and ran from the kitchen.

I stared at the smashed cup, then at the door Betty had vanished through.

It was a relief to step outside.

The morning was already starting to warm, but the air was still cool and smelled clean and rainwashed. The bricks of the terrace were dark and damp, the potted shrubs glittering with raindrops. A puddle near the iron table reflected a weathered-looking rainbow. Gray-olive eucalyptus rose in a windbreak to the west of the house, the grass under it littered with broken branches and leaves from the night's storm. Elsewhere the lawn looked ragged, marred by patches of brown fungus and devil grass.

I followed the curve of the terrace to the back of the house and walked down to the garden. The situation was no better here. Once carefully primed and weeded, the flower beds were a tangle of thorns. Wild mustard, chickweed, and ragwort grew rampant, all but engulfing the heirloom roses and peony bushes that once had so delighted generations of Mrs. Bancrofts. Here and there, above the sea of meadow, a spindly bush waved a tentacled branch in disinterested greeting, blown and fading blooms scattering their petals like bedraggled confetti. The garden had a dusty, moldering scent, like dead things were buried there.

In the center of the upper garden stood a small dusty fountain, the basin clotted with leaves and browned blossoms. A moss-stained and muddy marble Diana, bow drawn, was as wide-eyed and indignant as if she'd been splashed by tires while waiting on a street corner.

I started down the brick walk leading to the lower garden but found the path ended in a tangle of weeds. Looking down the hillside, I saw that the maze, an intricate pattern of hedges covering an acre of ground, was as neglected as the rose garden. Good luck finding your way out of there now. The shrubs, which had always been clipped to geometrically precise forms and whimsical topiaries of deer and lions, were now unkempt blobs. New leaves poked through iron ribs like pale, green tongues. The smooth velvet lawns that had rolled like a carpet down to the swimming pool were dotted with yellow dandelions.

What the hell was the excuse for this? Okay, Aunt H. and Liana were currently living like nuns, but what did their lack of social life have to do with the upkeep of the grounds?

I turned back toward the house, cutting through a break in the vegetation. Turning the corner, I spotted a man leaning on a hoe and staring intently at the house. He wore one of those brown felt Aussie hats, and though it was still early and cool in the shade, he was shirtless. Though his back was turned to me, I knew he was a stranger. Presumably the new gardener, who wasn't afraid of ghosts. He had an exceptionally nice back— lean and lithe. Wide shoulders and narrow hips. What was he looking at so intently?

The gardener must have heard something because he turned suddenly, studying me with a hard, blue appraisal. Or maybe I imagined the hardness, because the next instant he was smiling cheerfully.

"Hey there. Lose your way through the woods?" He was about my age, his voice friendly.

That broad, white grin was hard to resist, like stepping into sunlight after miles of deep shade. My spirits rose for the first time since my return to Green Lanterns.

"Nope. I'm Artemus Bancroft, Mrs. Hyde's nephew."

"Ah." He cocked his head, his gaze quizzical. Really, his front was just as appealing as his back. In fact, he was unexpectedly good-looking in a rugged, dirt-under-the-fingernails way. His eyes gleamed in his sunburned face. His dark stubble looked almost fashionable. "Right. Ulyanna said something about you visiting. Well, I'm Cassidy, the head—and so far only—gardener."

"Nice to meet you, Cassidy."

To be honest, he was not like any gardener I'd ever met before, a feeling reinforced as he reached automatically to shake hands but then realized his were stained with mud. Not that I'm a big believer in the Upstairs-Downstairs paradigm, but I'd never known one of the gardeners to try and shake hands before. I stared at his hand. His fingers were long and slender, his palm newly blistered.

"I was weeding the dahlias," he said.

I glanced down at his feet. He wore boots, which were firmly planted in the midst of a clump of flowers he had been weeding. "Those aren't dahlias," I said. "They're begonias. Or were."

His brows knitted. He gazed down at the flowers, hastily removed his feet from their necks, then offered that grin again. He probably got a lot of mileage from that expression. "You say potato, I say potahto."

"Oh? Because it seemed like you were saying tomato," I retorted.

He laughed. "Nobody told me you were a horticulturist."

"Nope, just a regular subscriber to *House and Garden*."

"Gotcha." He continued to smile at me. "What is it you do, then?"

Again, I couldn't ever recall a gardener—or any employee at Green Lanterns—asking me what I did for a living. It wasn't that I minded him talking to me like a peer—he *was* a peer, if we were going to get philosophical about it—but it wasn't typical behavior.

"Theater critic."

His brows rose. "You don't say."

"Sure I do." I had the funniest feeling he'd already known what I did for a living before I answered.

He continued to give me that direct blue stare. Not just direct. Admiring. It had been a while since anyone looked at me like that. And while I can't say I minded, this too was kind of odd coming from the new gardener.

"So you're out here taking your morning constitutional?" he inquired. There was a little edge of mockery in his tone.

I responded in the same tone, "Surveying my domain."

"It's Mrs. Hyde's domain, isn't it?"

"True."

"Your aunt's a late sleeper, is she?"

"Not really. She didn't use to be."

"And the other lady. Mrs. Hyde-Kent? On the eccentric side, I've heard."

Yeah, not like any gardener I'd ever met.

"Where did you hear that?" I inquired.

He shrugged. "I've heard she holds séances."

I stared back at him. Said nothing.

His eyes flickered. "Well, duty calls." He lifted his hat in a parody of servility. I wouldn't have been surprised if he'd tugged on his forelock. Assuming he had one under that wide brim.

"Uh-huh," I said.

His eyes continued to search mine, and disconcertingly, I saw a smile lurking in those blue depths. "I'll see you around."

My momentary irritation vanished. Rude, impertinent, odd, whatever, there was something inexplicably likable about Cassidy.

"Like it or not," I said.

The smile was back. "I do like it," he said.

I decided to get the last word by saying nothing.

As I went up the stairs to the front portico, I couldn't help considering Cassidy. He was attractive, no question, but there was something…off about him. Kind of like his clothes. It wasn't that they were wrong—although I'd never seen a gardener in one of those Akubras before—but they reminded me of a costume rather than work clothes. That was it. Something about Cassidy reminded me of an actor playing a part—and a slightly miscast actor at that.

Never mind not knowing the difference between a dahlia and a begonia. Shouldn't a gardener, someone who worked day in and day out in the open, be a lot more weathered-looking? He was as sunburned as any frat boy on the first day of spring break. And surely, if he used garden tools over any length of time, his hands would have become hardened, calloused, stained. They weren't. He had blisters.

The way he spoke too. Not merely the choice of words. His very voice. He sounded, well, more educated than was usual in the gardeners I'd known through the years. And a hell of a lot nosier. Not just nosy—there had been a certain assumption of authority. Like he thought he had the right to ask questions. No, not even that he *thought* he had the right, because no thought was involved; he simply took it for granted he had the right.

Interesting.

And strange.

And…I was making a mystery out of nothing. Gardeners went to college too. Gardeners had to suffer through their first job like anyone else. Finally, why *wouldn't* he be curious about Liana? Who wasn't?

I was.

CHAPTER THREE

Liana was a changed woman.

I guess that could have been a move in the right direction, but in this case—and considering the implications for Aunt Halcyone—no.

After all the discussion of Liana's reclusiveness, I was surprised when later that morning Aunt H. informed me Liana wanted me to visit her in her crib. I think it was the uncharacteristic timidity with which my aunt conveyed the royal summons that persuaded me to march upstairs forthwith. The idea that Aunt Halcyone was tiptoeing around her own home infuriated me.

I suppose Aunt H. was afraid of a confrontation because she hotfooted after me, not speaking, but hovering almost nervously as I rapped briskly on Liana's sitting-room door.

A muffled voice asked me to come in, and I opened the door.

The room was in deep gloom, the only light radiating from a couple of small accent lamps. It smelled of incense and dust. Liana stood by the bay window. She hadn't been looking out, though, because the drapes were drawn tightly shut. A small table was positioned between two velvet-upholstered wingback chairs. Cards covered the tabletop. Though I was too far away to make out their faces, I was pretty sure Liana had not been playing solitaire.

I was prepared to see a change, but Liana's haggard, disheveled appearance came as a shock. She had always been so consciously, calculatedly elegant—from the shining tips of her manicured toenails to the feathery ends of her blue-tinted hair, everything about her announced (in cultivated tones, naturally) the kind of style only money can provide. *This* woman looked like *that* woman's bag-lady sister. She wore a shapeless silk dressing gown of indeterminate color. Her sallow face was bare of any makeup, and her gray hair frizzed around her face and shoulders. There were pouches beneath her eyes and grooves of anguish carved into her crepey skin. No question she was suffering, and I was a little ashamed I'd doubted she had that much capacity for genuine feeling.

Which didn't change my belief that she was an unhealthy and worrying influence on my dear old auntie, and needed to exit stage left STAT.

"Artie, oh, Artie," Liana said in a tearful voice, stumbling forward to meet me. She threw herself into my arms and began to cry. Those harsh sobs raised the hair on the back of my neck.

"It's all right, Liana," I said. Idiotic, because of course it wasn't all right.

"My dear, dear Ogden is *gone*."

"I know. I'm sorry." It was kind of bewildering because we'd already covered this at Ogden's funeral. Maybe she didn't remember I'd been at the funeral. Maybe she didn't remember *she'd* been at the funeral. Either way, it was disturbingly déjà vu.

Aunt H. came to the rescue, stepping forward and capably, kindly transferring Liana's limpet-like clutch from me to her.

"Liana, you really must pull yourself together, my dear. After *all*." Her worried eyes met mine over Liana's bowed head.

"It's just so *unfair*…"

"I know…"

I shook my head at Aunt H., and she shook her head back at me, although we were telegraphing very different messages to each other.

"That life should be so cruel…"

Aunt H. sighed and continued to pat Liana's bony back.

I took a couple of unobtrusive steps toward the bay window, and yep. Just as I feared. The colorful, macabre faces of tarot cards were spread across the small table in a large cross.

As though aware of a sudden drop in temperature—possibly emanating from my part of the hemisphere—Liana gave a couple of final gulps and wiped her face. She pulled out of Aunt H.'s supporting hold and blinked her red, watery eyes at me. "I'm sorry, Artie. You must think me a total fool. It's just that seeing you again reminded me of all our happy times in this house."

Uh…yeah. No. Maybe happy times for Liana. Maybe even some happy times for my aunt. But from the moment Ogden had moved into Green Lanterns, my happy times had ended. Not that I blamed Liana for that. In fairness, I couldn't even really blame Ogden that things had changed. A certain amount of change was inevitable. Even necessary.

"Of course," I said. "I understand."

Her pained grimace was a shadow of her old smile. "Of course you do. Such a sensitive, thoughtful boy you were."

"I had my moments."

"You must tell me what you've been up to these past months. I want to know everything." She kept a ruthless grasp of Aunt H.'s hand, leading us toward the table and chairs by the window. "Come and sit with me."

"I'll just ring for coffee." Aunt H. gently freed herself.

I tried to communicate with my gaze that she not leave me alone with Liana.

"Yes, do that." Liana seated herself and gazed across at me with unnerving intensity. "Are you back for good, Artie?"

"Me? Oh, no. *No,*" I said quickly, unable to hide how appalled I was at the idea.

Liana's face fell. "*No?* But I thought—"

"Liana, dear," my aunt interjected quickly, "Artie's life is in New York now. You know that."

"Oh. Yes. Of course." Liana looked unconvinced. Her gaze fell automatically to the cards spread out on the table in front of her. I stared down too and spotted a skeleton knight riding a skeleton horse. At the bottom of the card was the word *Death.*

Naturally. What else?

She continued to study the cards as she said, "How do you like New York?"

"I love it."

"But you loved it here too?"

"Well, yes, but… My job is in New York."

Liana began to slide the cards out of formation and into a small pile. Still not looking at me, she said, "Jobs are a dime a dozen for a handsome, talented young man like you."

"Uh…not really."

"I'm sure you're wrong, Artie. The cards say otherwise." She looked at me then, and there was something oddly alive and alert in her previously dull eyes. "Will you let me do a reading for you?"

"That's nice of you, but I don't believe in that stuff."

She smiled. It was a stranger's smile, and it did little to transform her drawn, colorless face. "Halcyone didn't use to believe either. She does now."

I'm not sure Aunt H. heard. Her back was to us as she stood in the doorway of Liana's bedroom, her attention caught by something beyond my sightline.

Liana patted the cards into a tidy rectangular stack, scooped them up, shuffled them in a manner more reminiscent of Vegas cardsharps than practitioners of the occult, and began to lay them out across the table.

The Magician.

The High Priestess.

"Things are changing in your life," she murmured. "The cards indicate that recent choices have brought you sadness and loss on an emotional level."

"Not that I'm aware of." If I sounded curt, it was because I guessed Aunt H. had mentioned to Liana the split between me and Greg.

Liana gave no indication she heard me. Her voice took on a dreamy quality. "But all that is changing. The cards show that a person has entered your life who will have great influence over your future."

"I see." I didn't bother to hide my skepticism.

"Ah, but you don't. You *don't*. A beautiful light illuminates your future, but you remain unaware. If you could only listen to the spiritual lesson of the cards and abandon these failed plans and false values, you would find yourself completely fulfilled alongside a man in whom you can place all your love and trust."

Sure. A tall, dark, handsome stranger, no doubt.

As though hearing my unspoken thoughts, Liana raised her head and stared past me. Her gaze had a distant, fixed look. Her lips parted, but she didn't speak.

"Liana?" I said, after an eerie second or two.

Nothing.

A little peculiar. Especially given that Liana had never shown any interest in mysticism prior to Ogden's death. A less spiritual person I'd be hard-pressed to name.

Was she on something?

Should she be on something?

I glanced around the room, only then noticing that Aunt H. seemed to have disappeared inside Liana's bedroom.

I turned back to Liana, who was still staring off into space, her hands seeming to deal cards of their own volition.

I said more softly, "Liana?"

"This man that the cards are highlighting will offer advice that could be crucial for the future…"

The lights were on, but nobody was home.

I rose, stepping away from the sitting area formed by the bay window, and went toward the door leading to Liana's bedroom. I could hear rustling sounds from inside the room. Even knowing it had to be Aunt H., something about that furtive sound made me uneasy.

I glanced over my shoulder, but Liana still sat rearranging cards on the table and mumbling to herself. I don't think she was aware I was no longer sitting across from her.

I took a quick peek inside Liana's bedroom with its pale furniture and filmy peach gauzes and glossy coral satins. From where I stood, I could see right past the bed into the en suite, and to my horror, I saw Aunt H. crawling around the bathroom tiles on her hands and knees.

My heart hit the soles of my feet as I had a momentary flash of the final scene of *The Yellow Wallpaper*.

I gulped. "What the…!"

Aunt Halcyone's head whipped up. She sat back on her haunches and put her finger to her lips.

I swallowed the rest of it and threw another uneasy glance back at Liana, who was now slumped back in her chair, apparently dozing.

"What the hell are you doing?" I whispered, tiptoeing across the pale tiles and helping my aunt to her feet.

"*Shhh.* Dearest, I know how it looks, but really, I can explain."

"Okay. Great. But what were you looking for?" I stared at the pink and gray marble tiles, the sunken bathtub, the long silver-framed mirror over the gleaming counter and sink fixtures. Everything looked perfectly normal, perfectly ordinary.

With the faintest hint of exasperation, my aunt replied, "Really, dear. *Not now.* We'll talk in your room."

I had to be content with that because not a word did I get out of her until we had silently crept out of Liana's bedroom, scuttled down the hall, and were seated before the fireplace in my room.

"If you're trying to scare the hell out of me, you're doing a good job," I said.

Aunt H. made a little face. "Of course not. Don't be silly, dear."

"What were you looking for?"

"Oh. Nothing in particular. I just wanted to make sure everything was all right."

"Like what? The plumbing?"

She gave a small laugh, almost a titter. "*Artie.*" Her expression was earnest, her eyes reassuringly sane. Somehow it was all the more worrying.

I think she could see it, because she said with a hint of her old briskness, "Come, Artie. You've seen for yourself how things are."

"Have I? I can see your plans to turn Green Lanterns into an inn didn't pan out. And I can see the house is falling into ruin, yes, but I still don't understand the reason for any of it. *Why?* Okay, Liana has slipped a gear—clearly—but Liana needs to go anyway."

"Artie, don't say that!" Aunt H. looked around wildly, as though she feared Liana had a drinking glass pressed to the other side of the wall.

"Come *on*, darling. Be serious. If she's not faking, which, in fairness, I don't think she is, she needs help. Seriously."

"It isn't what you think. Liana believes she's channeling the spirits."

"That's *exactly* what I think!"

"Artie, if you could only open your mind. The line between the material and spirit worlds may be so much *finer* than any of us previously realized."

"Even if I did believe that, I don't buy Liana as some kind of spiritual tour guide. The only spirit she's channeling is Maria Callas in Pasolini's *Medea*."

My aunt opened her mouth in protest. I went on, "But okay, let's shelve the question of Liana's psychic powers for the moment. Let's get back to practicalities. You two should not be here on your own right now. What if you were to offer twice what anyone else around Russian Bay is paying? At least for a time. If you could get a few people to stay—"

Aunt H. shook her head. "I tried that. I offered to double both Cora's and Mabel's wages. They refused. They said no amount of money was worth it."

"Worth *it*? What *it*? What does that even mean?" I was practically stuttering in astonishment and anger. "They actually said that to you?"

Aunt H. nodded miserably.

"I can't believe that!"

I did believe it, though, because I'd never known Aunt H. to lie. She wasn't even prone to exaggeration.

"I couldn't either. At first. I thought…well, I'm not sure what I thought. It doesn't matter, because we're offering more per hour than anyone in the county, but we still can't get anyone to stay. Not more than a night or two."

"And what's their excuse for leaving?"

Her troubled gaze met mine.

I tried to soften my tone. "Tarrant said people were talking about ghosts and-and hauntings. Do you think that's what's happening here? Is someone, er, spooking the help?"

"No. No, of course not. Who would do such a thing?"

"Tarrant?"

Aunt H. looked shocked. "Never."

"Are you sure?"

"Of course I'm sure. Tarrant has been with me forever. Ulyanna was born in this house. He would never do anything to harm any of us."

I made an unconvinced noise. "He doesn't seem like the old Tarrant to me."

"No, he doesn't, but it's very difficult for him and Ulyanna. They have to do the work of four now, and Tarrant is not young—nor is Ulyanna in good health."

"Well, something is sure as hell going on in this house."

The frightened look was back in her eyes. "Yes."

"Well, what is it? You can't just keep dropping alarming hints. Tell me what you think is happening."

"It isn't any one thing. It's a host of things."

"Fine. Go on."

"Every night I hear footsteps. A man's footsteps walking down this hallway."

I ignored the sudden chill that slithered down my spine. "Tarrant's, probably."

"He denies it. And I believe him. There isn't any reason why he should be walking around upstairs in the middle of the night. It's true Tarrant's grown eccentric, but he hasn't lost his mind."

"If you say so."

"I do say so. Whatever is behind this, it isn't Tarrant."

"Okay, it isn't Tarrant. It also isn't a whatever. It's a *who*ever."

To my dismay, she didn't answer.

"Tell me the rest of it. There's obviously more."

Aunt H. licked her lips, her face suddenly without color. "It doesn't matter where the footsteps start. Sometimes I hear them overhead. Sometimes I hear them downstairs. Eventually they start down the hall and walk toward my room. They always stop in front of my door." She clenched her hands.

I took those cold little fists in mine. "Darling, you're losing your nerve. When you hear those footsteps, why don't you open the door to see who it is?"

"I *did*, Artie. Of course I did. The first few times. There was never anyone there. Now…"

"Now what?"

"I'm afraid whatever is on the other side is going to open the door."

I let out a long breath.

Fucking marvelous. Crackpot servants, mysterious footsteps in the night…what next?

I tried to keep my tone neutral. "You know, with Liana next door playing third crone from the right, no wonder your imagination has started to get the better of you. I'd be freaked out too."

She said nothing.

"Is it possible you could have dreamed the footsteps? Or maybe mistook some creaking floorboards for something else?"

"No. Certainly not." Aunt H. sounded like her old self when she said tartly, "I'm not a fool, Artemus. I've lived in this house my entire life. I know every creak of its old timbers."

I smiled at her. "Fair enough."

She smiled back, but the trouble had returned to her gaze. "It isn't just the footsteps. There've been other incidents."

"Like?"

"Three days ago, there was a pool of oil on the floor of Liana's bathroom. She slipped in it and nearly knocked herself out."

"Wait. What are we talking about here? Spilled bath oil? Really?"

My aunt shook her head. "No. It wasn't an accident. It wasn't bath oil. It was *motor* oil."

Once again, I had the sensation of an icy, pointy fingertip running down the length of my spine.

"Who says it was motor oil?" I demanded.

"I say it was! I know what motor oil smells like, and it was motor oil spilled on Liana's floor."

"Okay. It was motor oil. What else?"

A flush stained my aunt's cheeks. "Last week someone tampered with my sleeping pills."

I'm not sure what concerned me more: the fact that Aunt H. was taking sleeping pills, or that someone had tampered with them.

Aunt H. hurried on, avoiding my eyes. "And before you ask, yes, I'm sure. I refilled my prescription on Tuesday. On Wednesday night, the bottle was only half full."

"Maybe Liana borrowed a handful."

"No. Liana has her own sleeping medication."

Of course she did. And if I stayed at Green Lanterns any length of time, no doubt I'd be popping Ambien too. And Xanax as well.

"That's…not good."

"No, it isn't. Roma says—" My aunt broke off at my expression.

"I can hardly wait. What does Roma say?"

"It doesn't matter."

"No, really. I want to hear it."

"Roma believes that the agency behind these events is… not human."

It took me a second or two to translate. When I did, I felt my temper rise. "Not human? Meaning…Ogden is doing these things? Ogden is sprinkling motor oil across bathroom floors and snitching your sleeping pills? He doesn't have anything better to do in the Hereafter?"

My aunt turned her hands in mine, gripping my fingers tightly. "My dear, I know how this must sound to you. But Ogden's death was so sudden, so…violent, it's not unreasonable to think that his spirit might be confused, lost, even angry."

"Angry with you and Liana? Then he's even a bigger fool dead than he was alive."

I hadn't meant to say it, but once it was out, there was no taking it back. My aunt let go of my hands and folded hers in her lap. She stared down at her wedding ring.

"I'm sorry," I said.

When she finally spoke, her voice was low but steady. "I know you didn't care for Ogden, but I won't have you speaking with such disrespect, Artemus."

"I know. I apologize."

She nodded tightly. I thought there was sadness in the gaze that finally met my own.

I said, "Look, darling, let's talk this whole thing out rationally. Let's say there is such a thing as ghosts. Do you really believe that a ghost would resort to household accidents and tampering with sleeping pills in an effort to, what? Wreak his revenge? Revenge for what?"

"Roma believes that Ogden might not understand that his death was accidental."

It was a struggle, but I managed to say calmly, "I see. So Ogden suspects either you or Liana—or maybe both of you—of murdering him? Is that it?"

My aunt nodded mutely.

"But why?" I asked. "What motive would either of you have?"

Once again, my aunt was avoiding my eyes. She shrugged.

"The spouse is always a suspect, and Ogden enjoyed reading mystery novels as I recall, but what would Liana's motive be? She's clearly shattered by his death. Wouldn't a ghostly presence notice that?"

"I don't think it works like that, dear."

"Why wouldn't it? If Ogden's trying to find out who's responsible for his death, he must be observing reactions and making deductions. Are you and Liana the only people experiencing these manifestations?"

"You're not taking this seriously at all!"

"On the contrary. I'm taking it very seriously. Has anyone outside Green Lanterns experienced anything?"

"I don't believe so." Aunt H. looked mostly offended by then.

"Of course, there's another possibility. Maybe Ogden hasn't returned from the grave. Maybe Roma is wrong, and the agency behind these mysterious happenings is human."

Aunt H. shook her head. "No. No, that's even harder to believe."

"Harder to believe than Ogden returning from the Great Beyond?"

"Yes."

I gave her a chiding look. She blushed, but her gaze was defiant.

"No one has anything to gain by harming me, Artie dear. Everything I have goes to you upon my death."

The conversation had taken a grim turn, and that was largely my fault, but it was a conversation that, in my opinion, had to be had.

"What about Liana? She has money in her own right, doesn't she? I always thought she inherited a bundle after her husband died."

"She had money, yes. Her finances seem leaner these days. I'm not sure about the terms of her will. I'm not sure Liana ever made a will. I am sure that before Ogden's death, she never gave a thought to such things."

"Does she have any other family?"

"No one. They had a younger brother, but he died in his teens. It must have been a terrible tragedy. She never spoke of it, and Ogden only rarely mentioned the boy. I had the impression it was all too painful to discuss."

"What about Ogden's will? I'm assuming he left a will?"

"Yes. But the sad truth is his publishing house was in financial straits. There could be no practical reason for anyone to want Ogden out of the way."

Maybe yes, maybe no. Given Ogden's roving eye, maybe someone had a motive that was practical but not financial.

I mulled all this over. "What does Liana think?" I asked at last.

Aunt H.'s shoulders seemed to slump beneath the weight of the world. "She believes Ogden is trying to contact us. That he has vital information he wishes to convey."

We were both silent for a few moments. Then I said, "Auntie H., if things are this bad—and they seem pretty damn bleak to me—why don't you and Liana pack up and go on vacation for a few weeks. Or even a month or two? Leave Ogden to work it out for himself."

Aunt Halcyone sighed. "Don't you think I've thought of that? When all this started, I begged Liana to come away with me. She refused. Since then, I've tried everything I could think of to get her to change her mind. She simply won't listen."

"Then leave her to it," I said. "Come back to New York with me. We'll have a nice, long, lovely visit. We'll catch a few shows, go shopping, dine at some great restaurants, check out some museums."

"I'd love nothing more, but I can't leave Liana now. Not like this. You saw her, Artie. She can't be left on her own."

I got up and walked to the window. Below me, the rose garden lay bathed in sunlight, a wild tangle of thorny yellows, creams, corals, pinks. I spotted Cassidy the gardener using a pair of loppers to attack the wave of greenery spilling over a stone wall.

As though feeling my gaze, he looked up, lowering the loppers and staring at the house. I didn't suppose he could see me with the sun hitting the windows, but he gave a jaunty little wave.

"Artemus?" my aunt called tentatively.

I turned from the windows. "Listen, me old darling." I went to sit down, gazing into her strained face. "Here's what I think. You and Liana—and the Tarrants as well—have been living a morbid, unnatural existence ever since Ogden died. At first, I think it was partly due to the shock of how sudden his death was. Now I think a lot of it is Liana's mood infecting the rest of you. I'm no expert, but I think she needs professional help. For all you know, Liana spilled that oil and took your sleeping pills."

"Oh, Artie." Aunt H. sounded truly disappointed.

"Hear me out. I know she loved her brother, but that… extremity of grief? It's not normal, and you must *know* it's not normal. The two of you need to get away from this toxic environment, and if Liana won't agree to leave, you need to go without her."

Aunt H. took a deep breath and slowly let it out. It made my heart ache to see her look so tired, so defeated. "You're right, Artemus. I know you are. You always did have a level head. That's why I wanted you here with me. Maybe…maybe you can talk to Liana. She might listen to someone else." Her smile was wry. "Especially if that someone else is a man."

"Then it's settled," I said.

I believed it too. But when I went upstairs to speak to Liana after dinner that evening, she refused to even open the door.

"It's no use, Artie." Her voice sounded thin and far away through the thick wooden door. "I know what you want, but it isn't possible. Halcyone and I must stay here for whatever time we have left. That's what Ogden wishes."

"Liana, at least open the door so we can discuss it."

"There's nothing to discuss. We can't leave. Not now, not ever."

It was all I could do not to punch the smooth, solid surface between us.

"That's cra— What are you talking about, Liana?" I called. "What do you mean?"

"Can't you *feel* it?" Her voice changed into a kind of wail, as though she was crouched down like an animal on the other side of the door. "He's here. He's back. Ogden's spirit has returned to Green Lanterns. Ogden has come *home*."

CHAPTER FOUR

I can't deny that Liana's stubborn refusal to leave Green Lanterns was aggravating.

And alarming.

I didn't give up, though. I figured it would just take a little time—and a lot more pressure.

But that night, the second night in my boyhood home, my certainty received a good, hard, swift kick.

I went to bed early, not so much tired—though I was certainly short on sleep—as emotionally worn out. For a time, I stared up at the shadowy ceiling beams, thinking about Aunt H., Liana, Ogden, Tarrant, Greg, even Cassidy the head gardener. Plenty to think about and too soon to draw any conclusions—about anything but Greg, and really, I hadn't had much choice there.

It seemed like I'd hardly shut my eyes when a violent *thump* brought me upright into a sitting position. My eyes strained the darkness. I could just make out the pale, rectangular glimmer of the door.

Had I dreamed it?

I held my breath, listening, held it so long, I thought my lungs would burst. The thump was not repeated. Slowly exhaling, I reached for the bedside lamp but stopped, hand frozen in midair at a new sound.

Footsteps.

Footsteps, deliberate, distinct, passing my room.

"What the fuck," I muttered and jumped out of bed, heading for the door.

The sound was already receding as I grabbed the knob and yanked open the door.

The hallway was dark, almost pitch-black. I stared in the direction of Aunt H.'s rooms, but nothing stirred in the gloom. I glanced back toward Liana's room, but again couldn't make out anything. No band of light shone from under either door. However, as I gazed past Liana's door, I saw…something. An indistinct shape. No. A *glow* slowly moving away from me down the corridor toward the staircase. I tried to make sense of that fuzzy light. Was the form male or female?

Was it even a form?

"Stop!" I commanded.

The glow did not stop. Did not even waver. It continued slowly, steadily, moving toward the staircase.

"Hold it right there!"

Hold That Ghost.

The phosphorescence dimmed, faded to a diffused grayness, vanished.

I ran after it. When I reached the landing, I could see the light had already descended halfway down the staircase. I heard the creak of steps. Heard something else too. The very soft rustle of cloth. Clothes.

Or maybe a winding sheet?

Okay, there was a creepy thought. Where the hell had *that* come from?

On the wall opposite the top stair, I felt around, fumbling for the light switch, but couldn't find it.

"Goddamn it." I couldn't waste time. I started down the stairs, blindly feeling for the bannister, using it as my guide.

The "ghost" continued unhurriedly on its way.

As it reached the foot of the stairs, the fuzzy light turned left, and with a floating bounce crossed the hall, paused before the drawing-room doors, wavered for a moment, then went through.

Wait. What had I just seen?

I froze on the stairs, trying to remember if I'd heard the turn of a knob, the whisper of a door hinge.

I had heard nothing.

Silence thrummed in my ears.

Was that because I was too far away to hear, or because there had been nothing to hear?

I wasn't sure.

Which is to say, I was pretty sure I had been too far away to hear. But I wasn't positive.

My heart beat in a funny, jerky rhythm as I stumbled down the last few steps and, guided by the opaque patch of fanlight above the outer door, groped my way across the parquet floor. I collided with a long table, nearly upsetting a vase of pale flowers…hearing the slosh of water, the chattering of glass on wood…before I found the handles of the drawing-room doors.

I threw the doors wide and went into the drawing room. This time I found the wall switch.

The light from the chandelier dazzled my eyes. I blinked as the mysterious white-sheeted inhabitants—chairs and cabinets—seemed to stare my way in affronted silence. Heart thumping, I scanned the room, half expecting one of those misshapen shrouds to come to life and jump at me—half expecting to see my glowing quarry standing in one of the corners.

Nothing moved.

Then I heard something.

A sliver of sound, like a *click*.

I spun around.

Nothing.

I listened tensely. The *click* repeated itself. The sound seemed to come from beyond the drawing room. I strode to the door on the far side of the room, flung it open.

Squares of moonlight shone through the Palladian windows of the music room, spotlighting a baby grand piano, a large standing harp, a painted fire screen, and several deep-cushioned sofas and chairs.

The room was empty. I could see that at a glance. What caused the hair on the back of my neck to rise was the whiff of tobacco smoke that reached my nostrils. *Fresh* tobacco smoke. The distinct incense-like aroma of Balkan Sobranie pipe tobacco. Ogden's brand.

Ghosts did not smoke pipes. That was a certainty.

But I had not imagined I was chasing a ghost.

The idea that a human agency was going to these lengths to fake Ogden's ghost wandering the halls of Green Lanterns was not all that much more reassuring. In fact, it kind of scared the hell out of me.

There was one more room on this side of the house—Ogden's study.

But when I pushed open the door and switched on the light, I found that room also empty. I gazed at the impersonal mahogany desk, the leather chairs, the floor-to-ceiling shelves lined with gilt-bound classics and the colorful dust-jacketed copies of Ogden's own published authors.

I took a couple of sniffs. The scent of Balkan Sobranie was unmistakable.

I went to the bookshelves and ran my finger along the edge, streaking the thick dust. There was no hidden door behind these shelves. No convenient secret passage. No handy-dandy hidey-hole. No one could have disappeared from this room. In fact, it didn't look like anyone had been in here at all since Ogden's death.

For a couple of seconds I stood motionless, considering the last few minutes. Did Tarrant smoke a pipe? I didn't recall. If so, he could very well have inherited Ogden's unused pipe tobacco. Even if it were Tarrant I'd been trailing—and that seemed unlikely—where had he disappeared to?

But if I hadn't been following Tarrant holding a flash-light…who *had* I been following? *What* had I been following?

I had not been dreaming. That I was sure of.

No, it had to be Tarrant up to something for reasons unknown. In the morning I would question him. And he'd better have a damned good explanation for these…shenanigans.

I turned off the light, and the sudden change threw the long French windows into relief, gauze-covered oblongs of grayish light. Framed in one of those pale oblongs was the silhouette of a man. A man with a large, misshapen head.

I sucked in a sharp breath.

Hold the hell on. *Not* a misshapen head. For God's sake. I was getting to be as bad as Aunt Halcyone and Liana. The man's hands were framing his face as he tried to peer inside.

Not that that was a lot better, and I'm embarrassed to say, I was paralyzed for a couple of vital moments as I tried to process what I was seeing. This couldn't be the figure I'd been pursuing, because that made no sense. Why would it—he—run outside to look inside when it had already *been* inside? So who was this, and what was he doing lurking outside the window of Ogden's study?

The dark shadow vanished.

Stop.

Not *vanished*. Withdrew.

I stumbled forward, parted the draperies, stared out.

I saw nothing but a strip of moonlit, cobbled terrace, and the silver-edged blackness beyond.

What the hell? *Who* the hell? Who had *that* been? A bum, a vagrant, a thief? Oh, hey. How about the new head gardener?

Was that—*he*—the same figure I'd nearly broken my neck pursuing through the dark?

I glanced down, only then noticing that the French doors were locked, the heavy brass bolt drawn across the slide.

No one had exited the house from here.

I strode down the length of the room, double-checking, but all the windows were locked. Locked from the inside.

CHAPTER FIVE

When I got back to my room, my aunt was waiting, sitting tense on the edge of the bed, her colorless face muffled in the collar of a beige velvet robe. "Well?" Her voice was uncharacteristically sharp. "You heard it too, didn't you?"

"Yes."

"Did you—did you see anything?"

"Maybe."

Aunt H.'s eyes widened.

"I've got a theory about who our 'ghost' is," I said, sitting down beside her.

Her lips parted. "Who?" she asked faintly.

"I'm not one-hundred percent sure, but what do you know about the new gardener?"

"*Cassidy?*"

I nodded.

"But... *Why?*"

I shook my head. "What's his story?"

"Well... He doesn't really have one. His references were excellent." She added slowly, "As was his timing."

"Did you actually *check* his references?"

She bit her lip. "Honestly, no. We needed someone desperately, and he seemed pleasant and intelligent. And he does *have* references, after all."

I said grimly, "We hope."

"I can't imagine Cassidy playing such silly pranks."

Silly pranks? No. Cassidy didn't strike me as a guy who went in for pranks. But whoever was creeping around this house was probably not doing it for laughs. Maybe Cassidy was point man for a gang of burglars and casing the place?

Or maybe not. That would be a pretty inefficient casing process. Nor did it quite line up with Aunt H.'s account of nightly pacing up and down the halls.

Okay, I wasn't convinced the ghost was Cassidy, but the idea of Tarrant skulking in the hallways with a flashlight in the middle of the night seemed even more unlikely, given how spry that mysterious glowing figure had turned out to be.

On the other hand, Tarrant was the one person who maybe had a legit reason for wandering around in the middle of the night. Maybe he'd heard a shutter banging? Or a raccoon frolicking in the attic? And Tarrant might ignore my call to stop just out of general cussedness.

Tarrant or Cassidy. Those were our two choices. Because what other rational explanation could there be?

Or was I being sexist? What if Betty was our ghost? Nah. That felt like a stretch. Her fear that morning had struck me as genuine. No way was Betty wandering around the house at night, candelabra in hand à la Mrs. Danvers.

So, who was left? Liana?

Hm.

Liana was certainly behaving oddly these days.

What if Liana was creeping around the place in an effort to keep Aunt H. in line by bolstering this fiction of Ogden returning from the grave?

I opened my mouth, but Aunt H. was watching me with a mix of anxiety and hope that stopped the words in my throat. Really, the last thing I should do was share my suspicions of the other members of this household. Aunt H. needed comfort, reassurance. She did not need to hear my theories about sinister servants, potential prowlers—ghostly or otherwise—let alone deranged in-laws.

"First thing tomorrow I want to have a look at Cassidy's references," I said.

"All right, dear," she said doubtfully. "Process of elimination, I suppose."

"Exactly, Watson. We have to start somewhere. We might as well begin with the newest member of Green Lanterns."

She smiled faintly, nodded, but was clearly unconvinced by my fake cheerfulness.

"Meanwhile, we both need sleep." I rose. "Can I see you to your door, madam?"

She managed another of those shaky smiles and stood, smoothing down the folds of her robe. "Yes, you may, kind sir."

I saw Aunt Halcyone back to her room, made sure she locked her door behind her, and then returned to my own chambers, where I spent what remained of the night wondering how the hell someone had managed to get out through Ogden's study while leaving the door locked from the inside.

I was up at first light. The house was still quiet and cool when I arrived downstairs. I hadn't expected to find anyone up and moving around yet, but when I went into the kitchen, the radio was blasting and Tarrant was pouring himself a cup of coffee.

"*A Russian Bay girl has earned over five thousand dollars selling lemonade this summer,*" announced the newscaster at KWTF.

"Morning, Tarrant," I said with determined cordiality. I had to raise my voice to be heard over the radio.

He responded, "Ulyanna is still in her bed." There was a note of accusation in his tone.

"I'm sorry to hear that. Is she ill?"

"Her blood pressure, it is always acting up." He divulged the information with a sort of grudging satisfaction. "She is not so young either. None of us are young here." Cup in hand, he moved from the stove to the pantry. When he came out of the pantry, he was holding a small white bag. He carried his coffee cup and the bag over to the table and sat down.

The announcer on the radio blabbed cheerfully on, like a host trying to cover an awkward moment between guests at a party. "*Fourteen-year-old Naomi Warfield says she is donating the entire amount to Rational Christians United!*"

"Does she take some kind of medication?" I found a mug in the cupboard and helped myself to coffee. "Does she need a doctor?"

"No." Tarrant reached in the paper sack and extracted a crusty, sugared ring of a doughnut. "She has got her pills. For all this good that they are doing her."

I leaned against the counter, observing Tarrant, and took a swallow of coffee. I almost spit it out again. It was lukewarm and bitter. At a guess, yesterday's coffee reheated. I set the mug on the counter beside me.

"Tarrant, do you smoke a pipe?"

His gaze grew suspicious. "What is it you are asking?"

"Just that. Are you a pipe smoker?"

"Sometimes yes. Sometimes no. Why is it you wish to know this?"

"I smelled pipe tobacco last night, that's all."

I thought his confusion seemed genuine. He continued to watch me with suspicion.

I tried to think of a tactful way to phrase my questions. I couldn't come up with anything, so I settled on the direct approach. "Did you happen to be upstairs last night for any reason? Like maybe checking a loose shutter or something?"

Tarrant heard me out, then gave a weird laugh. "Now it is you who are hearing ghost."

"No. Whatever that was, it was no ghost." Maybe an argument for ghostly manifestation could be made for the scent of pipe tobacco, but the boards on the staircase had squeaked beneath someone's weight. I had heard the rustle of clothing. Those were indicators that the nocturnal wanderer had been corporeal. Not that I had really doubted it.

Not for more than a couple of crazy seconds when the figure had seemed to float through the drawing-room doors.

His brows rose in not so polite disbelief. "You are so sure?"

"Yes, I am so sure."

Tarrant broke off a wedge of doughnut, dipped it into his coffee, and held it over his cup. "Maybe it is better for all if you leave."

"I beg your pardon?"

He shrugged his bony shoulders, popped the bit of soggy doughnut into his mouth.

I felt an unfamiliar rush of temper. "Whether I stay or go is my own affair, Tarrant. I don't recall asking for your opinion. If you can shed some insight on whoever was moving around the house last night, I'll be glad to hear it. Otherwise—"

"Otherwise you wish me to be shutting up?" He glared at me with open hostility.

Pretty much. Yep. I managed not to say that, though. "Otherwise," I said in what I hoped was a cold and quelling tone, "I wish you to behave in a polite and professional manner, which is what my aunt pays you for."

Far from being quelled, he rose, knocking against the table and upsetting his coffee cup. "Yes, it is your aunt who pays me. Mrs. Bancroft, *she* is my employer. Not *you*. You have no right to come here and be ordering us around. *Do this, Tarrant! I say do that, Tarrant!* Who are you to come back here and play great lord?"

I'm pretty sure the word that best described me was *gaped*. I gaped at him.

"The great… What the hell's gotten into you?"

Tarrant gave another of those weird, unnerving laughs. "You do not like to hear truth, do you, Mr. Artemus? Always you are spoiled and pampered boy having your way. Until Mr. Hyde comes. Then it is all so different. Then you do not like it. Then you run away. Now you are thinking you can come back and have everything as it was, have your way again—"

"Are you kidding me?"

"Mr. Hyde, he will not have it!"

"You're about to talk yourself out of a job, Tarrant." I'm not sure how I managed to say it so calmly because my heart was hammering in my chest and the muscles in my neck and jaw clamped so tight, I felt like a marionette trying to chop the words out.

He shut up but continued to blaze silent rage in my direction.

"I don't understand your attitude at all. Whatever has happened to change you, you can't blame on me. I haven't said more than ten words to you since I got back. I sure as hell haven't been ordering you around."

His face was still flushed, but his expression grew sullen, secretive.

"Aunt H. has always looked on you and Betty as part of the family."

Okay, wrong thing to say. Because no, Aunt H. did not consider the Tarrants part of the family. She viewed them—valued them—as loyal retainers, but that's really a very different thing than family. I was rattled, though.

Tarrant turned several darker shades of red and burst out, "Family? Is this so? No! I say no! Servile toady, that is for what Mrs. Bancroft wishes. Bowing and scraping and smiling. That is for what she is requesting. Years and years we have been putting up with it. *Yes, ma'am. No, sir.* My Ulyanna bent over that damned stove in hot weather and cold, her ankles swelling, her hair turning gray. She has grown old in this house. Why? Why? To feed bunch of rich, greedy hogs. Family? We are *slaves*!"

I was flabbergasted, and I'm sure it showed. "I— If that's the way you feel, why don't you get— Why do you stay?"

"Where is it we would be going? I am old man. Ulyanna, she will soon be old woman. No. Here we will stay, and when it is over, we will be collecting our pension." His eyes met mine in open defiance before he turned and left the kitchen.

It was a surprise to find the sun shining and birds singing when I walked outside a few minutes later.

Frankly, I was shaken by my exchange with Tarrant. That outburst wasn't the result of a sudden flash of temper, nor indicative of any recent change of heart. He had to have been harboring his resentment for years. How long exactly? Before Ogden had come on the scene? Or after?

Did it matter?

Regardless of when or why Tarrant's attitude had changed, changed it had.

"When it is over, we will be collecting our pension."

When *what* was over? What the hell had he been referring to?

For all I knew, the reason Aunt Halcyone could no longer keep staff was Tarrant. Even if he wasn't actively faking ghostly activity, that black attitude would scare off any reasonable person.

Under normal circumstances, I'd have gone straight to my aunt and told her she needed to dispense with Tarrant's services. Or, if she wanted to be more merciful than I felt, award him a gold watch and his pension on the spot. But given the difficulty in hiring these days, she couldn't afford to lose even Tarrant, let alone Betty, who was only too likely to take her father's side in a labor dispute.

Since I was already batting a thousand with the help, I decided to have a chat with our new head gardener. I knew his apartment was over the garage. I decided to walk down there and see if he was part of the proletariat uprising as well.

As I headed across the freshly mown expanse of lawn, I had to give Cassidy credit. He might not know his flora from his fauna, but he could cut a mean swathe of grass.

The ivy-covered garage had begun life as a carriage house and was large enough to contain a small fleet of cars. At one time the upper story had provided living quarters for the chauffeur, but there had been no chauffeur at Green Lanterns since Aunt Halcyone had been old enough to drive.

As I approached the long white building, I saw that two of the overhanging black doors were wide open. The lighted interior revealed a shining row of cars and, in the far corner, a winding staircase leading up to the overhead living quarters.

There were four cars parked on the floor of the garage: a 1927 Silver Ghost Rolls Royce, Aunt H.'s 1957 baby-blue Chevrolet Bel Air, which she'd been driving as long as I could remember, the green station wagon provided for Tarrant and Ulyanna's use, and a white MG. The MG threw me. I was expecting to see Ogden's silver BMW—before remembering it had been smashed to bits with Ogden.

Did that mean our mysterious new gardener drove a vintage classic car?

I ducked into the garage and was halfway up the circular staircase when I heard a loud *clang* and then the reverberation of a heavy metal object hitting cement.

"Hey there!" I called after the echo had died down. "Cassidy?"

A second later his muffled voice answered, "Yo!"

I jogged back down the stairs and strode down the length of cars until I came to where the MG was parked. A pair of brown leather boots and blue-jean clad legs protruded from beneath the chassis of the car.

I couldn't help thinking that those boots did not look like they had spent a lot of time in mud and muck. I also couldn't help thinking Cassidy had nice, long legs.

I was still dwelling on those legs as Cassidy suddenly rolled out from beneath the MG on a creeper. My gaze traveled the lean length of him, from narrow hips to his broad shoulders, before self-consciously rising to meet his brightly curious blue eyes.

He winked.

It was such a cheeky, knowing signal, I felt my face heat. I made a disapproving sound.

Cassidy sat up, wiping at a smudge of grease on his cheek—and making it worse. "Well, well. It's the lord of the manor."

His hair was dark and springy. He was grinning, his teeth very white against the frame of that *GQ* stubble, but after the argument with Tarrant, I didn't find the "lord of the manor" crack all that funny.

"Uh, yeah," I said. "Not really."

"What can I do for you, Artemus?" He got to his feet, wiping his blackened hands along his Levi's.

He was taller than I remembered, a few inches taller than I was, and for some reason, having to look up into his eyes threw me. As did the fact that he called me by my first name.

Who *was* this guy?

I said, "You're from New York? I didn't realize."

I thought I'd imagined that hint of Staten Island in his delivery.

His eyes narrowed. He followed my automatic glance toward the front of the car and its license plate, and he gave me a wide, practiced smile. "Me? No way. This baby originally belonged to a transplanted New Yorker." He tilted his head inquiringly. "What was it you needed?"

It belatedly occurred to me that what this situation required was a little finesse. The pricy classic car and New York license plate seemed to confirm my suspicion that Cassidy was not what he seemed. Or rather, he seemed like a lousy gardener and probably was that, but he was something more too. Something he didn't want us to suspect. Something it might be better to pretend we didn't suspect.

Which wouldn't be hard since the vaguest suspicion was all I had so far.

"Uh… I wanted to know if you're happy here," I said at random.

That caught him by surprise. "If I'm *happy*?"

"Right." I scrambled for solid ground. "That is, it's been so hard to keep help over the past few months, I—my aunt—we wanted to make sure everything is going all right for you so far."

I could see him thinking that one over and deciding that *maybe* it made sense, given that we were all a bunch of kooks. He relaxed a fraction, and until that instant, I hadn't realized he was on guard.

"Sure," he said. "I don't have any complaints."

"The others didn't have complaints either. They just suddenly left."

His eyes lit with interest. "True. Come to think of it, I do have a couple of questions if you have a minute or two." He moved as though to usher me by the elbow, then remembered the grease on his hands. "Maybe we could go upstairs so I can wash up?"

I hesitated. Not that I thought Cassidy was up to anything nefarious—not in broad daylight—but I could feel my control over the conversation rapidly slipping away.

As though he recognized my hesitation, he coaxed, "What do you say? We can have a cup of coffee and a chat before I begin my duly appointed rounds."

There it was again. The feeling that he was enjoying a private joke at my expense. At the same time, I didn't sense any malice or meanness in him. He was smiling at me with that unexpected twinkle in his eyes.

It was hard not to smile back, and actually, not smiling back would defeat the purpose. I wanted him disarmed. I wanted him to open up to me. Right? I gave him an answering smile, my charming best, and watched him blink in the radiance.

"Sure," I said. "That would be great…er, I don't know your first name."

"Seamus." He continued to gaze into my eyes, then seemed to recollect himself. He turned to the staircase.

"That would be great, Seamus. Betty wasn't feeling well this morning, and Tarrant was reheating yesterday's coffee."

He glanced back at me. "Who's Betty?"

"Ulyanna. Long story."

"Oh, right."

We reached the top of the stairs, and he opened the door to a large sunlit room.

I couldn't remember the last time I'd been up in the chauffeur's quarters, but it hadn't changed much. White walls and built-in bookshelves and fireplace. A row of large windows with swoops of white dotted-swiss curtains. Comfortable battered chairs and sofa in a blue and white cabbage-rose print. There were a couple of framed so-so watercolor landscapes circa the 1950s, which, according to legend, had been painted by the next to last of the chauffeurs.

"Excuse me," Seamus said. "Have a seat while I try to get some of this grease off."

While he was busy in the bathroom, I glanced at the mostly empty bookshelves. *Cults in Our Midst: The Continuing Fight Against Their Hidden Menace*; *Cults, Conspiracies, and Secret Societies: The Straight Scoop on Freemasons, The Illuminati, Skull & Bones, Black Helicopters, The New World Order, and many, many more*; and finally, *Cults That Kill: Probing the Underworld of Occult Crime.*

If it hadn't been for a dog-eared copy of *Cooking with Booze: From Beer Batter to Vodka Jelly, 101 Recipes from the Liquor Cabinet*, I'd have been genuinely alarmed.

Okay, so maybe our gardener was escaping from a cult. Maybe he was planning to start a cult. Maybe he just liked to read himself to sleep at night with the kind of thing that gave most of us nightmares.

Something on the fireplace mantel caught my eye. A small wooden-pipe display rack. I stepped over to get a better look. Five beautifully carved pipes rested on the rack. Seamus Cassidy, the guy interested in cults and the occult, also smoked a pipe.

Interesting. What was his tobacco of choice? Balkan Sobranie?

I jumped as Seamus said from the doorway behind me, "I was thinking of growing a beard; now I'm not so sure."

I turned. Above his beard, his face was scrubbed clean. His cheeks were pink, and his dark hair was slick and shiny and wet. He certainly seemed to enjoy his cleansing ritual.

"What do you think?" He walked toward me.

I said warily, "About?"

"Beards."

For one crazy minute I thought he must know something, that he was making some oblique reference to me and Greg. I stared at him. He was rubbing his bristly jaw and smiling ruefully, and as I gazed into his eyes, I understood that no, he was not talking about Greg, nor did he want my views on facial hair—his or anyone else's.

"No opinion," I said. "I see you're a smoker?"

He had been in the process of reaching for me—body leaning in, lips parting—but that brought him up short.

He straightened imperceptibly. "Um, not really. The occasional weed to relax."

I'm embarrassed to say that because of his gardening gig, I was momentarily confused. I had an instant and befuddling image of dandelions on fire.

My puzzlement must have shown because Seamus said helpfully, "Grass."

Which didn't help either.

"*Pot*," he said in the tone of one starting to have his own suspicions.

"*Oh*. Right. Of course." I nodded to the pipe rack. "But you smoke a pipe, don't you?"

It was his turn for confusion, but then he shook his head. "That's not mine. It was here when I moved in. I kind of like it, though, so I left it."

"These aren't yours?" I wasn't a pipe smoker, but Ogden had been, and I knew quite a bit about expensive pipe tobacco and even more expensive pipes. Nobody would deliberately leave pipes like these behind. The least expensive one on there had probably cost sixty dollars.

Seamus was eyeing me oddly. "No. I don't smoke. Not cigarettes and definitely not a pipe."

CHAPTER SIX

Had he said that last too casually? I wasn't sure. In fairness, I was the one who'd brought up the subject of smoking and pipe tobacco.

I studied him doubtfully. He studied me back.

"How do you take your coffee?" he asked finally, when the conversation continued stuck in idle.

"Coffee? Oh. Black."

"Me too." He winked as though that was some kind of in-joke and motioned to the blue and white flowered sofa. "Have a seat. I'll get the coffee."

He stepped into the kitchenette, and I walked over to the row of windows. Seamus had a perfect view of the back of the main house—including Ogden's study—from his own easy chair. I considered that for a moment or two, absently listening to a yellow bird singing sweetly in the branches of the nearby apple tree.

"It's so quiet out here," I said. "Do you mind being this far from the house?"

"I like it." Seamus returned with two fat, red cappuccino cups of steaming black coffee. He handed one to me. "Anyway, it's not that far away. Did you want to sit down?"

I glanced at him and then moved over to take a seat on the sofa. I swallowed a mouthful of coffee. It was very hot and very good. I took another appreciative sip. The world began to seem less sinister.

"Sorry if I seem like I'm being forward here, Artemus"—Seamus folded into one of the club chairs opposite the sofa—"but it seems like maybe there's something you need to get off your chest."

"You could say that." And he just had. "Can I ask you something?"

His brows rose. "Sure. Anything."

Anything? Probably not. But I intended to start small and build up.

"Why exactly did you take this job?"

Seamus looked surprised. "Because I needed it."

"I see."

He smiled quizzically. "Why? Is there something wrong with the job? Something I should know about?"

"No. Well… No."

He laughed. "That's reassuring."

Smart-ass. I decided to be forthright. "I hope I'm not being forward either, but you don't really seem like any gardeners I've known."

"You don't seem like any theater critics I've known," he retorted.

"See? That comment right there." I pointed at him. "That is not the way gardeners talk. Not even gardeners from New York."

"I'm not from New York."

"Still."

Seamus shrugged. "I can't help it if your experience with gardeners has been limited up to now. Mrs. Bancroft-Hyde didn't seem to have any problem with my references."

He was still smiling, but as he delivered that line—gazing right into my eyes—I knew without a doubt that *he* knew Auntie H. had not checked his references. How? How could he possibly know that—unless his references were faked?

I smiled back at him. "As a matter of fact, she hasn't checked your references yet. I was going to do that today."

His smile grew slightly less pleasant. "Check away," he said.

"Anything you'd like to declare for customs?"

He gave a funny laugh. "Nothing to declare. You'll find my papers are in order."

"Ha." I tilted my head consideringly. "I wonder. How do you sleep at night?"

At that, he looked taken aback. "Sorry?"

"We had a prowler last night. But maybe on second thought, it wasn't a prowler after all. Tell me, Seamus, do you enjoy long walks in the moonlight?"

"A prowler," he repeated slowly.

I knew I wasn't imagining the guarded look that crossed his face.

"That's right. Last night, around midnight, maybe a little after, I was in my—the late Mr. Hyde's—study when I spotted a man peering through the windows."

"You did?" He set his cup on the coffee table between us. When he glanced up, his expression was rueful, his smile winning. "I'm embarrassed to admit it, but that was me."

"No!"

He threw me a doubtful look, but Seamus wasn't the only one with experience at playacting. I blinked at him in astonishment.

He said, "Um, yes. Sorry if I startled you. I didn't realize anyone was up at that hour."

To be honest, I'd been prepared for evasion, defensiveness, even denial. Frank admission sort of threw me. It took me a moment or two to recalculate.

Seamus said into my silence, "It never occurred to me anyone saw me." He sank back into the chair. I could practically see his nimble hands working the loom as he spun another web of lies. "By coincidence, I did have trouble sleeping last night, so I decided to go for a walk in the garden. And while I was strolling around, falling over rakes and wheelbarrows, I happened to spot a light go on downstairs."

"I see." That first light would have been the drawing-room chandelier.

He nodded absently, as though gazing inward at some memory. "A minute or two later, I spotted another light go on two rooms over."

That would have been when I turned on the lamp in Ogden's study. He had certainly memorized the layout of the house. How? No, more to the point, *why*?

Seamus was still blithely running along, telling his tall tales. "Of course, I know the Tarrants occupy the other wing of the house, and it was hard to imagine the old ladies running around in their nighties at that hour." He gave me an apologetic smile. "I'd forgotten all about you."

That was payback for dodging his kiss. I smiled blandly, as though nothing pleased me more than to be instantly forgettable.

"Naturally, the first thought that popped into my head was a burglar."

"Naturally," I said. "Because the first thing burglars do is turn the lights on."

"Since I happened to be standing right next to the terrace, I ran up and had a look in the window. I recognized you, of course, but then the light went out. I felt like an ass racing around peering through windows in the dead of night, so I took myself home to bed."

"Yeah, of course," I said. "What else could you do?"

Seamus gave me a narrow look.

I said, "You didn't go inside the house for any reason?"

"No."

"If you were chasing burglars—"

He said shortly, "I didn't go inside the house. Not for any reason. Not at any time."

"Hm."

I believed him, but I pretended not to be convinced. Seamus retorted, "Anyway, if you saw me, why didn't you wave or yell or send smoke signals or something?"

Again with the smoke.

"I was otherwise preoccupied."

"With what?"

"Chasing a ghost."

He stared at me. "A ghost? Whose ghost?"

"Now that's a very interesting question. According to local gossip, my aunt's late husband. He died about a year ago. You may have heard something about it."

"Right. A fatal car crash."

"Yes."

He was looking at me as though he couldn't quite make his mind up about something. "What happened? Last night, I mean."

"Last night? Not much." I gave him the whole story, from the thump on my door to the dead end—no pun intended—of Ogden's study. Seamus heard me out in silence, his alert gaze never leaving my face.

When I finished, he said casually, "You don't believe in ghosts, then?"

"No. Even if I did, I don't believe in pipe-smoking ghosts who apparently have enough earthly body left to make stairs squeak."

He smiled faintly. "I see your point. You never actually got a good look at him—or her?"

"No. I was never close enough to know for sure whether I was chasing a man or a woman."

"Any guesses as to who your haunt might be?"

"I assume it's supposed to be Ogden. As to who it really is floating around after-hours? No. There's a limited cast of suspects."

He grinned. "Including me."

"Including you." Even as I said it, I knew it was unlikely. I believed him when he said he hadn't gone inside the house the night before. And I believed the friendly mockery of that grin. He found the idea of himself as lead ghost highly amusing.

"What would be the point, though?"

Good question. The question I kept coming back to.

I said, "I don't know. If the ghost is Tarrant—and I have to say, that seems a bit *Scooby-Doo*-ish—I guess he could be pretending to haunt Green Lanterns in order to sabotage Aunt H.'s idea of running an inn. No more inn means he and Betty have a lot less work to do. But then again, the inn is all but officially closed now anyway. And Tarrant and Betty would have less work if we could keep more staff, so from that perspective, pretending to haunt the place is the last thing he'd want to do."

"It does seem illogical."

"Same lack of motive applies to Betty. Plus, she's genuinely afraid. Which, come to think of it, is another reason against Tarrant being behind the haunting. If there's one person in this world he cares for, it's his daughter. I can't see him deliberately frightening her."

"True. Who does that leave?"

It left Liana, who was behaving so weirdly these days, I didn't put anything past her. Even so, the idea of Liana floating around the halls of Green Lanterns seemed a stretch. But then the idea of *anyone* floating around the halls of Green Lanterns was a stretch.

I glanced at Seamus, who was regarding me with that bright, attentive gaze. He raised his brows in inquiry.

It occurred to me that I was sitting there confiding in him like we were friends—or at least on the same team. And the truth was, we were neither of those things. Which didn't change the fact that Seamus Cassidy was surprisingly easy to talk to. Surprising, because I really did not trust him. Was quite certain he was up to something. Probably not flitting around the halls of Green Lanterns pretending to be Ogden, but…something.

I gave him my best party smile and rose. "It leaves you," I said. "And I shall do the same."

CHAPTER SEVEN

I spent the better part of the morning checking Seamus Cassidy's job references despite Aunt Halcyone's nervous reminder that we couldn't afford to fire him even if he had faked his résumé.

"At least we should know what we're dealing with," I told her, and she reluctantly agreed.

But what we were dealing with remained an enigma. To me, anyway.

Apparently, Cassidy had spent three years working for the city of San Francisco in what was termed a Gardener 2 position. According to his former supervisor, his duties had been to maintain lawns and flower beds—including applying fertilizers, pesticides, and herbicides—participate in greenhouse cultivation and transplanting operations, supervise employees by assigning duties and checking work for completion, and perform other duties as assigned.

Three years of that and he couldn't tell a begonia from a dahlia? Three years of that and he didn't have a respectable callus to call his own?

But according to the Recreation and Parks Department Director of Operations James Rosario, Cassidy had performed his job with knowledge, ability, and skill.

"So you'd rehire him?" I asked.

"In a heartbeat," Rosario assured me.

I remained skeptical.

Before working for the city, Cassidy had been employed by a Mrs. David Honeycutt of Honeycutt House in Pacific Heights. Mrs. Honeycutt remembered Cassidy very well. She said he had spent one year as an Under Gardener (Did they still make those?) and, after the retirement of her Master Gardener, had taken on that position. Mrs. Honeycutt praised Cassidy's knowledge, ability, and skill.

Was there an echo in here?

"The job sounds perfect for him. Why did he leave?" I asked.

"Seamus wanted to work for the city," Mrs. Honeycutt replied promptly. "Higher wages and better benefits than we could offer. Unfortunately."

"Would you rehire him?" I asked.

Mrs. Honeycutt gave a little trill of laughter at the very question. *Of course they would! In a heartbeat!*

"Then it's good news," Aunt Halcyone said when I reported back to her.

I didn't know if it was good news or not. I didn't like the fact that Mrs. Honeycutt and James Rosario seemed to be reading from the same script. But seeing the relief on my aunt's face, I kept the thought to myself.

"It could be worse," I admitted.

Auntie H. laughed and patted my hand.

My next move was to phone a locksmith. By the end of the day, we had brand-new locks on all the windows and doors of the ground floor.

My aunt was unconvinced this was a move in the right direction.

"I'm afraid Tarrant is going to be offended you didn't even consult him, dear. He's so…sensitive these days."

I said blandly, "I hated to bother him with this kind of thing when he's already had to take on so much extra work. Anyway, I'm sure he'll be in favor of anything that helps Betty feel safer at night."

Aunt Halcyone grimaced. "I don't believe Ulyanna is any more afraid of burglars than I am."

"Well, *I'll* feel safer," I told her, and she shook her head.

I did feel better after the locks were changed. For a little while, anyway.

Until the séance.

The day after I had the locks changed, Aunt H. informed me Roma Loveridge would be conducting a séance that very evening in the dining room.

"I guess it's Taco Bell for me tonight," I said. I was kidding—about eating at Taco Bell, anyway—but gave it up at her look of real dismay. "Now don't look like that. If you want me there, I'll be there. I just thought nonbelievers messed with the celestial vibrations."

"You could *try* to keep an open mind," Aunt H. said.

"I could. That's true."

"It means so much to Liana— Dear, don't roll your eyes like that. You're not eleven years old, after all."

I grinned and kissed her cheek. "For you and only you, I'll try to keep an open mind."

I was lying about keeping an open mind, though. Not that I didn't believe there might be more to the afterlife than earth and worms. I freely admit there's plenty of things beyond my simple comprehension, from man buns to the Standard Model. I'm undecided on the power of prayer, but one thing I'm pretty sure of is that paying a professional medium to act as go-between for you and your dearly departed is the equivalent of throwing money in a wishing well.

Regardless of my private feelings, no way was that séance taking place without me being there to observe the famed Ms. Loveridge in action.

Aunt Halcyone had confided to me that Roma Loveridge preferred to have at least nine people present at her soirees because, according to the Bible, nine represented finality and the last judgment—or something like that. It was all moot because Liana didn't want any "outsiders," i.e., former friends who might question what the hell the two of them were thinking, so they'd dispensed with the idea of nine attendees and relied on using the Tarrants to help fill out the sitting.

I could finally see where Tarrant might have a legitimate complaint about work conditions.

"Since we're still a few bodies short of a full séance, why don't we invite Cassidy to sit in?" I suggested. I'm not exactly sure why the idea occurred to me, beyond the uneasy feeling that if something went wrong, I'd be pretty much on my own. I might not trust Cassidy, but I did think he'd be a good man in an emergency. Unless the emergency had to do with knowing toadstools from mushrooms or something like that.

My aunt's eyes lit up. "Oh! Do you think he might be willing?" The next instant, the light died out of her face. "No, never mind. Liana wouldn't want a stranger to attend."

"I have no idea if he'd be willing or not, but it wouldn't hurt to ask. As for what Liana wants or doesn't want, this is *your* home. *You* get to decide who attends the parties here."

"Of course, dear. It's just that when Liana works herself into a state, it's…rather exhausting."

I was ashamed of my impatience. It was easy for me to say Liana could like it or lump it. Auntie H. was the one who had to deal with the woman.

"If you want Cassidy, I'll ask him," I told her. "If you don't want to risk Liana coming unglued, we'll forget about it."

"Maybe next time, dear," she said apologetically, as though she imagined not having Cassidy there was going to be particularly disappointing for me.

I shrugged. "Sure. It was just an idea."

* * * * *

Roma Loveridge arrived promptly at eight o'clock.

We were waiting for her in the drawing room. The dustcovers had been whisked away for this special occasion, but somehow the room still felt like something left wrapped for years in mothballs. Tarrant and Betty hovered uncomfortably near the windows. He looked much put-upon (and I couldn't blame him). Betty's eyes were popping in anticipation. Liana, wrapped in a flowing black kaftan, sat before the Italian-marble fireplace, her face shuttered as she gazed at the cold, empty grate. Ogden seemed to stare down benignly on her from his portrait above the mantel.

Weirdly, it was left to my aunt to escort the evening's guest of honor to the drawing room. Aunt H. was saying in a bright, slightly breathless voice, "Of course, you know everyone with the exception of my nephew. Artemus, dear, this is Roma Loveridge."

I said, "How do you do?"

I'm not exactly sure what I was expecting. Someone straight out of central casting? A modern variation on the theme of Maria Ouspenskaya? A new incarnation of Miss Cleo? In fact, Roma was an attractive fortysomething. Tanned, trim, and blonde. She wore a classic black sheath—and she wore it well. Despite the black mantilla shawl draped over her slim shoulders, she looked like a successful lawyer or the CEO of a lucrative female-centric startup. She did not look like someone trading in the occult. I wasn't sure if that was a relief or not.

We shook hands, and her grip was warm and firm. She smiled straight into my eyes. "How very kind of you to make time to join us, Artemus."

"I wouldn't miss it," I said, which was quite true.

A little smile trembled on her lips, as though she understood me perfectly.

"Oh, Roma!" Liana interrupted, rising and twisting her hands. "Do you think tonight will be the night?" Her voice wavered.

"It's not up to me, Liana."

"The night for what?" I looked uneasily from Roma to Liana.

"Perhaps we should get started," Roma said, not bothering to reply to my question.

"Everything is prepared in the dining room," my aunt said, and Roma smiled graciously.

"Thank you, Halcyone."

Without further ado we adjourned to the dining room, which was certainly an elegant setting but kind of an odd choice. Weren't these affairs typically conducted in small rooms with black curtains and spirit cabinets?

Here too the dustcloths had been removed, though the room still felt stuffy and closed off. That was partly due to the windows being shut and the heavy brocade draperies drawn, despite the warmth of the night. All the leaves had been removed from the long, gleaming tortoiseshell table, presumably so that the six of us could gather round, and it looked weirdly diminutive in the large room. Two tall silver candelabra sat on either end of the sideboard. A crystal water carafe and several goblets sat in the center. As refreshments went, I'd have preferred something a little stronger.

On the bright side, holding the séance at Green Lanterns ensured there could be no piped-in creepy music and no rigging of special effects like ghostly lights or floating tambourines and trumpets—assuming that was the kind of thing Roma went in for. (My idea of séances was very much influenced by old movies.)

We took our places around the table. I sat on Roma's left, and Liana took the seat on her right. My aunt sat next to me. Betty sat next to Liana. Tarrant took the foot of the table.

Roma turned to me. "This is your first séance, Artemus?"

"Not counting taking the occasional Ouija board for a spin in college."

Roma permitted herself another of those tiny smiles. "And you consider yourself a skeptic."

It was not a question, but I answered anyway. "I think most people would consider me a skeptic."

She nodded as if in approval. "Diderot said: 'Skepticism is the first step on the road to philosophy.'" Her pale gaze wandered to the foot of the table. "Mr. Tarrant originally believed himself to be a skeptic as well. Isn't that so?"

Tarrant glowered at me—why me?—and said nothing.

"Perhaps you believe that endeavors such as ours are something good Christians should avoid?"

I said sardonically, "Like no tattoos and not eating shellfish? I'm not unduly worried about what participating in tonight's festivities will do to my immortal soul."

"Artie," my aunt murmured in soft protest.

"The séance is a facet of spiritualism, and spiritualism emerged out of Protestant Christianity; however, many Christians are uncomfortable with spiritualism these days. I can assure you that I do not consider myself a practitioner of the occult. My gifts, such as they are, do not arise from the demonic. I am a priestess, if you will, of the light."

"Okay," I said tersely. I didn't trust myself to say more.

She studied me. "While it can be challenging to work with hostile sitters, it can be done. I only ask that you empty your mind and keep your thoughts as neutral as possible."

"Roger wilco."

She scanned our small square, her gaze resting on Liana. "Be calm, Liana. Have faith."

Liana fluttered her hands and said, "I'm trying."

Roma smiled at her. She unhurriedly removed the mantilla from her shoulders, shook out the folds and gracefully draped the lacy veil over her head. As an on-the-fly costume change, it was peculiarly effective.

When she spoke to Aunt H., Roma's voice sounded subtly different, distant. "Will you lock the door, please?"

I held out my hand, and Aunt Halcyone handed me her key. I rose, locked the door, and gave back the key, which Aunt H. slipped into the pocket of her pantsuit. She gave me a tentative smile. I smiled back.

"Tarrant, will you please turn down the lights?"

Tarrant rose and went to the wall switch. The room was plunged into darkness. A few faint sparks seemed to crackle in the globes of the crystal chandelier overhead. Betty emitted a squeak. The darkness wasn't complete, though. Silver moonlight sliced through the narrow gap where the draperies did not quite join.

Tarrant muttered beneath his breath as he shuffled his way back to the table. Static electricity caused little blue sparks beneath his feet.

Aunt Halcyone's cold fingers crept into mine. I squeezed them reassuringly.

"Are we ready to begin?" Roma asked. There was a murmur of assent. "Let us join hands."

Her hand, a pale blur in the gloom, reached out to me. I took it. Her grip was steady as a rock. Across the table Liana did the same, taking Roma's hand and then reaching impatiently for Betty. Betty joined hands reluctantly. Her eyes looked white-rimmed and enormous in the gloom.

Roma said quietly, "Close your eyes and empty your mind of all negative thoughts. Be at peace. We are safe here."

I stared at her. She met my gaze and then closed her eyes. I glanced around. The others all appeared to have obediently shut their eyes as well.

I looked back at Roma. Beneath the lacey shadow, her face was thrown into strange, exaggerated relief by the band of moonlight, enlarging her elegant nose, deepening her eye sockets, shadowing her cheeks so that she looked disturbingly crone-like. A sense of foreboding crawled down my back.

I waited for her to open her eyes and take a peek around. She did not. Her eyes stayed firmly shut. Her chest rose and fell in deep, even breaths.

Everyone else followed her lead. The silence was total; no one stirred beyond those deliberate inhalations and exhalations. I grimaced and went back to watching Roma.

Aunt H.'s fingers quivered in mine. Liana let out a shaky breath.

Roma uttered a hoarse, strangled moan. I jumped—and so did she. Her body seemed to jerk upward. Her face contorted, her head fell back, and she began to mumble.

I couldn't quite understand the words. It took me a second or two to identify them as non-English.

Oh, right. Because Roma's spirit guide was a disgraced ancient Egyptian vizier named Rekhmire. Although, if that was 18th Dynasty Egyptian, I was Mortimer Brewster.

With a shuddering sigh, Roma's body relaxed. Her head, eyes still firmly closed, rose to face the rest of us. She said in normal tones, "Are you there, Lord Rekhmire?"

In the pause that followed, Roma tilted her head and listened attentively.

"Do you have a message for any of those present?"

Another inquiring tilt of the head. Roma said dreamily, "Is there one here whose name begins with the letter *A*?"

My aunt's hand jumped convulsively in mine. I gave her a squeeze.

"I'm here," I said. I was slightly amused, slightly disgusted.

"There is someone with Lord Rekhmire. A young man. Hardly more than a boy. His hair is red. No, chestnut. He wears glasses. He says you must not blame yourself. There was nothing you could have done."

I was no longer amused, and disgusted didn't begin to cover it.

"I see, Spirit," I said coldly. "And you are—*were*…?"

Aunt H. gulped. Roma communed with the spirits. She said in a talking-in-your-sleep kind of tone, "He says you know who he is. He says he's Tony."

Aunt Halcyone gasped, tightening her grip on my hand. I was too angry to speak.

"Tony!" Aunt Halcyone whispered.

By then my eyes had adjusted to the dark. I saw Liana open her eyes. She looked from me to Aunt H. "Tony? Was that the boy who…"

She didn't finish it. No one answered her. There was a prolonged silence. Then Roma moaned. "He's gone."

Someone echoed that moan. Betty?

My heart was beating so loudly in my ears, I wasn't sure if anyone spoke or not. I couldn't remember the last time I'd been that furious.

I had to give Roma credit for doing her homework. Tony had killed himself over a decade ago. I didn't even think Ogden, let alone Liana, had known about it. It had all happened before their time. But it was a small town and people gossiped.

Roma's head dropped forward as though she was dozing. I thought about rising and turning on the lights. But no. I wanted to find out exactly how far the fake medium was willing to take this.

After a minute or two, Roma lifted her head and stared blindly before her. She said in a faint, husky voice, "Another spirit has joined Lord Rekhmire."

Liana whimpered. Aunt H. sucked in a breath.

Roma intoned, "This presence is very strong. Male. He has spoken to us before."

"Ogden!" That cry was from Liana.

"Yes," Roma whispered. "*Yes*…Ogden."

"Ogden," Liana said. "Oh, Ogden, I'm so glad you've come! I *knew* you would. I *knew* tonight would be the night."

Listening to her babble, I felt a weird mix of pity and revulsion. She really did believe this nonsense. Really believed in Roma Loveridge's psychic abilities, believed Lord Rekhmire had found gainful employment in the afterlife as a spirit guide, believed Ogden Hyde had returned from the dead to chat with—

My thoughts broke off as a deep, masculine voice somewhere to my right suddenly spoke.

"Liana…my dearest sister…"

A cold wave washed over me. I *knew* that voice. That was not Roma speaking. That was not mimicry or ventriloquism. No. I didn't want to believe it, told myself it couldn't be true, but I recognized the familiar silky baritone, the precise enunciation that was characteristically his.

I knew Ogden Hyde's voice when I heard it, and *that* was Ogden Hyde speaking.

CHAPTER EIGHT

I surfaced from my shocked thoughts to hear Ogden still speaking in that faraway voice. "Is Halcyone there? Are you there, my dearest?"

Aunt H. spoke so faintly, I'm not sure her words were audible to anyone but me. "I'm here."

"I miss you, my dearest. I'm so lonely here without you."

Liana chimed in. "I miss you too, Ogden. So much." Her voice was filled with yearning. Embarrassing and unnerving.

"Dearest Liana. My two best girls…"

Whoa. Rein it in, Artemus. That *had* to be a recording. Right? Yes. Absolutely. That was the only reasonable explanation. So far "Ogden" hadn't said anything that couldn't have been preprogrammed.

But when would such a recording have taken place? *Why* would it have taken place?

Someone said, "What do you want?" in a hard, flat voice. I realized it was me.

It wasn't that I expected an answer. I was just thinking out loud, but after a pause, Ogden's disembodied voice spoke again.

"Who is there? Who is speaking? Is that you, Artemus?"

Jeez, couldn't *he* see through the blackout either? I mean, *come on.* This was farcical. It was ludicrous. And offensive—although apparently, I was the only one who thought so.

Yet even as my rational mind rebelled against what we were witnessing, I knew part of my anger and outrage stemmed from fear. Because his response to me had not been—could not have been—prerecorded. And the voice *was* Ogden's. I had a good ear, and as faint and faraway as that disembodied voice sounded, I still recognized it, like it or not. And I did *not* like it.

I could barely bring myself to respond but managed a terse, "Yep. It's me."

"Artie." Aunt H. gulped. I could see the gleam of alarm in her eyes.

"What's he doing?" Liana gasped from across the table. "What is he saying? Artemus, what are you doing? You mustn't speak like that to…him."

Everyone's eyes were open now, and they were all looking my way with various degrees of dismay. All but Roma, still shrouded in her black lace, head bowed forward as though she had dozed off.

Ogden chuckled, and I felt my hair stand on end.

"Same old cynical Artie. You spoiled him, my dearest Halcyone."

Aunt H. murmured protest, but Liana burst out, "Oh, Ogden, why? Why did it have to be *you*? Why did you go out that terrible, terrible day?"

Ogden soothed, "Dearest Liana. How could you guess? It wasn't *your* fault. I know that now…"

If my hair wasn't already standing on end, it would have prickled like porcupine quills at that. I didn't think I misheard that faint inflection on "it wasn't *your* fault." Meaning it—he—thought the accident was someone else's fault?

I studied the outline of Roma's limp figure. Her head lifted a fraction from its forward position, but there was no movement of her throat, and her lips were still. Anyway, even if she was the greatest mimic ever, the voice wasn't coming from Roma. In fact, it didn't seem to be coming from any fixed direction. It seemed to float as if Ogden's spirit was slowly circling the table.

Pretty creepy, in all honesty. My eyes ached with the effort of probing the gloom. My heart skipped. Was there a darker shape standing behind Liana's chair?

My thoughts were disrupted by Aunt H.'s sudden, faltering, "It was an accident." She repeated more steadily, "An accident."

I said, "Of course it was an accident."

"Halcyone, dearest…don't. Our time together is too short…"

What the hell did that mean? Was this supposed spirit about to accuse Aunt H. of knocking off Ogden?

I wasn't the only one thinking it either. There was a shocked quality to the profound silence that followed the drone of Ogden's words. The room seemed to grow even darker, as though a black veil had settled over all of us.

I shivered at the chilly gust of exhalation against the back of my neck—it felt like someone standing behind me had moved away. But no one had been behind me.

"Ogden!" Liana's cry pierced the hushed silence. "Ogden! Are you here? Please, don't go! Don't leave me!"

"I will return…" Ogden's voice sounded very faint.

Liana moaned, a sound that was echoed by Roma. I glanced at Roma but was distracted by Betty's gasp. The sound was one of pure terror. I looked around in time to see a cloud of milky-white substance drifting behind Tarrant.

Tarrant stayed rigid and still in his chair, as though afraid to look over his shoulder. "What is it?" he whispered.

No one answered. We all stared as the nebulous form continued to swirl behind him, growing larger and denser. It took on a phosphorescent glow like the figure I had chased downstairs two nights earlier.

"What is that?" Betty gulped.

Liana breathed, "Oscar?"

Oscar?

That was almost funny. Were there supposed to be two ghosts in the house now?

My aunt said nothing. Her breathing sounded faint and shallow.

The roiling white mist gradually resolved itself into the indeterminate outline of a man. The arms, the shoulders, fuzzy as if seen under clouded glass, emerged…and at last, the head began to form.

Ogden Hyde.

Shock—which was three parts unadulterated irrationality and one part primordial fear—held me frozen. I did not believe in ghosts, and in particular, I did not believe in Ogden Hyde's ghost, but there was no pretending that for a few vital seconds I was no longer Artemus Bancroft, sometimes cynical and occasionally witty theater critic and man about town, but a blue-painted primitive crouched in my cave, trembling at an approaching horror. The dark on the other side. Death.

The manifestation spoke, but the voice was no longer Ogden's. It was hoarse and weirdly vicious, a stranger's voice. "I will never rest until you have paid for what you did."

"Ogden…" my aunt breathed.

I pulled free of her and Roma both, shoving my chair back and starting around the table toward the ghostly figure.

The misty outline was already beginning to fade.

Liana wailed, "Ogden, don't leave me!"

Before I could reach it, the mist seemed to evaporate and vanish. I stumbled to a stop, then jumped at a strangled shriek—followed by the *thud* of a falling body.

My instant and instinctive fear was for Aunt H. "Get the lights," I ordered Tarrant.

He must have already been in motion because he half rose, backing his chair into me. The wooden leg planted heavily, painfully on my foot.

I yelped, swore, pushed the chair and Tarrant away, and dived back around the table where everyone still sat babbling and turning this way and that.

Tarrant was also swearing. In Russian.

"Whatever's happening? Whatever's going on?" Betty cried.

Liana was still wailing for Ogden or Oscar or whoever—whatever—the hell that had been.

With relief, I heard Aunt H. call above the din, "It's Roma, Artie. I think she's fainted."

"Are *you* all right?"

"Of course, dear," she replied staunchly, betrayed by only the smallest wobble in her voice.

Tarrant finally bumbled his way to the light switch. The chandelier blazed on, and the gabble of voices cut off as though a switch had been flipped on them as well.

Liana breathed, "Oh no. No. *Roma...*"

Roma lay in a crumpled heap on the floor. Her eyelids were twitching, her face had an alarming greenish cast.

Aunt H. knelt beside her. "Water. Artie, quick. Get some water." She began to chafe Roma's long, pale hands.

Liana came to stand over Aunt H. and the fallen medium. "Is she..." She looked at me, and her gaze sharpened with accusation. "You did this. *You* broke the circle, Artie! You must have known it's very dangerous!"

"None of that now, Liana," Aunt H. said impatiently. "Roma? Roma, can you hear me?"

I turned to the sideboard, but Betty was there before me. With a shaking hand, she poured water from the carafe and passed me the brimming goblet, which I brought to my aunt. She was still kneeling beside Roma, rubbing her hands and speaking quietly to her.

Roma's eyelids were half-open, the whites staring blindly up—pretty unnerving, frankly.

"Does she have a pulse?" I asked.

My aunt's head jerked up, her eyes wide. "Of course she does!"

I could feel the others staring at me. I wasn't sure why I'd said it. Why the idea had popped into my head that Roma must be dead.

Aunt H. raised Roma's lolling head and put the glass to her bloodless lips.

After what seemed like forever, the color came back to Roma's face. She stirred, choked down a sip of water. Her eyes fluttered open.

For a moment she stared up at us. No one said anything. Roma's gaze traveled from face to face. She licked her lips, said faintly, "We made contact, then?"

"Yes." Liana's expression was…well, worrying. Her eyes were too bright, her face too red. She looked exultant. "You did it, Roma. You brought him back to us."

"Did I?" Roma murmured. I thought there was a hint of speculation in her eyes.

Liana clasped her hands together. "Yes! Ogden was here. Not just his voice. *Ogden.* Ogden was *here*!"

CHAPTER NINE

"Liana's gone to bed," Aunt H. said when she joined me in the music room. "I tried to persuade Roma to stay the night, but she insisted she wanted to go home."

I nodded absently. "I bet."

It was about an hour after the séance had ended. I had retreated to the music room once it was clear Roma was not in any immediate danger. I needed to think, and I couldn't do that while Liana was gleefully reliving the evening's haunted highlights for the rest of the stricken attendees.

Aunt H. was clasping and unclasping her hands, an uncharacteristic and, I knew, unconscious sign of nervous tension. "The poor thing was so exhausted. I offered to have Tarrant drive her, but she declined."

I said, "Speaking of exhaustion, you look beat, darling. You should call it a day."

No lie. Aunt H. looked white-faced and haggard. There were dark shadows beneath her eyes and lines around her mouth. So much for my reassuring presence. She looked even worse than the night I'd first arrived.

"I will. I wanted to talk to you, Artie." She took the matching rose-and-silver wingback chair across from my own, sinking onto it wearily. Her expression was a mix of anxiety and reproach. "You shouldn't have done it, dear. It's not like you to be so…so foolhardy. Suppose you had managed to grab hold of-of that *thing*. It might have… Who knows what might have happened!"

"Aunt H., you *can't* really believe—"

She didn't let me get any further. "I blame myself. I shouldn't have sent for you. I wouldn't have if I'd thought you'd take such an intolerant…sneering view of the situation."

After a moment, I said, "Well, that hurts. And I don't think it's fair."

It did hurt. And it did feel unfair.

"What you did tonight… There could have been *terrible* consequences."

"All right, I admit that in the heat of the moment I forgot the rule about not breaking the circle. Which, considering how many times I've seen *The Legend of Hell House*—"

"You're still joking about it!" Aunt H. cried. "It isn't funny!"

"I'm joking because the fact that you seem to believe this…*nonsense* is scaring the hell out of me." I reached for her hands. They were ice-cold and rested unmoving in my own. "Aunt H. Think about this rationally. Do you honest-to-God believe Ogden showed up in the dining room this evening?"

She didn't answer. She just sat there staring at me with that troubled gaze.

"Roma Loveridge faked the whole thing. I don't know how she did it—yet—but I know she did."

"How can you *say* that?" Aunt H. protested. "It was Ogden's voice. You know it was. We both know that was Ogden. And it couldn't have been a recording. He answered you. He responded to you. No one could have anticipated you would be there tonight, let alone what you would say."

It was reassuring to know she had thought it through, even if she had come to a different conclusion than me.

I was trying to think of how to respond without further putting her back up, and into my hesitation, she said, "Artie, have you considered that perhaps your resistance is…perhaps you're afraid to believe?"

I sighed. "No. It isn't that. I'm willing to consider the possibility that ghosts exist. I'm even willing to consider the possibility that ghosts return to haunt the living. But what happened tonight? I don't buy it. Starting with the guest appearance of Tony Clarke."

Her expression altered. "Yes. That was…odd."

And by odd, she clearly didn't mean supernatural, spooky odd. She meant she'd also sensed something off.

"Did you ever mention to Liana what happened with Tony?" I asked.

"No." Aunt H. was definite. "But I did tell Ogden about it. I thought one reason you settled for Greg was you were afraid to get involved with someone vulnerable again, as someone who truly loved you, truly cared about you would be vulnerable."

I was too startled to know what to say, and eventually came up with a lame, "Greg loved me."

"Maybe. In his own way. Not enough to actually divorce his wife."

No. Not enough to divorce her. And what a good thing, since it had simplified matters when he'd decided to return to her. Well, a bird in hand is no doubt worth more than waiting maybe decades for your boyfriend to inherit.

I said shortly, "I don't want to have this conversation. The point is, Roma somehow found out about Tony and used that knowledge tonight to try and buoy the idea that Lord Reckmore or whatever his name is—was—and his cast of thousands was legit."

"Lord Rekhmire."

"Like I said, I'm not buying it."

Aunt H. shook her head as though I'd disappointed her once again. "You'll never convince me that Roma was faking. She truly believes in what she's doing."

"Maybe. Her faint seemed genuine. I guess a trance state is a form of self-hypnotism."

"Even if Roma did incorporate a bit of local gossip into the session, it's not a reflection of her powers," my aunt said. "I think it's perfectly natural a medium might repeat information they've picked up. It's probably unconscious." She gave another of those little head shakes. "Artemus, I don't see how you can dispute Roma's extraordinary gift after everything that happened this evening."

"I can dispute it because I don't believe in what happened this evening. Speaking as a theater critic, I give tonight's performance a C+."

She sighed, pulled her hands free, and rubbed her temples.

I watched her for a moment. "Have you heard Ogden's voice before during one of these séances?"

Aunt H. opened her eyes. "Yes, once before. In one of the first sessions."

"Wait. *Yes?* You didn't think to mention that before?"

Twin spots of pink appeared in her colorless face. "It never happened again—and we never actually saw him until tonight."

She leaned forward, clasping her hands tightly. "Do you realize what a miraculous thing that was?"

"You know, I hate to be a spoilsport, but that filmy figure could have been anyone."

"You know that's not true."

"The voice, yes, I admit the voice sounded like Ogden. That figure was too…too nebulous to be able to identify with any certainty."

"Artemus, you're approaching this like a film critic objecting to the quality of a particular print. The point is not the aesthetic merits of the manifestation. The *point* is that tonight we witnessed a true manifestation."

"Maybe we did. But isn't the quality of the print—if you want to put it like that—part of how we can determine whether what we saw was real or—"

She didn't let me finish. "Wait. I want you to really consider for a moment, Artie. With Roma's help, Ogden not only materialized, it was managed without any apparatus. No spirit cabinet. No spirit slates. Roma didn't use so much as her Ouija board!"

I made a face. "Does *anyone* use that stuff nowadays? Wouldn't the special effects be done with lasers and wireless? The kind of thing you're talking about was used to simulate a lot of hocus-pocus at the turn of the last century."

"No. That's not correct. Roma inherited her gift through her mother, who inherited her ability through *her* mother. In fact, the Loveridge women have worked as mediums since the heyday of the spiritualism movement. Very often Roma does use her great-grandmother's old spirit cabinet to make contact. But early on she said Ogden's presence was so strong, so vital, we might not need the cabinet."

None of that reassured me. And the gleam in my aunt's eyes reminded me all too much of Liana's feverish glare.

"That first contact with Ogden—where you heard his voice—did that happen here or at Roma's…place of business?"

My aunt wrinkled her nose in distaste at the idea of a "place of business." She said, "Roma doesn't have a shop in a strip mall like some sleazy fortune-teller, if that's what you imagine. She invites people to her home."

"Okay. She works from home. That first séance where Ogden—"

Aunt H. cut in, "Yes, the first time we heard Ogden speak, it was at Roma's home."

"I see."

"Roma did use the cabinet on that occasion. The way I understand it, the cabinet affords the medium a dark, enclosed space in which to build up her power so that the ectoplasm—that's that white, milky mist we saw tonight—can form. Even though Ogden did not appear that time, Roma said his spirit was so powerful—and it's obvious her own gift is so strong—that moving forward we could dispense with the cabinet. Even so, it's taken this long for Ogden to materialize."

"Auntie H., do you honestly believe that…cloud…was Ogden?"

"Yes," she answered without hesitation, her blue eyes meeting mine steadily. "I do. Do you honestly believe it wasn't?"

I turned my head away and did not answer.

Until this evening, Aunt Halcyone had appeared to at least consider the possibility that some human agency was behind the "haunting" of Green Lanterns. Now she seemed to have bought in completely to the idea that Ogden had returned from the Great Beyond.

"Do you or don't you?" Aunt H. repeated.

"I…" I let out a long breath. "I don't deny I attended the séance with a certain amount of bias, and I'm still skeptical. But there was something…eerie in that room tonight."

"Eerie! I think tonight's manifestation qualifies as something more than *eerie*!"

"Okay, spooky. I'll give you spooky. It wasn't just the dark or the silence or the weird atmosphere, although all those things were part of it, of course. There was something…not right."

Aunt H. opened her mouth, and I said, "Yeah, I don't mean that, though. I mean I could feel a tension, an undercurrent in that room."

Menace.

I had felt a strong sense of menace. From whom or toward whom, I was unsure, but I was *not* unsure in my belief that something malignant was at work. Call it instinct, call it intuition, but I was sure something—no, *someone*—intended ill.

"I will never rest until you have paid for what you did."

Until that moment, Ogden's comments had been fairly innocuous. But that final declaration—and the venom in the spirit's tone—had been very different. That had been a threat. Plain and simple. It could have been directed at Liana, but I didn't think so. I didn't think I'd imagined the hints the ghost had dropped about Ogden's accident. Motor oil on the floor of Liana's bathroom or not, the ghost had pretty much cleared her of suspicion tonight.

"It wasn't your *fault."*

The "ghost" had been standing behind Tarrant at the time, so maybe the comment had been directed at Tarrant, but I didn't think so. And I didn't think anyone else at that table thought so. Was Aunt H. really oblivious to what had been suggested during the séance? Or did she not want to acknowledge the implied accusation?

Or—

No. I refused to consider that possibility. Refused to consider the idea that the "ghost's" veiled accusation hadn't registered with Aunt H. because…it was true.

I said, "Maybe there's life after death, maybe not. But you'd think if Ogden had something important to say, he'd spit it out. If he thinks his accident was no accident, why doesn't he just say so? If he blames someone for his death, why not speak up?"

She bit her lip. "You take such a…a utilitarian view of the afterlife. It isn't like this world. It takes so much energy to cross over, and, after all, a spirit doesn't have an actual brain to reason with."

"No comment."

She frowned but, much like one of those overextended denizens of the afterlife, didn't seem to have the energy for another scolding.

"Have they all gone to bed now? The still-living attendees, I mean."

Aunt H.'s gaze was puzzled. "Yes. I suppose so. Why?"

"I want to examine the dining room for myself."

She shook her head. "There's nothing there. You know there isn't. What could there be? A hidden projector? A hidden microphone?"

"Maybe."

"When would Roma have planted them? Especially since you had the locks on the doors and windows changed."

"I don't know, but I want to look that room over. There's got to be a scientific explanation for what we saw tonight."

My aunt nodded once, solemnly, granting permission. She remained motionless in her chair by the unlit fireplace as I went through to the dining room.

The room seemed strangely unchanged.

Yes, the chairs were in disarray, the crystal carafe had been moved to the table. A half-filled goblet sat beside it. In the old days, I had never seen so much as a side table out of formation. That wasn't the kind of change I meant.

After the events of the evening, I was expecting, well, not ectoplasm dripping from the chandelier, but something to confirm the weirdness of earlier. But beyond the scattered chairs and water carafe, there was nothing to indicate anything untoward had occurred.

I studied the long room as though seeing it for the first time. Gilt-framed oil paintings lined the walls, the brocade draperies were still drawn across the windows. The furniture was the same rickety antique tortoiseshell stuff Bancrofts had been dining on for generations.

There were no convenient alcoves, nooks, or cubbyholes to conceal recording devices or a fog machine. No closet or cupboard someone could hide inside.

I went to the windows and drew back the drapes, looking out at the moonlit terrace. Half the garden was still overgrown and wild. The other half was efficiently if not elegantly chopped back into submission.

I tested the new bolt on the window frame. It held firm. No one had gained access from outside.

The leaves of the eucalyptus trees glinted and glittered in the moonlight like silver coins. Through the wind-tossed trees I spotted the light shining from the chauffeur's quarters over the garage. I fingered the brocade curtains for any telltale lumps made by wires but found nothing. I turned away from the cheerful twinkle of the carriage-house windows.

From there I moved to the table, crawling beneath and checking for bugs—the listening-device type—wires, speakers, anything. There was nothing. No hidden drawers, nothing taped to the underside, no hollow legs. Same with the chairs. They were just ordinary…dining room table chairs.

I crawled out from under the table and went to examine the sideboard and twin servers. The drawers and cupboard doors all seemed solid and well made. I couldn't find any wires or electronic devices.

I dusted my hands and rose. I was starting to lose hope, but no way was I ready to give up yet. I moved to the walls of the room. If there were hidden doors or secret passages at Green Lanterns, I'd have surely discovered them during my Hardy Boys phase. But it was still worth a try. The house had been built in the late 1800s by Alexander Bancroft, a wealthy coal baron from Victoria, British Columbia, as a wedding present for his American bride. It had plenty of nooks and crannies, so maybe a long-lost secret passage wasn't out of the question. A lot of wealthy families had built hidden rooms during Prohibition to conceal their private bars.

I ran my hands over the smooth, forest-green walls, seeking… Well, honestly, I didn't know exactly what I was looking for beyond a seam or edge where one didn't belong. Sadly, there was no handy bookshelf with a fake-book lever or a faux fireplace with swiveling andirons. I could find no suspicious cracks, no ridges, no hidden hinges.

Pulling my shoes off, I climbed onto the table and checked every arm of the chandelier. I felt around the ceiling medallions. Nothing. There was no ceiling trapdoor, no access panels.

Strike three. Or possibly eleven.

The only thing left was the floor. I started at the far end of the room and went over the parquet floor, square by square, running my hands around each and every groove. I shoved the table and chairs to the side of the room, rolled the faded green-and-gold silk Isfahan rug out of the way, and went over that section of floor too, but there were no loose blocks, let alone a hitherto unnoticed trapdoor.

Defeated, I climbed wearily to my feet. My hands were filthy, and the knees of my jeans were dusty. There was a tickle in the middle of my forehead as my sinuses began to protest breathing all the dirt and dust accumulated over the months while Betty had been left to try and deal with the entire house on her own.

I pushed my damp hair back with a grimy hand. So that was that. Whatever the hell was going on, the room had not been rigged. It was disappointing, but not really a surprise. Wiring the room for sound, setting up projectors, would have required the cooperation of someone inside the house, and that was nearly as hard to believe as Ogden's spirit wandering the halls of Green Lanterns, pointing the finger of suspicion at all and sundry. All and sundry being Aunt H.

I wandered back to the windows, gazing out at the light still shining through the trees. After a moment, I pulled the curtains.

What if I was wrong? Was cynicism blinding me to one final possibility? The possibility that Ogden Hyde really had come back from the dead?

As I let the idea sink in, a chill went through me. It was a completely atavistic reaction. Even when you don't believe in ghosts…well, you can't know for sure. No one knows for sure. I don't believe in demonic possession either, but the Catholic Church apparently does, and they're a pretty big, well-established organization. So there you go.

For a few seconds I stood motionless, just…absorbing the feel of the room. It seemed cold for a summer night, and the sense of menace I'd felt earlier was back. But was that the room, or was that imagination getting the better of me? Because it was all too easy to start imagining something lurking in the shadows, watching us with hollowed eyes as we stumbled around in panic. I could almost visualize a grinning skeleton standing across the room from me.

Ohhh-kay. Enough of that.

I went to the French doors, slid the bolt, and pushed the doors wide. The summer breeze wafted in, dispelling the stale scent of dust and old candles and furniture wax. A distant pale balloon floated past the moon and disappeared behind the trees. The night smelled of eucalyptus and sounded like a symphony of crickets and frogs. Moonlight gilded the ornate iron furniture—and picked out the gleam of eyes of someone standing in the shadows.

CHAPTER TEN

"**W**ho's there?" I demanded.

The sharpness in my tone couldn't quite conceal the fear. *Mostly*, I was just startled—especially after the evening I'd had—but not entirely. My nerves were not as steady as I'd have liked, and I did feel an instinctive and irrational flash of alarm at the glimpse of that shadowy, unknown figure.

Except, embarrassingly, I *did* know—or at least was pretty sure—who had to be lurking outside on the terrace, even before Seamus said quietly, "It's me, Artemus."

He stepped into the long oblong of light from the dining room, and—unnervingly—I had the strangest, strongest urge to throw myself on his manly chest and pour out my tale of haunted happenings so that he could wrap his muscular arms around me and assure me there was no such thing as ghosts.

Which I already knew, and which would be pretty weird since I didn't know or trust the guy as far as I could throw him.

I reacted instead by shouting, "*Jesus Christ*, you scared the life out of me! What are you *doing* out here?"

Seamus answered, "Watching you search the dining room."

"You... What? How were... *Huh?*"

"What happened tonight?" he asked. "What were you looking for?"

I snapped, "How is that any of *your* business?"

He closed the distance between us with a step, pulled me to him, and covered my mouth with his.

That's not the kind of thing that happens to me, and for a very long second or two, astonishment held me openmouthed and wordless as Seamus's firm, warm lips pressed insistently against mine. Everything seemed to stop. My heart. My head. The very breath in my lungs. Nobody had ever kissed me like that. I didn't know there *were* kisses like that—sweet, hot, hungry—outside of movie theaters.

Then I came back to life with a jolt, like a surgeon had slapped defibrillator paddles to my chest and jump-started my heart. I felt the piercing, unexpected delight of that kiss in every fiber of my being—right down to the unraveling threads and overstrained seams.

Like the hymn says, *Awake, my soul, stretch every nerve; and press with vigor on.*

And holy smoke, I did indeed want that vigor to press on. My lips parted, my hands—flattened against the broad planes of his chest—slid caressingly up to lock behind Seamus's head to pull him still closer. I molded my lips to his, kissing him back with a passion I didn't think I still possessed for anything outside opening night on Broadway.

I was thinking about dragging him into the rose bushes, when somehow, from somewhere, sanity reasserted itself. I stopped pulling, started pushing, and Seamus let me go with a suddenness that sent us both staggering.

"Sorry," he said huskily. "I didn't plan that."

"That would be some plan," I agreed, equally unsteady.

"It's just—" He broke off.

"Exactly," I said. "Twelve months at sea is a very long voyage."

He blew out a hard breath and shook his head like a punch-drunk boxer, then asked in a brisk, businesslike tone, "Are you going to tell me what happened here tonight?"

Was I? I was tempted to—though I wasn't sure why. Or rather, I knew why I was tempted, but not why I thought giving in to that temptation would be a good idea.

Instead, I hedged, "What makes you think anything happened?"

"I saw the Loveridge woman tear out of here like demons were after her."

"Happily, demons were not part of the evening's festivities. At least, I don't think so."

"She held another séance?"

"No, no. She dropped by for dinner. It turns out she strongly dislikes apple crumble for dessert."

Seamus made a sound that fell somewhere between amusement and exasperation.

"Artemus."

"Seamus."

"You know, you can trust me," he said.

I was momentarily distracted by the sight of another colorless balloon—actually a pair of them—drifting toward the tall wall of eucalyptus. Weird.

I turned my attention back to Seamus, who was waiting for me to say something. "Unfortunately, I *don't* know that," I replied. "I'm pretty sure you haven't been entirely honest with either me or my aunt."

He seemed surprised. "Didn't my references check out?"

"Yes, your references checked out."

"Then I'm not sure what the problem is."

"Neither am I," I admitted.

Seamus said lightly, "Do you think maybe I faked my résumé?"

"Yeah, I do," I said. "No offense."

That clearly threw him. After a startled moment, he said, "How would I? And *why* would I do something like that?"

I shook my head. "But I notice you don't deny it."

Belatedly, he noticed the same thing and said, "Of course I deny it. It's so…out there, I didn't think I'd *have* to deny it. Not in so many words."

I sighed. "And *this* is why I don't trust you. Because you're lying."

I have a trained eye. I can spot bad acting in all its forms, and lying is just another type of acting.

He was silent. "Have you shared your suspicion with your aunt yet?" he asked finally.

"Yes."

Again, he seemed to have no response.

I said, "I'm not sure if she believes me or not. Good help is hard to find, and frankly, I don't think she cares that you're a fake so long as you mow the lawn, weed the flower beds, and don't murder us during the night."

"She's not planning to fire me?"

"I doubt it."

The set of his shoulders relaxed. "Good." He added, "I promise I mean no harm to you. Or Mrs. Hyde."

I wasn't crazy about the fact that Auntie H. was clearly an afterthought. And not a very convincing afterthought.

"But you can't—or won't—tell me what you're really doing here?"

"I'm *really* working in the garden." Seamus held out his palms for me to witness his blisters. "As you can see."

"Okay. Have it your way."

I turned away to go through the French doors, and he said quickly, "Artemus?"

I glanced back in inquiry.

"If you change your mind—if you decide you need someone to talk to, I'm here."

I quirked an eyebrow, though I doubted he could see in the indistinct light. "Hopefully by 'here,' you don't mean *here*," I said. "Because it was pretty creepy walking outside to find you lurking behind the potted plants."

Seamus opened his mouth, but I firmly closed both doors, bolted them—and pulled the drapes shut.

To my relief, Aunt Halcyone had abandoned the music room by the time I returned. I hoped she had retired for the night, though I couldn't imagine any of us sleeping soundly in this house ever again.

On impulse, I went through to Ogden's study, switched on the light, and looked around for a sign. Not a sign from the Great Beyond. Definitely not. A sign of human agency at work. Dropped ash, muddy footprints, a matchbook, a missing button, a monogrammed hankie… How about a signed confession? That would have been useful. There was nothing. Not a single clue. The thick, springy carpet held no trace of anyone's passage, not even my own.

I examined the crowded bookshelves. I'd always been skeptical of Ogden's publishing business. He had been vague about the details, but I'd gathered it was some kind of hybrid vanity press devoted exclusively to nonfiction. Nonfiction, but not scholarly or academic work. In fact, Ogden had seemed to prefer authors who specialized in being crackpots and eccentrics. From crazy diets to weird science to peculiar religions, no topic was too uncommercial for Hyde Publishing. If any of Ogden's titles had turned a profit, I'd never heard it mentioned.

I suspected a lot of Aunt H.'s financial resources had gone into propping up Hyde Publishing, but she'd never discussed it, and certainly had not complained. Nor was it my business how she chose to spend her money. It was *her* money.

Ogden's shelves included tomes on sharing the joys of solo sex, supercharging quantum touch, a diet based on Gertrude Jekyll's garden design, and how to meet and date on the astral plane.

The funny thing was Ogden had never struck me as particularly imaginative or spiritual. Not the kind of man who would have an interest, let alone choose to encourage belief, in astral planes and new religions. He had been conservative to the point of stuffiness.

I turned from the bookshelves, studying the room. His sanctuary, he'd called it. It was exactly what one would expect from a guy who wore yachting leisurewear without irony.

Leather club chairs. Framed prints of perplexed pheasants and dead hares, varied golf trophies on the side table, a marble bust of Julius Caesar on a pedestal near the bookshelves, assorted pipes in a carved, circular rack.

I sat down in one of the leather club chairs and switched on a small lamp.

Sanctuary. Sanctuary from what? I wondered. What had Ogden been hiding from in this room? What the hell had he thought about all those hours he had spent alone in here?

The lamp seemed to throw a spotlight on the large, immaculate desk, reminding me of an overpriced stage prop. Had Ogden actually done any work in here? I didn't know. At the time, I had been more interested in avoiding Ogden than observing him.

I rose and went to the desk, taking the tall leather chair and swiveling slowly around to scrutinize the room from Ogden's perspective.

Originally, the study had been the domain of Aunt H.'s first husband, Edwin. The framed maps and encyclopedias were all from Edwin's era. In fact, other than the introduction of golf trophies and the bust of Julius Caesar, it hadn't changed much from master to master. In fairness, it probably hadn't changed much from generation to generation.

I didn't remember Edwin well, but he had always seemed pleasant and even-tempered. He had been kind to a grieving child and patient with a moody, touchy teenager. I don't suppose his marriage to Aunt H. was a great love match. They'd known each other all their lives. But I did remember Aunt H. and Edwin laughing a lot and always having something to talk about. It had been a very different house then.

But then Ogden had been a very different husband.

I reached out to finger a crystal paperweight shaped like a globe of the world. That too had been Ogden's. The crystal globe and the bust of Caesar seemed very much like things

Ogden would have owned. The publishing company devoted to New Agey, spacey philosophy and religion? Not so much.

I leaned back, resting my head against the leather cushion. How late was it now? Well after midnight for sure. Beyond the long French windows, the black night was salted with bits of cracked and chipped stars. As I stared, another of those pallid balloons floated past, ambling its way across the heavens.

What the hell with the balloons? Was the circus in town?

No, there had been something on the news. Something about a show of balloons to get the media's attention for some cause or another. Hopefully not the air-pollution crisis.

The uneasy shadows around the periphery of the lamp seemed to quiet, settle down.

I closed my eyes. I was tired. Completely drained. Something was very wrong at Green Lanterns, but I had no idea what it was or how to fix it. And sitting here worrying about it wasn't solving anything. I should go to bed. I would in a minute.

I might have drifted off. In fact, I must have. Because when I opened my eyes again, the room was in complete darkness. I blinked in confusion, still seeming to hear the echo of a sharp, distinct *click*.

I sat up straight, listening tensely.

Nothing.

It was so quiet, I could hear the dust falling.

Had I imagined it? Maybe I'd been more deeply asleep than I realized.

Click.

There it was again!

I had some vague idea that a secret door was about to swing open, and I leaned forward, gripping the arms of the chair, watching for motion in the gloom.

Nothing happened.

I continued to sit in straining, rigid silence, waiting…

Someone laughed. A soft, deep chuckle that seemed to come from right behind me.

I jumped out of the chair, knocking something from the desktop. I heard the smash of glass on the floor—the crystal paperweight landing between the edge of the carpet and the wooden floor. I could just make out small shattered chunks glittering in the moonlight as I backed away from the desk.

No one stood behind the chair.

At least…not that I could see. And what the hell was I doing standing here in the dark?

I reached out, ignoring the fact that my hand was not steady, and snapped the lamp on.

There was no one else in the room.

Of course not. Because I had dreamed the whole thing up. I was probably dreaming now.

I did not feel like I was dreaming, though. I didn't feel remotely sleepy. My heart was thundering in my ears, and every muscle in my body was tense and ready to jump.

Even if I had imagined the laughter, who had turned out the lights?

CHAPTER ELEVEN

I had no intention of telling Aunt Halcyone about my unsettling experience in Ogden's study.

For one thing, after a good night's sleep I was inclined to think my nerves had gotten the better of me. The séance had shaken me—as it had shaken everyone in the house with the exception of Liana, who had been almost giddy with excitement—and naturally, I'd been predisposed to believe something else might happen. Understandable then that I'd dreamed something else up in the form of mysterious clicks, ghostly laughter, and lights turning themselves on and off.

And if I *hadn't* dreamed it, then someone in this house was deliberately, maliciously trying to terrify the rest of us. To what purpose, I couldn't guess. But I was pretty sure that person was Vadim Tarrant.

Anyway, I wasn't going to worry Aunt H. with any of that, but unfortunately, she caught me in Ogden's study the morning after the séance, replacing all the books I'd dragged from the shelves and dumped on the floor in my quest to find the entrance to the secret passage I was convinced—or had been at two o'clock in the morning, anyway—must exist.

"*Artemus!*"

I wheeled.

"What on *earth* are you doing?" Aunt H. stood in the doorway, her expression horrified. "Why are you in here? What's this about?" She pointed to the books strewn helter-skelter across the carpet and balanced in precarious stacks on the desk. Books were everywhere, some open, their spines cracked, some resting face up. I'd been pretty ruthless about clearing the shelves.

I said tersely, "I'm looking for a secret passage."

"You're…" Her expression changed. Grew stricken. "*Why?* Why in here? Why now?" The color drained from her face. "Did you—?" She swallowed. "Was it…*him?*"

"Him? Him who? No. I didn't hear *him*. I heard something." I looked back at the partially filled bookshelves. "I heard a clicking sound."

"You're lying," Aunt H. said in a wondering tone. She took a couple of steps forward to better examine my face. "You *did* hear something."

"I told you what I heard." I shoved another volume back onto a random shelf.

I don't think she heard me. "And it frightens *you*," she said. Her tone was incredulous.

"It doesn't frighten me. It makes me mad. This is all bullshit, Aunt H. I don't know what the point of it is, but I plan to find out. Has anyone made an offer on the property recently?"

"No. Of course not. Nothing would convince me to sell this house. The house will go to you and your children one day."

I said shortly, "I live in New York. I *like* New York. I'm sorry, but I don't see myself moving back here—nor do I see children in my future. So if you want to sell this place and move to a healthier clime, I say go for it."

"Sell Green Lanterns!"

"Yes." I added ruthlessly, "That's all I'd do if I had possession of it."

She repeated in that same stunned tone, "*Sell* Green Lanterns!"

"Aunt H., you yourself told Liana my life was in New York now."

"Yes, of course. *Now.* But you're still young. Things change. This house is part of your inheritance. This house is part of your family legacy."

"*Has* someone made an offer on Green Lanterns?"

"No."

"Is that the truth?"

"Of course it's the truth!" she said indignantly.

"What about the adjacent properties? Is the old Carter School House still for sale?"

Built in 1873, the Carter School House had served as the local elementary school for generations of Russian Bay kids, though it had been abandoned by the 1960s. The property had been purchased by out-of-towners, who began construction to turn it into a single residence, but after a year or two the plans had been scrapped and the structure once more left to rot. Local rumor was that the building was haunted. A far more likely explanation was the new owners had run out of cash. Renovating a very old house in the middle of nowhere is a costly proposition.

The property had not been inhabited since.

"No," Aunt H. said. "It was purchased a few months ago."

"Was it? By whom?"

I was thinking farming conglomerate or some other evil corporate entity out to annex Green Lanterns as part of their final game plan, but Aunt H. said with a tinge of exasperation, "By Reverend Ormston. What on earth does the Carter School House have to do with you tearing apart this room?"

"Nothing, as far as I know. I'm trying to think of a reason someone might want us all out of Green Lanterns."

Aunt H. began to splutter. She's not a woman for spluttering. "You prefer to believe that there's some complicated criminal conspiracy to drive us from our home rather than accept that Ogden's spirit might be restless and wandering?"

"Yep!" I snapped. I don't often snap at Aunt H. "I do."

"Do you hear yourself? You're willing to entertain the idea there's a sinister plot to drive down the price of Green Lanterns—when no one has shown any interest in purchasing the house or land—over even *considering* the possibility that what ails this house is rooted in the spiritual."

"You're not talking about the spiritual. You're talking about the supernatural. I don't believe in the supernatural."

Not exactly true. I didn't think I had all the answers when it came to the afterlife. As much as I preferred a rational approach to life and death, when it came to heaven, hell, ghosts, spirits, and haunted houses, I had my share of questions. I think most people—somewhere deep down—suspect there's at least a possibility ghosts might exist. Or if not ghosts, an afterlife of some kind.

Aunt H. said, "I'm genuinely shocked that you, of all people, would be so closed-minded."

"I don't know why me *of all people*," I protested. "There's open-minded, and then there's gullible."

Aunt H. drew herself to her full height—which, frankly, was still pretty petite. "I'm sorry you find me gullible simply because I'm not willing to dismiss the evidence of my own ears and eyes. It's only fair to warn you that Liana is hoping to persuade Roma to return this evening for another session. Assuming she's fully recovered from last night. If you would prefer to dine out or meet friends, I'll completely understand."

"Are you kidding me? *Again?*"

"I am not joking," Aunt H. said grimly.

"Then I'll certainly be here."

Aunt H. opened her mouth, and I said, "And don't worry about my negative energy interrupting the cosmic flow since I clearly couldn't stem the tide last night."

She closed her mouth, nodded, then turned and left the room.

I resumed banging books onto empty shelves.

Shortly before lunch I drove into Russian Bay to meet a couple of old friends at a pub called Hops and Barley. I hadn't realized how oppressive I found Green Lanterns until I was having my second microbrew and catching up with Cyril and Deedee over the best fish and chips on the West Coast.

"Last man out alive," Cyril said mockingly as we clinked mugs. "Congratulations."

"Come off it," I scoffed. "You guys could leave anytime you wanted. You just didn't want."

Cyril cocked an eyebrow. "Didn't I? Don't I?"

"*Do* you?"

Cyril shrugged. He was a tall, lanky towhead, mildly cynical but mostly amiable. In high school he'd had dreams of someday winning a Pulitzer. He was currently working as the lead reporter for the *Russian Bay Navigator*. It wasn't the *Washington Post*, but there was something to be said for being the big fish in a little pond.

"Cy's right," Deedee said. "You got out just in time, Artie."

Deedee, pretty, popular, and always top of our classes academically—well, to prevent Deedee from leaving for the big-city lights, her father had bought her a local boutique, which she was apparently turning into quite a success. Not exactly the career in fashion design she'd hoped for, but she too seemed to be making a go of it.

I said, "Yeah. Well."

Cyril gave me an inquiring look. I shrugged.

Deedee said, "That's right. You didn't get on with your uncle. That's why you left so suddenly."

"He was *not* my uncle," I said, and they both laughed.

"Good thing you weren't around when Ogden went over—" Cyril swallowed the rest of it as Deedee directed a death stare his way.

I said, "It's okay. I already know there's gossip about Aunt H. cutting Ogden's brake lines."

"There was nothing wrong with the brakes of his car," Cyril said.

Which was true. Ogden's car had skidded out of control and gone over the edge of a cliff on the seacoast road. The official verdict had been Accidental Death. A lethal combination of high speed and bad weather.

At the same time, Deedee said, "Nobody with a brain believes that."

"I don't know. Something sure as hell put the kibosh on Aunt H.'s plans to turn Green Lanterns into an inn. Maybe guests were afraid they'd find ground glass in their Beef Wellington."

"Your aunt doesn't do the cooking," Cyril objected.

Deedee rolled her eyes. "I don't think it was anything to do with the inn or with people believing Halcyone killed Ogden Hyde," she said. "To be brutally frank, I don't think most people would have *cared* if she'd bumped him off. It wasn't just you. He wasn't very popular around here."

"It's her ruthless streak I like best," Cyril said of Deedee. She grinned back at him.

They'd dated in high school, but it turned out they clicked better as BFFs than sweethearts. It had been a relief at the time. I'd felt very much like the odd man out when they were experimenting with falling in love. Now I hoped they'd meet the right person, but they both seemed to have as much trouble settling down as me. Though at least they'd avoided the trap of falling for someone who was already married.

I said, "I guess you've heard there's a medium visiting the house regularly. I was at a séance just last night."

Deedee shuddered. "Roma Loveridge. She gives me the creeps."

"She does?" Cyril seemed surprised. "She seems pretty normal to me."

"That's what feels so creepy about it!"

Cyril and I laughed.

Deedee protested, "Seriously. Between the Loveridge woman's sudden rise in popularity with respected citizens like your aunt, and the return of RCU, it's like we're being taken over by pod people."

"RCU?"

At my look of puzzlement, Cyril said, "She's referring to the new and improved Rational Christians United. Which, for the record, I don't think Roma Loveridge is in any way connected to."

"Are the Rational Christians still around? I thought they died out after Reverend Hornsby was caught hey-diddle-diddling Edna Popov."

"They're back," Cyril said. "Hornsby died a couple of years ago, and they've got a new head man who, by all accounts, has completely turned things around. They've got a trendy acronym now and properly filed tax-exempt status. I did a story on them last month for the *Navigator*."

"They're a cult," Deedee said. "I don't care what they call it. It's a cult."

Cyril grinned at her. "You think the Catholic Church is a cult." To me, he said, "They're not a cult."

"You wouldn't know a cult if one kidnapped you," Deedee retorted. She said to me, "They're going to be your new neighbors."

"Now that you mention it, I think I do remember hearing something about Rational Christians and zoning permits."

"That's right," Cyril said. "They just got the go-ahead to turn the old Carter School House into a learning center."

"Great. Waco, here we come."

"That's right," Deedee said grimly. "Except the word is *wacko*!"

CHAPTER TWELVE

"Ulyanna isn't feeling well enough to attend the séance tonight," Aunt Halcyone informed me over dinner.

"Isn't she?" I glanced at the double doors through which Betty had just disappeared. She had seemed fine serving dinner—and as usual, it had been a delicious dinner. Herb-basted chicken, fluffy mashed potatoes drizzled in a rich, brown gravy, and garden-fresh roasted vegetables.

"She says not." Aunt Halcyone sighed. "I think Tarrant may have forbidden her to attend. She was very upset last night."

"Yeah. Well."

Aunt H. ignored that. "Anyway, I've asked Cassidy to join us this evening, and he's agreed."

That got my attention. "You're kidding."

"Not at all. He said he always wanted to attend a séance." I couldn't help feeling there was a note of accusation as she added, "He seems both intellectually curious and open-minded. I know you're suspicious of his motives, but there's something about him I like."

"Good for Cassidy," I said casually. To be honest, I was kind of relieved. Regardless of my suspicions, I thought

Cassidy would be a useful guy to have in a crisis, and I could only too easily imagine another crisis occurring tonight.

I said, "Seriously. Do you think all this—this business of recalling Ogden—is good for Liana?"

My aunt said with grim candor, "I believe it's the only thing that keeps the poor thing going."

That was probably true, which, in my humble opinion, was a good reason to pull the plug. But sadly, no one was asking for my humble opinion.

A little before eight, Tarrant appeared in the drawing room in full oppressed-proletariat mode: sullen-faced and dark-browed. When Aunt H. inquired after Betty, he informed her haughtily he had forbidden his daughter to attend, so Aunt H. had guessed right.

"She is having her head all full of trash," Tarrant informed Aunt H., "like you other females." He looked from my aunt to Liana to me in what I imagined was supposed to be deliberate challenge.

I raised my brows. Like I'd never heard that one before? What did he imagine my next move was? Challenge him to a duel? Fire him on the spot? I said, "I'm sure last night didn't help her blood pressure."

"No," he said grudgingly. "It did not."

"We certainly wouldn't want Ulyanna to attend if she's feeling ill," my aunt said. "Mr. Cassidy has agreed to make up our number."

Liana gave a little gasp. "The gardener?" She had dressed for the occasion in a bright turquoise robe-dress, the wide sleeves richly embroidered in varying shades of blues and greens. The wild snarl of her hair had been combed into submission, and I noticed a shaky attempt had been made to apply pink lipstick to her mouth.

Aunt H.'s choice did not meet with Tarrant's approval either. He clucked his tongue. "That one!"

"Do you have something against Cassidy?" I asked Tarrant.

"He snoops. That one, he is snooper."

"I think so too," Liana said.

My aunt looked taken aback, but before she could question either of them further, the snoop in question ducked his head around the doorframe.

"Here you all are," Seamus said cheerfully. "No one answered the kitchen door, and I felt odd going to the front."

"But not odd walking in unannounced?" I inquired. I was smiling, though, because like Aunt H., there was something about him I too just couldn't help liking.

Seamus grinned unrepentantly back at me.

"Thank you so much for joining us, Mr. Cassidy," my aunt said, going to meet him. "It's so very kind of you to stand in for Ulyanna."

"Whatever I can do to help," Seamus said gallantly.

He'd showered and changed into black jeans and a black V-neck sweater pulled over a white T-shirt. It was a warm night outside, but maybe he was anticipating a cold spot or two.

"I believe you know everyone," Aunt H. added, waving vaguely at the rest of us.

Seamus nodded pleasantly to Liana, which for some reason confirmed my belief that he'd heard himself being discussed.

"Would you like a drink?" I asked.

"Sure," Seamus said. He smiled into my eyes, and I smiled back.

Liana cut in. "No alcohol!" she exclaimed. "Spirits interfere with the—"

"Spirits?" I suggested.

She frowned.

I didn't give a damn whether Liana approved of drinking while contacting the other world or not, but by then it was exactly eight o'clock. The front door bell rang, and Tarrant went to admit Roma Loveridge. Liana cooed with excitement and rubbed her hands together as though she could hardly contain herself.

Seamus smiled at me again—and again I smiled back. No point in pretending I wasn't glad to see him, though I was a little surprised at how glad I was.

Roma appeared, still stylish but looking a little wan this evening, and we moved to the dining room, which had been prepared once more for the festivities.

"Please be seated. Are you a believer, Mr. Cassidy?" Roma asked as she took her place at the head of the table.

"It depends," Seamus said.

"I only ask because Mr. Bancroft is not a believer. It is difficult overcoming his negative energy."

"I've heard the same thing from a number of theatrical producers," I said, and Seamus laughed.

Roma was not amused. Actually, *only* Seamus was amused. The look my aunt directed my way was affectionate but chiding.

Roma huffed, "Exactly. So if you too are aggressively skeptical, we may not have the best conditions for contacting the other side."

Liana made a sound of dismay.

Seamus said, "I like to think I'm always willing to learn something new."

He sounded more cheerful than earnest, and Roma sighed. "I suppose that will have to do." She draped her black mantilla over her head. "Will you please join hands?"

Liana snatched at Roma's hand. "Will we see Ogden again tonight?" Her haggard face was flushed with excitement.

"I can make no promises." Roma threw an automatic glance my way. "It's going to be challenging."

I tried to look suitably soulful. She did not seem reassured.

"I've prayed," Liana told her. "I've prayed all day."

I was vaguely uncomfortable at the idea of Liana praying for Ogden's appearance at a séance, although maybe that was me being narrow-minded again. Roma had made her case the evening before for spiritualism as an offshoot of religious movements of the mid-nineteenth century.

"Good," Roma told her curtly. She nodded to Tarrant. "Please douse the lights."

Tarrant, standing by the door, flicked the light switch, and darkness folded around us once more.

I listened to Tarrant shuffle his way to the table. Tonight I was determined not to be distracted by my aunt's nervousness or anyone else's reactions. All my focus was on listening for some telltale sight or sound that would confirm my belief that last night's supposed manifestation was rigged. Which didn't alter the fact that I was acutely aware of Seamus sitting opposite Aunt H. It was too dark to see much of anything, but I could smell his soap and Bay Rum aftershave. I could hear Tarrant's slightly wheezy inhalations and Liana's breathy gulps. And I could feel the rigid, ice-cold tension in my aunt's grip.

On my other side, Roma was breathing softly, evenly, her hand cool and dry. She said in a singsongy voice, "Close your eyes and empty your mind of all negative thoughts. Be at peace. We are safe here."

The room was absolutely silent.

I glanced around the table. I could just make out the alert gleam of Seamus's eyes. Once again, I was reassured by the simple fact of his presence.

Seconds ticked by. They felt like minutes. Then minutes passed, and it began to feel like hours.

Liana whimpered in frustration.

I turned my head to stare at Roma through the gloom.

As if on cue, her breathing grew deeper, harsher. She began to shake as though experiencing her own personal earthquake. Her head fell back and then forward. I glanced around the table and again caught the gleam of Seamus's eyes. Everyone else continued with bowed heads and closed eyes as they concentrated on making contact.

Roma slumped forward in her chair. After an unnerving moment, she raised her head and whispered softly, "Lord Rekhmire comes."

No one said anything.

"Lord Rekhmire, do you have any messages for Seamus Cassidy?" Roma asked.

"The *gardener*?" whispered Liana in protest.

Beneath the lace veil, Roma tilted her head attentively.

"Lord Rekhmire says you must be careful. They are watching you, Mr. Cassidy…"

Seamus said, "Thanks for the warning. Who is watching me exactly?"

Roma said nothing. Maybe she couldn't hear over the spirits all talking at once. Maybe she was waiting for an answer. If so, it didn't come.

Seamus asked, "Okay. Well, is there anyone there who wants to speak to me?"

Aunt H., Liana, and Tarrant all opened their eyes and turned their heads to stare at him in surprise.

I swallowed a laugh.

"It doesn't work like that," Liana said.

"Why not?" I asked.

There was a momentary pause, and then Roma said in a dreamy voice, "Yes. There is someone here. A tall man with iron-gray hair and blue eyes. He has a beard. He's wearing a plaid flannel shirt and blue jeans. He carries an ax… John… Jonathan… No. John yet not *John*…"

Seamus didn't say a word.

"Does this mean anything to you?" Roma asked. "Does the name John mean anything?"

"Could the name be Sean?" Seamus asked, almost unwillingly.

Roma took a moment before confirming, "Sean. Yes. Your grandfather."

Seamus said nothing.

Roma said more confidently, "Yes. Your grandfather. He wants to know if you are still so sure about Mary Kate."

Seamus gave a strange laugh. "I'm sure."

Silence.

Was that it?

We all studied the shadowy form of our tour guide to the spirit world.

After a moment or two Roma began to hum. The tune was familiar, but it took me a moment to recognize "Too Ra Loo Ra Loo Ral." I think it took Seamus a minute too.

"How do you…" He sounded genuinely astonished. He looked across the table, and his words seemed directed to me—as one skeptic to another? "He used to sing that to me when I was in my crib."

His surprise—not just surprise, there was a hint of something like alarm in his voice—was unnerving. I felt the prickle of hairs on the back of my neck. How the hell could Roma possibly know so much about Seamus? I knew that part of the medium gig was to do research on marks, but she had no way of knowing Seamus would take part in tonight's session. And these were difficult things to research anyway. The reference to Mary Kate? A childhood lullaby?

It was weird. I hated to admit it, but it was uncanny. And I could tell by Seamus's reaction that he thought so too.

Suppose, just suppose… My mind tottered for an instant before I yanked back from the edge. With a name like Seamus Cassidy? It would be safe to guess there might be a Mary Kate in his life. And "Too Ra Loo Ra Loo Ral" was an American-Irish classic. Not magic. Not spirits. Just a calculated guess.

Liana's petulant voice sliced through the humming. "Where is Ogden? Aren't we going to speak to Ogden?"

Roma broke off humming and returned to business. "Ogden is here. Ogden, Liana wishes to speak to you."

"Oh, *please*." Liana's voice was tearful. "Please, *yes*."

There was a lengthy pause. Maybe Ogden had dropped the phone. Maybe it was a bad connection. I opened my mouth.

"Liana, dear," Ogden's strong, deep baritone spoke, and the words dried in my throat. *Where is that voice coming from?* I couldn't pinpoint it. I half turned in my chair, and Roma's hand tightened on my own.

Ogden droned on. "And Halcyone. Halcyone, dear love, are you there too?"

Aunt H. made a strangled sound, lost beneath Liana's, "Oh, Ogden! Oh, it's you at last!"

"Liana… So loyal. So true…"

So totally and completely unbalanced, if you asked me.

A sob tore out of Liana. "My dear, dear, dearest brother…"

"Halcyone," Ogden said, switching gears. "My loneliness grows."

Aunt H. said faintly, "Ogden… I…"

"I cannot rest while we remain apart."

"*The hell*," I said and tried to rise.

Aunt H. clutched my hand as I pushed back my chair. "*No. Artie. No. The circle mustn't be broken*—"

I managed not to pull away from her, but I was so angry, I was shaking. I stared into the darkness beyond the foot of the table and could just make out a dark shape—or was I imagining it?

I blinked again and again, and inky spots began to dance across my retina. It was impossible to make out anything for sure in that Stygian blackness.

"Ogden, don't go. Don't go!" The words were wrung from Liana's throat.

A long silence followed. There was only the sound of breathing in the blacked-out void.

Then, as on the previous night, a tiny puff of milky-white substance, no larger than a fist, appeared. Tarrant sucked in a hoarse breath and swore something in Russian as the small cloud began to grow.

Suddenly, a horrible, wild scream ripped the silence. Roma tore her hand from mine, thrashing about in her chair, all the while screeching like a wounded animal. I felt that terrible high, piercing shriek slice through me like the ragged edge of a knife.

"*Jesus Christ,*" I exclaimed and freed my hand from Aunt H.'s desperate clutch. "Roma? *Roma?*"

I couldn't see her!

Everyone began to talk at once. Beneath the panicked babble, I heard the sound of a chair going over and crashing to the floor. The next minute the lights blazed on overhead. Tarrant stood near the doorway, fingers on the light switch. He looked both frightened and outraged.

Roma lay writhing on the floor behind the head of the table. Seamus bent over her. "Get some water," he told me.

I got over to the sideboard and poured water from the decanter into a glass. I carried the water to Seamus and knelt beside him.

"Thanks," he muttered, taking the glass.

"Is she having a seizure?"

"Maybe. I don't know."

We watched as Roma's frantic movements slowed, then finally ceased, and she lay motionless and waxen.

I gulped. "Uh... Is she—?"

"No." Seamus lifted Roma's head and pressed the glass to her colorless lips. The liquid dribbled down her chin.

I said uneasily, "You're sure she's not—?"

"I'm sure," he said grimly. He pressed the rim of the glass to her mouth again, and a little liquid spilled between her lips. "I think she's coming around."

Behind me, Liana broke off sobbing with a gasp. I turned. Aunt H. stood in the center of the room, staring as though hypnotized at the black leather glove she held.

"It was lying on the floor," Aunt H. said. She sounded like someone talking in their sleep. "What can it mean?"

No one said a word.

Roma suddenly sat upright—which was nearly as disconcerting as her fit had been. She said hoarsely, "Someone broke the circle. Who?" Her feverish eyes raked our small, shaken group.

"It was Mr. Cassidy," my aunt said slowly. "I saw him rise. He was sitting across from me."

Seamus looked nonplussed as all eyes turned his way. "Well, yes. In the heat of the moment, I did leave the table."

"The heat of the moment?" Roma's voice was cold, her gaze hard. "You came intending to trick and deceive the rest of us with a false hand."

"With a *what*?" I asked.

Roma pointed at my aunt, who held up the black glove with a guilty air.

"Wait a minute," Seamus said, looking from Aunt H. to Roma. "That's not mine."

"From the first, you planned to break the circle," Roma said.

"Look, I don't deny I broke the circle." Seamus was speaking to Aunt H., not Roma. "Strange things have happened in this house lately. I thought I saw someone standing behind the table, and I did leave my chair. But that's not my glove."

"How would a glove pass as a fake hand?" I asked Roma.

Roma pushed to her feet, and Liana and my aunt went to support her on either side. She glared at Seamus. "I've seen such tricks before. You're not the first nonbeliever I've encountered."

"I don't know what you're talking about."

She wasn't listening—though I was, and I believed him. Seamus seemed genuinely bewildered.

"I could understand and sympathize with honest skepticism. I have no fear of sincere, bona fide investigation." Roma's voice wobbled. "I've cooperated in several studies conducted by the American Society for Psychical Research, the results of which have been published in their journal. I'd be happy to share those articles with you."

"I'd like to see them," I said.

Aunt H. shot me a reproving look. Roma pretended I hadn't spoken.

"But *this*." She had to stop and compose herself. "This kind of cold, deliberate deception is intolerable. You intended to trick and trap me with that ridiculous prop. *Me*."

Seamus's mouth opened to protest, but she rushed on. "Your behavior is not only a personal affront, it's an insult to my entire family and my calling." A pulse began to beat at her right temple. "I won't tolerate it."

"I sincerely apologize for breaking the circle," Seamus said. "But that's the extent of my crime. That glove isn't mine. I didn't bring any kind of prop."

Roma ignored him, turning to Aunt H. "I will not conduct another session in this house if Mr. Cassidy attends."

"I understand," Aunt H. said.

Without another word, Roma turned and left the room. Liana made a sound of pain, sank into her chair, and put her face in her hands.

Tarrant followed Roma from the room. He had recovered from his earlier shock. In fact, I thought he was smiling. Certainly, he looked smug.

Aunt H. said, "Why on earth would you pull such a ridiculous stunt, Cassidy?"

"Mrs. Hyde, I swear I didn't deliberately disrupt the séance."

"Are you saying you dropped the glove by accident?"

"No! I'm saying that glove doesn't belong to me."

"Wait a minute," I interjected. "How the hell would *that* pass as a fake hand? It's not stuffed. As far as I can tell, it's just an ordinary leather driving glove."

Aunt H. followed my gaze to the glove she still clutched. As she stared at the glove, her expression altered. She shoved the limp leather fingers into the pocket of her trousers. "Anyway," she said briskly, "what's done is done. Let's not belabor the matter."

At this abrupt change, Seamus and I glanced at each other.

"I don't think it's belaboring the matter to allow Cassidy to defend himself," I said. "May I see the glove?"

"No," Aunt H. snapped.

"*No?*"

She threw me a harassed look.

Unexpectedly, Liana came back to life. She lifted her head and sat up straight, staring at Seamus. "Whether you intended to disrupt the session or not, your behavior was dangerous, irresponsible," she told him. "You could have killed Roma! You very well may have severed the tie between Ogden and the rest of us forever with your reckless, disrespectful actions." She turned to Aunt H. "He *must* go, Halcyone. You can't allow him to stay on after this."

"Okay, let's all take a deep breath," I began as Seamus's eyes widened with alarm.

Seamus said, "Mrs. Hyde, you can't fire me for something I didn't do. Please—"

Aunt H. shut him up with a glance. She wrapped her arm around Liana's shoulders, helping her to her feet.

"Hush now, Liana. Don't upset yourself. Everything is all right. Let's have a nice, quiet cup of tea." She gave me a look I couldn't quite interpret and guided Liana, who had resumed whimpering, from the room.

As the door swung shut behind them, Seamus muttered, "Well, that could have gone better."

"Oh, do you think so?"

He glanced at me and scowled. "I didn't drop that glove. And that's all it was. *A glove.* You saw it yourself. That was no fake hand."

"I know."

"What kind of moronic trick would that be anyway? You'd need two fake hands to pull it off in this setting, and I kind of think the people on either side of me would notice if I got up from the table and left them each holding a stuffed glove."

I snorted in amusement at the image that conjured. "I agree. Do you think Roma was pretending to believe you tried to sabotage the séance?"

He hesitated. "She didn't fake that faint. She had some kind of reaction to the circle being broken, and I'd swear it was genuine."

"Yeah." I thought back to Roma's dramatic collapse. "And when she recovered, she was genuinely furious at the sight of that glove."

"Yes." He scratched absently at his stubby beard. "I assumed she'd be a fraud, but…"

"Now you think she's the real deal?" I had the same mixed feelings about Roma. I wanted to believe she was faking, but I wasn't sure.

He shrugged. "Maybe. I guess it's possible." He added reluctantly, "I think it's possible she's actually unaware of what's going on while in a trance. Maybe Lord Rekhmire is some aspect of her subconscious. Maybe she's got a split personality which emerges during the séance."

"Maybe," I said noncommittally.

He studied me. "You searched this room from top to bottom. I watched you do it. You didn't find anything. If she's faking, how does she do it?"

"I don't know."

Seamus said, "Sometimes a medium will conceal a wad of treated gauze in her mouth, or a bag of luminous dust on her person, dispersing it in the dark. There are all kinds of tricks. But I couldn't find anything."

I was astonished—and impressed. "You patted her down while you were delivering first-aid?"

He squared his jaw as though bracing for more censure. "I did."

I beamed at him. "Well done!"

Seamus's answering smile was cautious.

"Here's what I don't understand," I said.

His brows rose in inquiry.

"Why did Roma instantly assume that glove was a fake hand?" I asked.

"She knows you're a skeptic. She's clearly encountered resistance, even hostility in her sessions."

"Right. She jumped to the conclusion that glove was a fake hand and part of a scheme to discredit her."

"So?"

"And yet anyone who really looked at it could see it was no such thing. It was an empty glove. An ordinary driving glove. Aunt H. saw it the minute I pointed it out." And she'd been horrified.

Why? Because she'd recognized the glove?

Seamus frowned. "I'm still not following."

"I don't know that many guys in California who wear driving gloves. But you know who did? Ogden. Ogden wore driving gloves all the time. No doubt he was wearing driving gloves the day he died."

Seamus stared at me. I could see him connecting the dots. "Why did Roma assume it was a trick?" he suggested.

"*Exactly.* If she's genuinely psychic, why did Roma instantly conclude that glove was a trap set for her? Why didn't she consider the possibility it was another manifestation? There've been plenty of them. So how did Roma know it wasn't another sign from Ogden?"

CHAPTER THIRTEEN

Somehow, despite never leaving the house, Liana managed to catch a chill the morning after the wrecked séance, and by lunchtime had taken to her bed.

That should have provided a much needed reprieve for the rest of us, but being Liana, she decided her time had come and informed Aunt H. that the "curse had come upon her," to quote the Lady of Shalott and proceeded to spend a couple of hours lying in bed, staring at the cobwebs on the ceiling, and waiting for the angels—or more precisely, Ogden—to claim her.

Naturally, that frightened the wits out of Aunt H., who, disregarding Liana's express wishes, phoned for the doctor.

I remembered Dr. Tighe from days gone by. He had been our family physician for as long as I could remember, and though he was clearly past retirement age, he remained tall and vigorous. His hair was white now, but his face was somehow still youthful. He had a wide mouth and grave dark eyes that I knew from experience could light with amusement or crinkle with unexpected mischief. He was not looking amused or mischievous that day, however.

"Good to see you home again, Artemus," he greeted me. "You're exactly what's needed in this house right now."

Personally, I suspected a handsome, eligible psychiatrist would be of more use than a gay theater critic, but I said all the usual things, and then Dr. Tighe and my aunt vanished upstairs to visit Liana on her deathbed.

Half an hour later they returned downstairs, and Dr. Tighe pronounced a nonlethal case of flu. He prescribed aspirin, rest, plenty of fluids—and handed Aunt H. a large bottle of vitamins.

"These are for you, Hallie. You need them more than she does," he said grimly. "I've never seen you look so peaked."

Aunt H. looked pained but took the bottle of vitamins without demur.

"What you *both* need is a complete change of scenery," Dr. Tighe added. "This moping about the house is doing nobody any good." To me, he said, "You take my advice. Book them a cruise this afternoon. Send them somewhere warm and bright and cheerful. Provence. Tuscany. Best thing for them."

"Sounds great to me," I said. The Riviera was more Liana's style, but I knew I had as much chance of persuading her to visit the moon as the Riviera, let alone Tuscany.

Aunt H. smiled faintly and patted Dr. Tighe's arm. "Thank you so much, Ed. I'm relieved to know it's nothing serious."

"I didn't say it was nothing serious," Dr. Tighe retorted. "This morbid fixation of Liana's is unhealthy in the extreme. And in my experience, liable to be contagious. If she refuses to take my advice about getting away for a few weeks, I want to know. I can recommend a good specialist."

"What do you think about having her committed?" I asked. "As a means of intervention."

Aunt H. gasped, but Dr. Tighe seemed to think I was kidding, and laughed heartily. "There's that sense of humor!" he said. "That's what you need more of around here." He instructed

Aunt H. to give him a call if Liana's condition turned "bronchial," and was on his way with a brisk and cheery goodbye.

"*Artie!*" Aunt H. exclaimed as the door closed behind the doctor. "You can't say things like that, even in jest."

"Who's jesting? He said she needed a change of scenery. I'm sure we could find some nice, trendy sanatorium with a spa and a singles' juice bar."

Aunt H. winced and cast an uneasy glance at the staircase. Following her gaze, I added, "Don't worry, we'd hear the stairs squeak if she was creeping down here to listen in."

Aunt H. winced again. "It's not like you to be so unkind, dearest."

"I'm reaching my breaking point," I said.

As I put it into words, I recognized the truth of it. After the events of the previous evening, I wasn't just worried; I was scared—and starting to feel desperate. I'd never seen Aunt H. look so wan and colorless. The lines I'd noticed first on my arrival had grooved themselves more deeply across her forehead and around her mouth. After a brief reprieve, the strained look had returned to her eyes.

"If you don't want to try to talk her into checking into a mental-health facility, then let me book that trip Dr. Tighe was talking about. Today. Now. You've got to get out of here," I said. "With or without Liana."

"I can't just *leave*."

"Of course you can."

"No," she said wearily. "Not after last night. It wouldn't do any good."

"What does that mean? You mean because you found Ogden's driving glove?"

I could see by her startled expression, I had guessed right.

"Tarrant dropped that glove," I said.

"*What?*"

"You heard me. Tarrant was the one sitting closest to where the glove was found."

"Did you *see* him drop the glove?" She looked momentarily hopeful.

"No," I admitted. "It was too dark to see anything clearly, but I've been thinking about it since last night. I spoke to Seamus—er, Cassidy—after you left us, and I believe him when he swears he had nothing to do with that glove being found in that room."

"No, I know," she murmured. "I didn't realize at first…"

"Roma was genuinely furious, so it wasn't her. It wasn't you or me. It might have been Liana, but it's more likely Tarrant is the culprit. He had a smirky look on his face when he walked Roma out last night."

"Oh, Artie. Do you *honestly* not see the truth?" my aunt said, and the gentleness in her voice alarmed me more than anything had yet.

"If by 'the truth,' you mean do I not see that Ogden has returned from the grave, then correct. I honestly do not see, and do not believe, that Ogden is haunting this house."

"But you've heard him yourself. You've *seen* him. You can't pretend you weren't shaken by the first séance you attended. I know you too well, my dear."

"I've seen and heard something. I'm not prepared to believe it's Ogden."

"Then what is it?" Aunt H. asked as though she were humoring *me*.

"I'm not sure yet. I haven't figured it out. But I will."

"What if I told you—" She stopped.

"What if you told me *what*?" I demanded.

She bit her lip. Shook her head. Her eyes were dark and… haunted. I felt the hair on my scalp prickle.

"What are you saying?" I asked.

She just stared at me with those wide, worried eyes.

"That you're somehow…" I couldn't finish it.

Aunt H. whispered, "I believe I am perhaps responsible—" She swallowed.

"No. *Bullshit*," I broke in, startling us both. "Bull. Shit."

"Artie. Your language." Aunt H. sounded a little more like her old self.

"I don't believe it. Not for a minute. Seriously? You're trying to tell me *you* sabotaged Ogden's car?"

"No, of course not. But…"

When she trailed off, I said, "Let me guess. You had an argument with him the day he died, and you feel somehow responsible—although if anyone should know Ogden loved himself way too much to commit suicide, it ought to be you."

She was silent. And studying her, I felt uneasy.

"Is that it?" I asked.

She hesitated. "Um, yes," she said finally—and unconvincingly.

"*Did* you argue the day he died?"

"Yes. I suppose so," Aunt H. replied.

I was truly perplexed. I'd been so sure I had the reason for Aunt H.'s guilty conscience figured out. Now I was less confident.

"What did you argue about?"

She sighed wearily. "The same things we always argued about."

I was silent. I hadn't realized they'd reached the stage of regularly scheduled arguments.

I asked tentatively, "*Do* you think he killed himself?"

"No." Aunt H. said it with complete certainty. "I don't believe that." Her gaze flicked to mine. "But he could have been upset, distracted. He always drove far too fast, and the cliff road is dangerous. Especially dangerous in bad weather."

"But that would still be an accident," I said. "You can't take that on yourself. People argue all the time. Married people argue all the time. So I've been led to believe."

"Edwin and I never argued." I don't think she intended to say it aloud, because she looked immediately uncomfortable.

"Okay, but still. You argued, then Ogden ended up having a fatal accident. I can see you might feel bad. Feel a little guilty. But Ogden always drove like a maniac. That wreck could have happened regardless."

"Yes."

I studied her face. Her expression was closed. No. More… cloistered. She was keeping secrets, and whatever those secrets were, they were intensely painful.

"I don't understand, darling," I said. "Do you…think it wasn't an accident?"

I could see by her expression I had somehow guessed correctly. She put her hands up as though about to physically push me back, although of course she made no such move.

"I hope it was an accident," she said. "But I believe—know—that either way, I'm in part responsible."

I opened my mouth, but she spoke over me. "That's all I'm going to say on the matter, Artie. I believe Ogden *has* returned, and I believe he has cause for…" She struggled to get the word out steadily. "Grievance."

She didn't mean grievance, though. I knew that much. She meant revenge.

* * * * *

Roma Loveridge lived in a white stucco two-story bungalow on a quiet, shaded street in Old Town. A white picket fence surrounded a charming rose garden. A cobblestone walk led past a blue birdhouse that perfectly matched the blue shutters and blue front door of the bungalow. It all looked so normal and pleasant, I half suspected I had the wrong Loveridge residence—until I spotted the black brass sign hanging next to the front porch steps.

Roma Loveridge, Spiritualist. Readings by Appointment Only.

I had phoned ahead, so Roma was expecting me, but I don't think it was with any great pleasure. She opened the door as soon as I rang the bell, and gazed out unsmilingly at me.

"Good afternoon," I said. "Thanks for seeing me on such short notice."

"Of course," she returned, leading the way through the foyer into a living room with bay windows and a large stone fireplace. "You sounded as though the matter was urgent."

She wore gray slacks and a white blouse and was as perfectly coiffed and groomed as always—or as always barring the occasional fit following a trance.

"Please, sit." She nodded at the flowered sofa in front of the windows. "Coffee? Tea?"

"Coffee. Thank you."

She went into the sunny kitchen, and I had a chance to look around the room. There was nothing remarkable about it. It looked like a comfortable room furnished in traditional style. The furniture was old but polished and well kept. The walls were bare of pictures or photos beyond a large portrait hanging over the fireplace. The painting was of four women in turn-of-the-last-century finery.

I was studying the portrait when Roma returned with a tray.

"My great-grandmother, grandmother, mother, and aunt," she informed me, setting the tray with the glass coffeepot and plate of cake on the low table in front of the sofa.

"They were also psychic?" I returned to the sofa and watched her pour coffee into small china cups.

"We prefer the term spiritualist."

"It's an old-fashioned word."

"Perhaps. However, it's the correct word. Cream? Sugar?"

"Neither, thank you." I took the steaming cup of black coffee from Roma.

Roma leaned back on the sofa, watching me over the rim of her cup. She looked cool, calm, collected—and utterly incurious.

That was suspicious right there.

"Are your powers—gifts—limited to contacting the dead?" I asked.

"Are you asking whether I can read minds? I don't need to be a mind reader to know you want to talk to me about Mrs. Hyde-Kent."

"That's right. My aunt and I are very concerned about her."

Roma permitted herself a dry little smile. "I'm sure you are."

"Right. Well, I don't know exactly how to put this, but I don't think these séances are helping her. If anything, I think they encourage her to wal—er, focus on her grief rather than move on with her life."

"The grieving process cannot be rushed. We don't all recover from loss at the same rate."

"No, I realize that, but it seems to me that perhaps Liana's recovery has, uh, stalled. And I think that the séances might be partly to blame."

She said mildly, "Mr. Bancroft, am I correct in my understanding that you're a theater critic and not a mental-health professional?"

Oh, touché.

I smiled grimly. "Correct, Ms. Loveridge. But Liana's doctor *also* seems to think she's suffering from a morbid obsession."

She sipped her coffee and considered. "You're not related to Liana, are you?" she said finally.

"No. Not really. And in the ordinary course of things, Liana's morbid obsessions are her own business—and possibly yours. The problem here is that Liana's mental state is starting to affect the entire household. Her unhappiness is making my aunt unhappy—and that *is* my business."

"I wasn't aware of that." Roma's face remained impassive, untroubled. "Your aunt has never given any indication that I'm not welcome in her home or that my services are not required."

By that point I knew I was wasting my breath, so I said nothing.

"It seems to me that our sessions are the only bright spots in Liana's life," Roma continued. "When one has suffered a great loss, it's a comfort to know the veil between this world and the next is so very fine, to know that one can still reach the beloved—"

"Yes, I appreciate all that," I interrupted. "Are you telling me you don't see the problem, the potential danger with 'Ogden' declaring someone has to pay for what they did—or those hints about not resting until my aunt joins him?"

It's possible that using finger quotes around Ogden's name was a bad move because for the first time Roma's mouth tightened.

"I am merely the vessel. The messenger, not the message. And under the circumstances, that message is not unusual. My understanding is your aunt and uncle quarreled the day he died. Ogden's confusion and hurt still tether him to this world. And after all, one day your aunt *will* join him. We all are destined to die eventually."

I was too shocked and angry to reply. I set the empty china cup down so hard, the handle broke off.

Roma's cool gaze moved from mine to the broken cup. Her mouth curved into a weird smile.

"Is your fear for Liana or for Halcyone?"

"Both."

"Liana's religion prevents suicide."

"Liana? Liana's not a religious woman."

"Perhaps once that was true. But I believe she's a follower of your local church."

"*My* local church? What church? Fisherman's Chapel? St. Teresa's?"

"Rational Christians United."

"RCU? You're kidding."

Roma did not bother to answer that. It should have been obvious she had never kidded about anything in her entire life. "I don't know if Halcyone subscribes to any particular faith. We've never discussed her beliefs. She's always struck me as a sensible woman, but if you believe your aunt is liable to self-harm—"

"*What?* No. I certainly don't believe any such thing."

If I was afraid of anything on those lines, it was of Liana deciding to carry out Ogden's not-so-subtle wishes.

Roma said, "I know the real purpose of your visit today was to ask me to discontinue my visits to Green Lanterns. I can't do that. I don't believe it would be kind or wise to break off the strong connection that now exists between Ogden and his loved ones."

"I see."

"No. You don't. But I do. I have a gift and a vocation. I must be true to my calling. As long as Liana requires my services, I must attend her. If you somehow persuade Halcyone to forbid my visits, then I will conduct the séances here, from my home."

"That's plain enough." I rose.

She unhurriedly set her cup aside and also rose. "I hope so."

We walked in silence to the front door. It had been a major mistake coming here. A strategical error for sure.

She opened the door, and I said brusquely, "Thank you for your time."

She did not reply.

I passed through the door into the sunny garden. Some instinct made me glance back.

Roma stood framed in the doorway, her hand on the knob as though she was frozen in place. She stared at me with a stricken expression.

"Second thoughts?" I asked.

She continued to scan my face with that unsettling intensity. "I know you're not a believer." Her voice was uncharacteristically strained. "But if I were you, I would leave Green Lanterns. At once."

I was not amused. "Is that a threat?"

Her eyes widened with surprise. "No. Not at all. Call it…a premonition."

Not what I would have called it. I said sardonically, "Let me guess. There's something written in my stars?"

Her gaze cleared. She gave me another of those strange smiles. "Yes. There is." Without another word, she stepped back inside the house and closed the door.

A chill rippled down my spine as I stared at the blue glossy and unrevealing surface of the door.

It's not that I believed in Roma's psychic powers—it was the fact that *she* believed.

CHAPTER FOURTEEN

A solitary police car was pulling out of the tall iron gates as I reached the turnoff for Green Lanterns.

As the blue-and-white-marked vehicle passed me, I thought I recognized Police Chief Kingsland, and felt a flash of unease. I remembered what Tarrant had said about local gossip the night I arrived. Did people really believe the investigation into Ogden's death had been cursory because the Kingslands were longtime friends of Aunt H.'s?

And was Kingsland taking another look at Aunt H. because of that gossip? Was he going to reopen the case? After Aunt H.'s vague comments about bearing responsibility in Ogden's death, the possibility seemed real—and alarming.

I returned Aunt H.'s baby-blue Chevrolet Bel Air to the garage and turned off the engine. Seamus came down the circular staircase as I was climbing out from behind the wheel.

"Hey there," he called in greeting.

"Hi," I called back briskly. "Was that Police Chief Kingsland?"

The briskness was because of the annoying way my heart jumped in recognition every time I spotted Seamus. I'd tried with only moderate success to forget all about that kiss we'd shared after the first séance. I did not want to be distracted when I already had so much on my mind—let alone be distracted by someone I didn't completely trust.

Completely trust? I didn't trust Seamus at all.

I did believe him when he swore he had not dropped the glove during the séance. And—maybe this was weird, but it was true—I believed him when he said he intended no harm to me. I was less certain about his intending no harm to Aunt H., partly because he hadn't sounded particularly convinced on that point. Seamus was definitely up to something. And it was enough of a something that he had government agencies like San Francisco's Parks and Rec Department willing and ready to help him fake his references.

Was he a cop? He didn't seem like a cop, but beyond Chief Kingsland, I hadn't had a lot of experience with the police. If he was undercover law enforcement, what the hell was he investigating at Green Lanterns? Ogden's death? Was he here to try and nab Aunt H. for doing away with Husband #2?

He came to meet me, saying, "She purrs like a kitten, doesn't she?"

"Who?"

He nodded at the Bel Air.

I appreciate a nice piece of well-oiled machinery, but I'm not what you would call a car guy. Also, I know when I'm being sidetracked. "Was that Chief Kingsland I saw pulling out the front gate when I arrived?" I repeated.

Seamus hesitated. It was fleeting, but it's my job to pay attention to dramatic beats, and there was most certainly a pause in the dialogue.

"Yeah, it was," he said very casually, meeting my eyes.

I didn't think we were having a particularly meaningful conversation, so it was a little disconcerting how hard it was to tear my gaze from his. *What the hell were we talking about again?*

He wasn't *that* good-looking, after all. Even if he was, since when did I go for the brawny, brainless type? Not that Seamus was brainless—or unduly brawny. I had no real idea *what* he was. It didn't seem to matter. That tug of attraction got stronger every time I saw him. At this point, it was close to a tractor beam.

Nor was the magnetic field all on one side. I could read awareness, attentiveness in his eyes too. Feel it in the way he crowded just a bit too much into my personal space, the way his hand seemed to reach automatically toward my own and then drop awkwardly back into place at his side.

"What did he want?" I asked, remembering we were supposed to be having a conversation.

"Who? Oh. Chief Kingsland? I— One of your neighbors reported seeing someone lurking outside the gates last night. He was just giving me a heads-up."

It was a plausible story. But Seamus's voice was too casual, his gaze too direct. Tiny cues that he was not telling the truth. Or at least not telling the complete truth. But so long as Kingsland had not come out to reinterview Auntie H., I didn't care. I much preferred prowlers in the night to a possible reopening of the investigation into Ogden's death.

"Our neighbors? Which neighbors? You mean the RCU?"

Seamus looked blank. "The what?"

"The church that bought the property to the north of here. They've set up camp in the old schoolhouse."

"Um, no. The residents to the south. The Chamberlains. They were coming back late last night from visiting their grandkids and thought they spotted a suspicious-looking character."

"I see."

Again, he trotted it out smoothly. It could have even been true. It would be like Kingsland to give the gardener a heads-up rather than worry Aunt H. with vague warnings about suspicious characters loitering. That didn't change my initial impression Seamus wished I hadn't spotted Chief Kingsland. Why?

Or maybe I was getting paranoid?

Aunt H.'s semi-confession earlier had shaken me.

"We'll keep an eye out," I said and turned away.

Seamus said quickly, almost urgently, "Artemus?"

I turned back.

"Would you want to—" He cleared his throat. "Get together? One night? Maybe have dinner? Or even just drinks. Whatever." He looked surprisingly serious. Even earnest.

My face warmed. My whole body warmed. My heart got all light and fluttery, like a bird belatedly noticing it was sitting on a tree branch with a cat.

I did want to. That was the problem. I wanted to a lot. I liked him. I found him attractive. Too attractive for comfort, frankly. Even if I hadn't been suspicious of him, that was a distraction I didn't need right now. Especially since I should surely feel a little more broken up about the way things had ended with Greg.

I opened my mouth to regretfully decline and was astonished to hear my own equally awkward, "Er, yeah. Maybe. Sure. Why not?"

His eyes lit. "Great! Tonight?"

What am I doing?

"Oh no. No, I can't tonight," I lied—and not very well.

He looked disappointed. Doubtful. "Okay. Well… tomorrow night?"

"Yes. Tomorrow night," my mouth said despite explicit directions from my brain to say otherwise. "I'd like to."

"Great!" Seamus repeated, cheering instantly. "Okay, then. Let's say seven?"

"Seven," I agreed, and I couldn't help smiling back at him.

* * * * *

"Artie, dear, I've been thinking," Aunt H. began over dinner that night. "Maybe it's time you returned to New York."

Liana was still sick in bed, so we were on our own, for once putting the dining room to the use God—or Green Lanterns' architect, anyway—had originally intended.

Betty fried veal cutlets, which she served with herb salad and mushroom rice. Whatever else had gone wrong at Green Lanterns, our Betty was still the best cook in the county. In a spirit of defiance, I raided Ogden's sadly neglected wine cellar and chose a bottle of white to go with our meal. I was drinking on my own, though. Aunt H. was not a wine drinker. She either drank sparkling water or cocktails—and that night she was sticking to water.

I put my wineglass down untouched. "Return to New York? With everything that's happening around here?"

"Yes, dear. I see now that I was wrong to drag you into my problems. You have your own life, and you must be anxious to get back to it."

"Sure, but you and Green Lanterns are also part of my life. And always will be."

Aunt H. avoided my gaze. "Yes, but… I'm sure your editor is wondering when you'll be back to work."

"Actually, if I showed up before my vacation was over, my editor would suspect I was an imposter."

Aunt H. did not so much as crack a smile. "All the same, dear. I feel you should book your return flight."

"Why?"

"I've just said—"

"No, the real reason," I cut in. "Why are you suddenly in a hurry to get rid of me?"

She raised her brows. "Really, Artie. *Get rid of you?*" She rarely resorted to the Grand Dame, but when she did, she did it well. Her tone—light and ironic—was perfect. As was her expression.

"Come on, Auntie H. What's changed?" As I studied her troubled face, realization dawned. I remembered Roma's oblique warning. "Are you worried about *me?*"

She didn't speak, but I saw at once I was right. I said, "Even if Ogden *is* haunting Green Lanterns, I'm not afraid of ghosts."

"But perhaps you should be," she burst out.

"What does that mean?"

"After you went out this afternoon, Liana did another reading of her tarot cards."

I snorted.

She ignored that. "Liana believes there's danger for you here. That if you stay, something…terrible might happen. I know you don't believe in any of this, but she wasn't play-acting. She was frightened."

I didn't laugh. For one thing, I could see Aunt H. was truly worried. For another, this warning coming so soon on top of Roma's did make me uneasy.

"What kind of danger?" I asked.

"I don't know. But I've been thinking. Ogden had his good qualities, but when he didn't get his way, when he felt thwarted, he could be difficult. Very difficult."

I thought there was a lot of painful history behind that rather terse comment.

"Okay, but—"

"I think his parents spoiled him terribly. As did his first wife. And Liana always catered to him. He isn't—wasn't— used to being told no. He didn't take well to what he would call obstruction. And if there is an afterlife, why would we be any different in character there than we were in this life?"

That was an interesting perspective. One I'd never considered. If there was such a thing as ghosts, did these shades retain their fundamental human traits? Or were they just shadows? Echoes of the past? Did spirits have free will, or were they simply running on autoplay?

"I see," I said. "And you think Ogden might feel thwarted by my attempts to keep him from ruining the rest of your life?"

She put her hand to her forehead. "You have such a-a way of putting things, dear."

"Okay, in your own words, then."

"I think Liana is right. At least, I think she's right that Ogden might resent your lack of...sympathy. I don't know what reprisals he could make—I don't understand how these things work." Unexpectedly, tears welled in her eyes. "But I'm not willing to risk *you*, my dearest boy."

I got a little choked up myself, and rose, going around the table to hug her.

"Look, me old darling." I had to stop and clear my throat. "I appreciate your concern. And I'm willing to concede I don't know how these things work either. But I'm not leaving you here to spend your days with Liana and her tarot cards and your nights with Roma and her séances. Something is not right in this house. And maybe it *is* Ogden acting out at finding himself inconveniently dead. But maybe it's something else."

"Oh, Artie. I thought so once. But what else could it be?"

"I know you're convinced otherwise, but I still believe the source of your problems is—could be—human." She opened her mouth, but I cut her off. "I know you think it's a stretch, but it's worth making sure, don't you think?"

Aunt H. hesitated, nodded reluctantly, and wiped her eyes.

I didn't sleep well that night.

Every time a floorboard squeaked or a panel popped or a gust of night breeze whispered down the fireplace, my eyes flew open and I spent the next few seconds listening intently to a silence that felt increasingly ominous.

But I must have finally drifted off, because around two o'clock I woke to the sound of footsteps overhead.

I blinked upward at the shadowy ceiling.

Were those footsteps, or was that a squirrel or a raccoon scampering around? For a moment I lay there, ears attuned. I was starting to think I'd been dreaming when I heard a muffled *thump*, as if something heavy had fallen over.

No, I was not dreaming, not imagining things. Someone was moving overhead.

A burglar?

Wouldn't a burglar be more likely to grab a microwave or TV set from downstairs and make his getaway?

Previously, the "ghost" had stuck to walking this floor. What was it up to on the third floor? I couldn't think of anything that would be of interest to a ghost, let alone a professional criminal. There were more bedrooms, of course, but no one slept up there. There was the ballroom, which had not been used since the fifties.

The attic was on the fourth floor, so that couldn't be the target.

Did the footsteps belong to Tarrant? At this point I could almost believe it. Given his open discontent, I could imagine him wandering around, pocketing a few stray collectibles and antiques to pawn.

Liana? Her behavior was erratic these days, to say the least. Could those muffled footfalls belong to Liana hunting for her dear dead brother's spirit among the mothballs and dust sheets?

Doubtful. Liana had been Nyquilized for the evening.

Aunt H.?

Even more doubtful.

There was another possibility. What if a tramp or a vagrant had taken up residence on the rarely disturbed third floor? They could live there undetected, safe and secure—and pretty comfortable, all things considered—emerging only at night to steal food, which would likely go unmissed, from the overstocked pantry and refrigerator.

By now two or three minutes had passed, and I could still hear that mysterious someone moving furtively overhead.

I threw the sheet back, grabbed my robe, shoved my feet into slippers, and let myself out of my room.

I stepped quietly down the hall and tiptoed up the stairs to the next level.

When I reached the third floor, all was silent. Had I missed my opportunity? I moved soundlessly down the hall until I came to the double doors of the ballroom.

I leaned my head against the wooden surface and listened. Nothing.

I reached down and noiselessly turned the knob.

The doors did not budge.

Hell. Was the room locked? That possibility hadn't occurred to me. As far as I could remember, the only locked doors at Green Lanterns had been Ogden's study.

I tried again, this time leaning my weight against the door. The wood creaked, but the hinges seemed remarkably silent as the doors slowly opened inward to a black void. I reached back to feel for the nearest hinge, and my fingertips brushed something slippery. I sniffed my hand. Household oil. My suspicions were confirmed. Someone had gone to the trouble of silencing the doors up here.

Using my smartphone's flashlight app, I stepped across the ballroom threshold.

The brilliant white beam bounced down a dusty vista of parquet flooring and dull, gilt-framed mirrors to a raised platform at the far end. Black plush chairs and small oak tables lined either wall, and above, suspended from the ceiling at intervals, hung three enormous amber chandeliers. Everything was festooned with cobwebs; the chairs and draperies, the chandeliers woven to one another in shrouds of gauze, intricate, hairy, shimmering in the phone's light beam.

It was both grand and creepy.

I advanced farther into the room. There was no sign that anyone had been there for years. The dust-blanketed floor stretched ahead like smooth, untrodden sand. Halfway down the long room, I spotted a brown, crumbling corsage resting on the seat of one of the chairs.

I turned and started back, my shadowy image reflected multiple times in the wall of grimy mirrors.

Once in the corridor, I listened again.

A complete and solemn silence met my ears.

Not so much as the rustle of a dust sheet.

The ballroom took up most of the floor, but there were a few additional bedrooms on this level. Murky, musty small rooms in various states of disuse. I had the vague idea these extra rooms had been used for household staff back when Green Lanterns ran a full stable of servants.

I took each room in turn, working my way down the main hall to the end and starting up the smaller corridor. The dust was not as thick in the bedrooms. The floors had been swept once or twice in the last year, so I couldn't say for sure no one had been through there. I didn't find any sign of actual occupancy: no crumbs, ashes, cigarette stubs, or discarded candy wrappers; no mussed bedclothes or disarranged pillows—no bedclothes or pillows at all. Some of the drawers were not flush to their dressers, and in a couple of cases, they even lay on the unmade mattresses. Maybe that meant something. Maybe it didn't. There could be any number of non-sinister reasons why empty drawers had been moved aside.

I was almost ready to believe I'd dreamed up those stealthy sounds, when I came to the final room on that floor. As I reached for the door handle, I heard a slight sound that raised the hair on my head.

No mistake. Someone was inside that room.

I put my ear to the door, and yes, I could hear the cautious slide of wood on wood.

Cabinets being opened, drawers being shut.

The sounds stopped. I heard the pad of footsteps. Then the scrape of wood on wood resumed.

Someone was searching for something—and I knew with sudden certainty who that someone was.

I yanked open the door and shone my phone flashlight in the direction of those secretive sounds. The blast of white light fell full upon the startled face of Seamus Cassidy.

CHAPTER FIFTEEN

"That's what I thought!" I said.

Seamus's face was a study in shock: mouth agape, eyes squinting as he winced in the glare of my phone's flashlight. But his recovery was quick. I had to give him that.

"You're up late," he said casually. "Can't sleep?"

"With you dropping armoires and chaise lounges overhead every few minutes? No."

He put his hand up to block the blinding beam. "Do you mind?"

"Do I mind that you're searching my aunt's home in the middle of the night? Yes. I rather do." But I removed the light from his eyes.

Seamus put his hand down and offered, "There's an explanation."

"I'd love to hear it." It occurred to me that we were both speaking softly. I could understand why Seamus would want to keep our encounter quiet, but why was I half whispering?

Seamus said, "You probably won't believe me, but I saw a light moving around up here and thought I'd come up to investigate."

I scowled. "You're right. I don't believe you. Try again."

"Well, what do *you* think I'm doing at two o'clock in the morning?" His tone was perfectly reasonable.

"I think you're systematically searching for something," I said.

He managed a grin. "The family jewels maybe? I wouldn't be looking in a dusty closet."

Was he seriously going to try and flirt his way out of this?

"I'll tell you what else I think. I think you're no more a gardener than I'm Noel Coward."

He stopped grinning. "Noel Coward, huh?" He was clearly giving himself time to think. "I'm not a thief. If you want to search me—" He linked his hands behind his head, mimicking someone in police custody, which only served to convince me I was on the right track.

"I don't think you're a thief," I said. "I think you're a cop."

That surprised him. Nonplussed him, in fact.

"A cop." He quit clowning around, studying me with narrowed eyes. "That's an interesting theory."

"And more interestingly, you don't deny it."

"Would you believe—"

"Nope."

Seamus grimaced. "Then I won't waste my time."

"Good." I held out my hand. "I assume you have some identification?"

That earned a rueful half-grin. "You're not very trusting, Artemus."

"No. I'm not. I've learned the hard way not to take things at face value."

Seamus muttered something, reached for his hip pocket, pulled out a square of leather, and handed it to me. "The married boyfriend," he commented.

It was my turn to be startled, which I tried to cover by opening his identification holder and studying its contents. I couldn't help saying, "You've done your homework."

"That's what they pay me for." He sounded less lighthearted.

The picture ID and blue-and-gold NYPD badge registered on my consciousness.

Sergeant Seamus A. Cassidy, Grand Larceny Division.

"NYPD. You're a long way from home," I said. I was thinking, *grand larceny*? "What are you supposed to be doing in our garden? Looking for counterfeit cabbage?"

"Ha. I'm working in liaison with SFPD's Financial Crimes Unit."

"Investigating what? Who? Er, whom?" Seamus hesitated, and I said in alarm, "*Aunt H.?*"

"*Shh.*" He took my arm. "We can't talk here."

I freed myself. "We can talk here as well as anywhere else. No more lies. Why are you at Green Lanterns? What are you looking for?"

Seamus looked pained. "Artemus—"

I wasn't having any of it. "Talk. Or go pack your bags."

Seamus studied my face, then groaned softly. "All right. But…keep your voice down."

"That's going to depend on future events. If you're after my dear old auntie, you're done here, Cassidy."

He made another of those pained sounds. "It's not… You're making this very difficult."

"I may soon make it impossible. What is it you think Aunt Halcyone has done?"

"Aside from knocking off her ne'er-do-well husband?" He said it almost lightly.

The lightness was both cue and clue. "You're not a homicide detective."

"True."

"What are you up to?"

His gaze searched mine, and whatever he read there caused him to capitulate. "I believe your aunt knows the whereabouts of the three million dollars your uncle Ogden embezzled when he fled New York six years ago."

"Three…million…"

"You heard me."

I sat down on the edge of the mattress and stared up at Seamus.

His face was stern and unfamiliar as he met my stunned gaze. No sign now of the easy-going, not terribly efficient, but definitely charming Master Gardener. This man was on a mission, and woe to whoever got in his way.

"Embezzled from whom? From where?" I asked finally.

"From his own company. Blue Moon Books."

My initial reaction was simple surprise. "Ogden ran a *successful* publishing company?"

"For a time. He was publishing soft-core porn and did very well financially until he branched out into filmmaking."

"*P-P-Porn* films?"

"Correct. He had a couple of big hits, but that was followed by a string of flops."

"Ogden was *producing* porn films?"

"Writing, directing, and producing, yes. Six years ago, Blue Moon Books was on the verge of financial collapse due to his pending divorce settlement, the poor box-office performance of his final film, *Hot Wet Mutant*—"

"Hot Wet *what*?"

"—and a lawsuit which halted the release of *Pink and Naked*. Foxworth embezzled over three million dollars from the Blue Moon bank accounts and vanished."

This was a lot to absorb. I latched on to the one thing that stood out. "Foxworth? And this Foxworth is supposed to be Ogden?"

"Oscar Foxworth is Ogden Hyde. Was. I was on his trail a long time. Despite the extensive plastic surgery, there's no doubt in my mind."

Porn films? Plastic surgery? Police investigations? What next? Where the hell to begin?

I said, "If you think Aunt H. was involved in any of that, you're nuts."

"I don't believe she was initially involved, no. There's no evidence to prove Foxworth knew your aunt before Ogden Hyde turned up in Russian Bay. But your aunt is a smart woman. Too smart not to have figured things out. Maybe she didn't kill Foxworth for that money, but I'm betting she has a pretty good idea where he stashed it."

Great. Maybe not a murderess. Just accessory after the fact. He believed it too! I said clearly, carefully, "You're out of your tiny little mind, Cassidy."

He shrugged. "Naturally, you're going to feel that way. You're probably not aware that keeping Foxworth in the style to which he was accustomed ate up a large part of your aunt's fortune. She's not broke, but she's not far from it. She needed the inn to be a success, but it wasn't. She could sell this house, but she won't. That doesn't leave her a lot of options."

I stood up, pugnaciously thrusting my face in his. Disconcertingly, I could see the flicker of his dark eyelashes and feel the warmth of his breath against my mouth. "My aunt is not some femme fatale in a neo-noir pastiche. There is no possible scenario in which Aunt H. would consider murder a viable option."

He opened his mouth, and I added, "I mean, where does Liana fit into all this? She would have to know the truth. What's her story? Is she even Ogden's sister? Maybe *she* knocked him off."

I remembered the first séance when Liana had called the ghost "Oscar." I'd thought I'd misheard or that it was a slip of the tongue or too many tranquilizers. Maybe it *had* been a slip of the tongue, but it had also been the truth. *Of course* she'd known Ogden's real identity the whole time.

"We're considering all possibilities," Seamus said in an official, stolid tone that made me want to conk him over the head with the nearest marble bust.

"You didn't answer my question. Is she his sister or not?"

We tried to stare each other down. He blinked first, admitting with disarming candor, "Artemus, I could get kicked off this case for what I've already told you. I can't—"

"You've told me too much to stop there, that's for sure."

"I can't force you to cooperate with this investigation, but if you lie to me, hide evidence, or act to hinder this investigation in any way—"

I snapped, "You mean by firing your ass and throwing you off this property?"

He stopped trying to appeal to my better nature and glared. "Don't try it. I'm warning you. You'll only make it worse for your aunt."

"My aunt is innocent. I'm not worried about that. I'm worried about the fact that she's surrounded by treacherous assholes who aren't who they pretend to be, starting with *you* and possibly including Ogden, who is *clearly* not dead."

"You're wrong there," Seamus said regretfully, apparently only hearing part of my speech. "Oscar Foxworth—Ogden, if you prefer—is dead all right. We've got the body to prove it."

Well, no. They didn't. Because what remained of Ogden—which had been little enough—had been since cremated.

"Burned past recognition. Did anyone bother to actually test for DNA?"

He looked both pained and patient. "Even if we had reason to believe Foxworth faked his death, given the state of his remains, the results of DNA testing would be at best inconclusive."

"So in other words, no."

"You're not listening to me."

"He pulled a runner once before," I said.

"He didn't try to fake his death. That's not an easy thing to do, you know. For one thing, it requires getting hold of a corpse—unless you're suggesting Foxworth also committed homicide?"

"Why not? You seem to think Aunt H. is capable of it!"

Seamus chose to overlook that. "Anyway, of course we investigated that possibility. No bodies were hijacked from local morgues or mortuaries or graveyards."

"What about missing persons? Anybody MIA?"

Seamus looked torn between sympathy and exasperation. "I understand how difficult this is—and how convenient it would be to pin everything on Foxworth. But Foxworth was not a master criminal. He was not a murderer. He was an embezzler—and not a very good one. And yeah, also a terrible filmmaker. But that's still a long way away from committing murder. Homicide would be skipping a few grades for a guy who had no record of violence."

"That you know of."

"He was the subject of an ongoing investigation for six years. There isn't much about Oscar Foxworth we don't know. Other than where he hid his loot."

"What makes you think he didn't spend it?"

"The money trail. Or, more exactly, the lack of a money trail."

"The kind of plastic surgery you're talking about is expensive."

"Not *that* expensive. It looks like Foxworth used just enough of his resources to…salt the mine."

"What does that mean? Salt the mine?" I had the unpleasant feeling I knew exactly what it meant.

"Foxworth bought a fancy car, a fancy boat, and rented a fancy apartment. He joined all the right social clubs and local business organizations so that he could meet…the right people."

"A rich widow," I said bitterly.

"Yes."

I thought it over. "None of that proves he couldn't have decided to strike out for greener pastures and pulled the plug."

"Why would he?"

"You just said he bled my aunt dry. He'd need a new mark."

"It would be a lot simpler to divorce your aunt than fake his death."

True. Ogden faking his death was tremendously more complicated—and risky—than just telling Aunt H. he wanted out. Plus, faking his death meant starting over completely, starting from scratch, rather than capitalizing on the social and financial network he'd spent time and effort building.

"Maybe he knew you were closing in on him. Maybe he didn't have a choice."

Seamus shook his head. "No. There's no way he could have known that because we *weren't* closing in. We weren't even sure we'd located him until shortly after his death."

I said stubbornly, "The guilty fleeth. Maybe he was paranoid. Maybe his criminal instincts told him it was time to pull up stakes."

"No. Trust me on this. No. Foxworth had dug in for the long haul. I believe he was completely invested in this identity. Even if he did decide to run, why not just disappear? Why attempt something as dangerous and problematic as faking his death?"

"Maybe he was more desperate this time around. How many times can he successfully fake a new identity? He'd already used the plastic surgery trick. You said yourself he expected to remain Ogden Hyde for a long, long time."

Seamus was shaking his head again. "You're arguing my case for me. Anyway, again, to fake his death, Foxworth would need a body, and where would he get that body? Violence was never part of his MO."

"You know whose MO has never included *any* crime of *any* kind? My aunt's." I didn't wait for his response. "You didn't answer me about Liana. What's her rap sheet look like? Maybe she's your femme fatale."

"She doesn't have a rap sheet."

"Is she really his sister?"

He hesitated.

"She's not, is she? Jesus Christ. So then who is she? His ex? His girlfriend?"

"I'm trying to be honest with you, but you've got to give me your word you're not going to do something stupid like confront—" He broke off, both of us freezing at the unmistakable sound of footsteps fading down the hallway.

We jumped for the door together, both jockeying for position and managing to get completely in each other's way. I settled matters by jamming my elbow into Seamus's ribs. He woofed out a breath like an outraged German shepherd but gave way, and I yanked the door open and shot into the drafty hallway.

Which was as dark as a dungeon and silent as a tomb.

I felt for my phone, nearly dropping it as Seamus lurched into me. We both stumbled forward, automatically steadying each other. I turned on my phone's flashlight and shone it down the long, empty corridor.

Where the hell had the owner of those footsteps disappeared to?

"Damn," Seamus muttered. "Tarrant. I wonder how much he knows."

"*Tarrant?*"

I felt rather than saw his nod. "He prowls this place at night."

"That makes two of you. At the least."

"I haven't been inside the house until tonight."

"Sure."

"That's the truth."

"If you say so."

"I'm telling you the truth. That wasn't me the evening you thought you were chasing a ghost. I was peering through the window all right. But I hadn't been in the house yet."

I tried to read his face in the gloom. "Then how do you know it's Tarrant wandering through the halls?"

"I've watched him. I've got a perfect view of the house from my front window."

"And a trusty pair of binoculars, presumably?"

He avoided that one. "Tarrant doesn't just stick to the main house either. He's been snooping inside the garage, the pool house, the greenhouse."

I said slowly, "He's looking for something."

"It seems so."

"Maybe your missing three million. Or whatever it's down to by now."

"Maybe." He sounded noncommittal. Why? Why wasn't Tarrant as good or better a possible villain as Aunt H.?

I said, "It wasn't Tarrant I chased down the staircase. And it wasn't Tarrant I heard laughing in Ogden's study. I don't think I've ever heard so much as a titter from Tarrant."

"What laughter in Ogden's study?"

Seamus and I had covered so much territory that evening, it only then occurred to me he didn't know about the eerie chuckle that had seemed to emanate from behind the walls of Ogden's study. I filled him in, sure now I hadn't dreamed up that ghostly laughter.

"Some kind of recording device," Seamus guessed. "Triggered when you sat down at the desk. Or when the light went off."

"But who turned off the light?"

"Could it be on some kind of timer?"

I scoffed, "Talk about an elaborate scheme. You can't suspect my aunt of faking the haunting of Green Lanterns."

"No. That seems pretty unlikely."

"And what's the point of it anyway?"

He shook his head. "I don't know. Yet."

I could feel his gaze. I met it directly.

Seamus said, "A lot of these Prohibition-era houses were built with secret rooms."

"I know. That was my first thought too. Aunt H. always insisted there were no such rooms at Green Lanterns. And frankly, if there *was* a secret room or a hidden passageway, I think I'd have found it by now."

"Those rooms were built to foil full-scale police searches, let alone one pissed-off theater critic with a tape measure."

I made a face. "Fair enough. The thing is, someone hiding in a place as large as Green Lanterns wouldn't require a secret room. If he's clever—and patient—he could cover his presence, sneak food from the pantry and larder, sleep in a different room every night. It could be done."

I could see this thought had already occurred to Seamus. Instead of answering, he put his hand on my shoulder and turned me in the direction of the staircase. "We should finish this conversation later. When there's no risk of being overheard."

"You may not be here later," I said grimly.

His hand closed tight, stopping me in my tracks. "I meant what I said, Artemus. If you hinder this investigation in any way—"

"Go. To. Hell." I glared back at him. "My aunt has the right to know she's got an undercover cop on staff—not to mention the fact that said cop is conducting what I'm pretty sure are totally illegal searches."

It was impossible to tell in the weird light thrown by my flashlight, but I thought his face darkened. I know it tightened into angry sharps and planes. "I confided in you so that you could pro—"

"You confided in me because I caught you red-handed," I burst in. "So don't try to pretend you were doing me any favors."

"I *am* doing you a favor," he snapped. "And your aunt as well. If I can find that money, if most of it is still intact, we might be able to come up with a believable story for its safe return that exculpates your aunt."

I stopped glowering. "What about the rest of it? The fact that you think Aunt H. murdered Ogden or whatever the hell his real name was."

He said bleakly, "I don't know if she killed him or not. I'm not a homicide cop. That case is officially closed. Who am I to second-guess the findings? I don't have any concrete reason to request the case be reopened."

As brief as our acquaintanceship was, I knew instinctively that halfhearted attitude was not typical for Cassidy.

"Why would you do that?" I asked slowly, suspiciously.

"I just told you."

"I don't believe you. You're up to something. Again."

A flicker of some emotion crossed his face. Irritation? Offense? Surely not *hurt*?

Seamus released a long, weary breath. "Because… Because you would never forgive me otherwise."

Now *that*, I did not expect. I was too confused to find it even remotely reassuring.

"You're right. But why would you care? How do my feelings come into it? You don't even know me."

"That's where you're wrong," Seamus said. "I know pretty much everything there is to know about you."

CHAPTER SIXTEEN

"Uh, possibly you don't realize how creepy that sounds," I said after an astonished moment.

"I do realize. Which is why I had no intention of telling you yet."

Yet?

"Tell me *what*?"

Seamus said almost desperately, "Can we *please* go somewhere we can speak in private?"

If Tarrant *was* wandering around up here, I sure as hell did not want him overhearing us. I nodded. "We can talk in my room."

But Seamus shook his head. "No. There's no place in this house where I trust we won't be overheard. Let's go back to my place."

I glanced down at my blue dressing gown and pajamas. "I'm not exactly dressed for social calls."

"It doesn't matter. It's not cold tonight."

No. True enough. It was a warm summer's eve. My reluctance was more about feeling…out of uniform. There's something sort of vulnerable about traipsing around in your PJs, and I did not want to feel vulnerable around Seamus.

I did not want to feel much of anything around Seamus, now that I knew whose side he was on. Or whose side he *wasn't* on.

I shrugged. "If you like. I don't plan on staying long."

I led the way as we crept down the stairs and went out through the dining room French doors. Though the night was warm, it was moist with humidity, mist rising from the newly mown lawn and cultivated flower beds.

The windows over the garage were dark, as were the windows of the main house. Seamus and I could have been the only two people awake in the entire world. It felt a bit like that. I had the impression he was marshaling his argument for the coming confrontation. I was pretty sure the evening was going to end with me firing him and ordering him off the property. The knowledge gave me no pleasure. I had liked him. Liked him enough that I had imagined there was maybe even potential for more.

And yeah, there probably had been—though I'd never pictured myself dating a cop—but it was all moot.

Though neither of us spoke as we picked our way across the dew-glistening grass, the night was alive with the sound of crickets and other insects. The full moon, drifting languidly as a lost balloon across the black canopy of sky, illuminated the empty drive and turned the garden silver, transforming it into something vaguely magical.

I was suddenly reminded of the night of the first séance and the pale balloons I had seen skimming through the purple-edged clouds. At the time I had been too distracted to do more than register the curiousness of so many stray balloons. Now, belatedly, I began to consider their significance. I vaguely recalled hearing something on the radio about an anniversary or a memorial service of some kind. I couldn't remember the details—and maybe I'd got it wrong anyway. Maybe I was clutching at straws.

We reached the old carriage house, and Seamus led the way around the side of the building. He unlocked the door, and we stepped into the dark, diesel-scented interior. He flipped the wall switch, and the tube lights overhead buzzed into gray-green life.

Seamus started for the metal staircase, and I said, "This is fine. We can talk here."

He said, "I don't know about you, but I need a drink," and continued up the stairs, his boots ringing on the metal rungs.

I hesitated.

He glanced over his shoulder and gave me a funny smile. "Afraid to be alone with me?"

I said in acid tones, "Yes, that's it. It's your animal magnetism. I fear I can't resist your charms."

Seamus laughed. "I meant, maybe you were still thinking I was one of the bad guys."

Oh, right. I felt my face turn red and hoped the poor light would provide adequate cover. I said curtly, "You *are* one of the bad guys," and started up the stairs after him.

When we reached his living quarters, he felt his way across the dark room, pulled down the window shades one by one, and then turned on one of the table lamps.

"Make yourself comfortable."

I raised my arm to illustrate I was already about as comfortable as one could get, and Seamus said admiringly, "That is *quite* a bathrobe. What is that, brocade? I didn't know people outside of old movies actually wore things like that."

"Ha. Ha. Anyway, it's a dressing gown." And a Christmas gift from Aunt H. I didn't actually swan around in brocade dressing gowns most of the time, but I'd figured if I was ever going to wear it, Green Lanterns was the place. "So what is it you have to tell me that couldn't be said back at the house?"

"Do you want a drink?"

I resisted the urge to shout: NO, I DON'T WANT A DRINK, and sighed loudly enough to be heard in the back row. "No," I said with exaggerated patience. "I don't want a drink, thank you. I want to know what the hell ever it is you think you know about me that's going to change my intention of tossing you out of here on your ear." And then, because there's a little bit of frustrated thespian in every theater critic, I swept over to the sofa, flung myself down, and crossed my legs. If I'd only had a foot-long cigarette holder, my performance would have been perfect.

"Well, I'm having a drink," Seamus said.

"Jesus. Then pour me one as well," I said irritably.

He brought back two tumblers and the bottle. We clinked glasses briskly. "*Sláinte*," Seamus murmured.

I downed half my drink. There's something really comforting about good whisky. This was Bushmills, my own brand—not to mention the brand of a few million other people—and I said, "What do you mean you know everything there is to know about me?"

Instead of answering directly, he said, "We met once before. A few years ago."

"When?"

"You won't remember. It was opening night for *Outside Mullingar*."

I frowned. "I go to a lot of opening nights. You'll have to be more specific."

Seamus offered a rueful smile. "My timing was off. Then and now. You were in the middle of arguing with your boyfriend."

Greg and I had argued a lot, so that didn't ring any particular bells either.

I shook my head. "Sorry."

"It was at the Samuel J. Friedman Theatre. I came up and introduced myself, told you I was a big fan of your reviews and essays in the *New York Magazine*, and then your boyfriend walked up, you threw your drink in his face, and exited stage left."

"Oh, *that* opening night," I said. I still didn't remember Seamus—or much about the play, for that matter—but now I knew why. That had been the night Greg broke it to me he was still technically married.

And even *then*, it had taken me another two years to figure out that whether Greg got around to divorcing his wife or not, there was no future for us.

"Anyway." Seamus shrugged. "When your name popped up in connection with the Foxworth case—"

"And why would that have been?"

"We were trying to figure out if there was some reason Foxworth chose Russian Bay of all places in the world to resurface as Ogden Hyde. You seemed to be his only remaining tie to New York. Or the theater world."

I opened my mouth, and Seamus said quickly, "It didn't take us long to see that the connection was purely coincidental."

His smile was apologetic. "It's no secret around town that you detested Hyde."

Huh. I thought I'd hid my feelings better than that. Apparently not.

"I see." That was overstating it a bit, but a picture was beginning to form.

Seamus said, "While we were assessing your potential involvement, I had to sort of…study you." He grimaced. "Which hopefully doesn't sound as stalkerish to you as it does to me putting it into words. Honest to God, it wasn't like that. It was my job to learn everything I could about you, and I'm good at my job. That's all."

I couldn't think of anything to say. The more he protested it was just his job and he hadn't been particularly interested in me personally, the redder and more self-conscious he got. Which, weirdly enough, was unexpectedly and disconcertingly flattering. He was so *pained* by the situation, it defused a lot of the voyeuristic element.

I raised my brows skeptically—mostly because I still couldn't think of a good response—and Seamus got still more uncomfortable-looking and burst out, "I mean, I did of course still find you attractive. But I wouldn't have dug into your background if my agenda hadn't been professional. I'm not a creep."

"Okay," I said mildly, because I did believe him about that part. "But assuming that's all true, I still don't see why you'd let Aunt H. slip through the dragnet simply because of me."

Seamus let out a long breath, like someone about to jump into a very cold lake. "It's not only because of you," he said, "although I admit I want you to like me and think favorably of me. My sister was in an abusive relationship. She's a smart, independent, beautiful woman, but it took a broken nose, blacked eyes, and three cracked ribs before she was able to call it quits. And then it took me calling in favors to get her the support she needed and protection from that asshole."

"I didn't— I'm sorry."

He nodded tightly. "I know firsthand that the system can fail victims."

"You think Ogden—Oscar—was abusive toward Aunt H.?" I shook my head. "He wouldn't dare."

Seamus looked sympathetic. *Sympathetic?*

I said, "I don't believe she wouldn't tell me. She would know she could come to me for help."

"There are all kinds of abuse," Seamus said. "But either way…victims *don't* always come forward, don't ask for help. For different reasons. The point is, I'm sympathetic to your aunt's situation. It's not my case. It's not my business. Okay? All I want is to close *my* case. I want to recover as much of the embezzled funds as I can—that's my job—and figure out whether—"

"What about Liana?" I interrupted. "Is she an accessory or what? If she's not Ogden's sister, who the hell is she?"

"Her real name—well, her real stage name—is Lacey Labanca."

I chose to overlook the real-stage-name conundrum. "Labanca? Seriously?"

"Yes. She starred in most of Foxworth's films. From everything I've been able to discover, they had just gotten involved when the bottom dropped out of Foxworth's finances. When he disappeared, she went with him."

"True love." My tone was acerbic.

Seamus shrugged. "Maybe. Or maybe it was the three million."

"Is she for sure an accessory?"

"No. We don't know exactly what she knew or didn't know when she threw in with Foxworth. It's possible she was crazy in love."

"She'd have to be crazy to agree to pose as his sister for years." I considered what had to have been going on behind Aunt H.'s back all the while she was married to Ogden. "Jesus." I drained my glass and set it on the table. "I'll have another, if you don't mind."

He took the glass, splashed another ounce or two over the ice, and handed it back. Our fingers brushed, and it was sort of comforting.

He said, "I know what you're thinking. You've got to promise not to confront Liana. Promise not to do anything that might interrupt or interfere with my investigation. I'm very close to breaking this thing wide open, but if you tip off Liana, you're going to fuck this up for everyone, including your aunt."

I sipped the whisky and brooded. For years—*years*— Ogden and Liana had carried on together under Aunt H.'s roof while Ogden bled my aunt dry. And after Ogden had— not a minute too soon—driven off the cliff road, Aunt H. had continued to provide a home and shelter for that treacherous bitch Liana. I wasn't sure I could contain my desire to throttle Liana—seeing that I'd wanted to throttle her *before* I knew the truth about her relationship with Ogden.

"Artemus," Seamus said quietly.

I glanced at him and scowled. "I understand. You realize that Liana is probably behind this whole fake haunting of Green Lanterns?"

"Yes. I have a theory she's working with Tarrant."

"Liana and Tarrant? Would this be a strictly business arrangement, or would she be Labonking the butler as well?"

Seamus had been in the process of taking a sip of his whisky. He choked, wiped the back of his hand across his mouth, and said, "I haven't yet determined that."

"I see. And you're sure Liana a.k.a. Lacey doesn't have a criminal record?"

"Yes. I'm sure. Unless you count her filmography."

I grunted. "I'll try not to clue Liana in. Personally, I think the ill-gotten gains will be long gone by now. Ogden always spent money like water."

"I hope not because that would complicate things. I'm relying on the recovery of the money to wrap up this case with the minimum of attention."

"What if you can't come up with the loot?"

His expression was not encouraging. "We'll cross that bridge when we come to it."

"Yeah. Great." Any way this played out, Aunt H. was going to be devastated. And I'd been thinking her being suspected of knocking off her husband was as bad as it could get.

I finished my drink, put the glass down. I was very tired. Very worried. And I didn't imagine that was going to change anytime soon. How much simpler life had seemed twelve hours earlier when I'd agreed—okay, maybe against my better judgment—to a date with Seamus.

A date? Dating was something that had happened in another lifetime. A safe, civilized lifetime where Ogden's greatest sin had been fooling around with Aunt H.'s gal pals. Where all I'd suspected Liana of was being a kook. Where it would never have crossed my mind Aunt H. could have been desperate enough to tamper with the steering column of Ogden's BMW.

I put my hands on my thighs, preparatory to pushing off the sofa.

Seamus said gruffly, "Wait."

I looked my inquiry.

He offered an uncharacteristically nervous smile. "It's just… You don't have to go."

Obviously, I didn't *have* to go. He wasn't throwing me out. But why wouldn't I go? What was left to say?

I must have shown my confusion because Seamus said quickly, "What I mean is, why don't you stay?"

"Why…"

He said with greater confidence, "Why don't you stay, Artemus? Please. I want you to stay."

CHAPTER SEVENTEEN

Actually, what he gulped out was, "I want you."

It sounded so unpracticed, so heartfelt. And unlikely or not, I seconded that sentiment. Passionately. Maybe it was the whisky. Maybe it was nervous tension. Maybe it was sexual tension. I'd been aware of and attracted to Seamus since I'd first spotted him gilded in sunlight and standing on a clump of begonias.

Maybe it was the fact that I hadn't had sex with anybody since Greg and I split up.

Whatever it was—and maybe it was a combination of all of the above—somehow this moment became right guy at the right time and the right place.

Without another word I opened my arms to him. And when Seamus's arms locked around me, pulling me close, it just felt right. In fact, it felt like relief. Like I had been swimming upstream for hours and I'd finally managed that last, monumental leap of faith.

He kissed me, whispered, "I've been thinking about this for so long," kissed me again, and stopped talking. It was with that second kiss that I started to pay attention.

As Seamus's warm, hungry mouth moved against my own, I realized for maybe the first time in my life that kissing was more than two sets of lips pressing against each other. A lot more. Seamus tasted of whisky, but he also tasted pleasantly…human. Like clover honey and bare skin and sun-dried cotton. Real. Alive. Immediate. Greg's kisses had been sophisticated and cinematic; the prelude to seduction. Seamus kissed like kissing was the *point*. He kissed me like someone yearning for connection, like someone who cared—and frankly, like someone confident in his kissing. A confidence that was well placed, as it turned out.

I liked the taste of him. I liked his warmth. I liked the feel of his smile against my mouth and the tiny kisses he interspersed between the long, breathless, moist stretches of osculation.

When Seamus lifted his head to gasp, "Would you want to—?" I gasped back—with maybe a hint of exasperation, "Well, *yes*. Of course."

His laugh cracked, and he pressed his mouth to mine again as if he couldn't get enough of kissing me—which I understood because I felt the same way. Like I had made some amazing scientific discovery and needed to keep verifying my test results.

Positive.

Still positive.

Positively positive.

By then I was out of the dressing gown, my pajama shirt… and was trying unsuccessfully to get my slippered foot through the cuff of my pajama pant leg—lust has a way of fogging the brain. Finally I gave my foot an impatient flip, and the slipper went flying only to hit the lamp, which crashed off the table, smashed on the floor, and went out.

"Oh *hell*," I said into the sudden blackout.

Seamus laughed. I liked the sound of that in the darkness. Soft, intimate, a little unsteady. Uncannily familiar. Not familiar in that we'd spent lots of nights like this. Familiar in my feeling I'd been *waiting* forever for a night like this.

"I like the way you move," he joked, lowering himself on top of me, and my hands fastened on his wide shoulders, appreciating the easy flex of muscle, the feel of his warm, smooth skin. Naked skin. He had been more efficient in scrambling out of his clothes. I slid my hands down his ribs, flanks, finding the hard, taut globes of his ass.

His chest hair tickled my nipples, and the beam of moonlight through a crack in the draperies silvered the line of his nose and the gleam of his teeth.

"I like you too," I said. It was true. I don't deny it went through my mind that having sex with Seamus was a good way of keeping him on my side, the side that was willing to do pretty much anything to protect Aunt Halcyone, but that wasn't why I was giving in to this. I wanted Seamus for his own self. And for my own self.

I took his unresisting hand, guiding it to the opening of my pajama bottoms, and Seamus needed no further invitation. His hand slipped through the slit of now slightly damp cotton and found me waiting. Hard.

Aching.

I wanted nothing as much in that moment as I wanted to feel Seamus's hand wrap around my cock. What he did was reach lower, find my balls, strong fingers closing around the twin sacs, caressing.

"God, you feel wonderful," he whispered, and squeezed gently.

The night changed color.

I let out a shuddering sigh, raising my hips instinctively. "Please…"

Seamus exhaled a long, wavering, "Why don't we try it this way," and we shifted gingerly, awkwardly against the cushions so that I could settle against him, half cradled between his legs, his cock bumping against my buttocks. Not graceful, not even comfortable really, but the right angle, and that was all that mattered.

His fingers wrapped around my shaft, a good solid grip that stopped short of a stranglehold, and I pushed up into his hold.

The darkness and unfamiliar surroundings made it easy, unreal, dreamlike. I found my rhythm, moaning softly as I tensed and thrust into that beautiful, steady slide of pressure and friction.

"Good, so good," I panted, pushing harder, faster…

"That's it. You're beautiful. So beautiful," Seamus urged me on.

"Oh God…oh God…" I let my head fall back against his shoulder. "Jesus, Mary, Joseph… Don't let this be a dream…"

Seamus's thumb feathered across the leaking tip of my cock, stroked the exquisitely sensitive underside of my foreskin until I saw lights sparking behind my eyelids and I began to come in hot, wet waves, spilling over Seamus's willing, waiting hand.

The fine, fierce relief of it, that release of tension like no other. Laughter bubbled in my throat even as tears stung my eyes. And he'd done it with just his *hand*. What the hell would it be like with lips and tongue and cock?

It really *was* better when you liked your partner.

Seamus's heart pounded against my shoulder blades. His cock was like a stalagmite prodding my backside. I was out of the habit of caring, but I cared about this. I cared that Seamus not regret tonight, that he got to experience not just the physical pleasure, but that sense of lift and near-liberation that was now sweeping me along.

I pulled out of his arms, turning on wobbly knees so that I could kiss him. His lips parted, and I slipped my tongue inside, flicking against his. I wrapped my hand around the rigid, painful pole of his cock, and his breath hitched.

I kissed him deeply, thrusting my tongue softly, enticingly as I tugged and stroked him, and Seamus made a helpless sound and began to thrust into my grip. Just a few hard shoves and he was coming too, coming in splashes of silver. Moonstruck, all right. Both of us.

He fell back at last, pulling me with him, and we lay in a surprisingly comfortable sprawl of legs and arms.

There were probably a dozen reasons we shouldn't have done it, but I couldn't think of a single one.

Seamus kissed the top of my head, settled, and began to breathe in the quiet, easy rhythm of sleep.

The pulled shades knocked against the windowsills like ghostly hands. The summer breeze sent the drapes gusting out, spectral-like, before flattening back against the walls.

It was not yet dawn when I left Seamus sleeping and started back toward the main house.

The air was damp, chill, with a thin, vaporish mist rising from the wet grass. Under the inconstant light of the half-shrouded moon, the untamed rose branches spiked upward from the shadows like grim, clawed tentacles.

I was thinking it would be better to sneak around to the back and go through the kitchen rather than head straight for the front door. It was too soon for Betty to be up, and even Tarrant had to sleep sometimes.

I was only a few yards from the kitchen entrance when I caught the glimmer of something pale out of the corner of my eye. I turned in time to see a filmy, white figure gliding slowly down the stone steps leading to the wilderness of the rose garden.

My heart stood still.

In fairness, with everything that had been going on at Green Lanterns, it was maybe natural that I might, just for a split second, believe I was witnessing something supernatural.

The words took form in my mind.

The ghost walks…

Except Green Lanterns was supposedly haunted by Ogden, and the figure that froze me in my tracks was definitely female. A woman in a flowing white gown.

The pale form descended down the steps and disappeared from sight.

Liana.

It had to be Liana. For one thing, no one else at Green Lanterns owned that kind of frivolous nightwear. Aunt H. had been wearing silk men's-style pajamas as long as I'd known her, and Betty? My vague recollection was Betty's nightwear was straight out of the *Dr. Quinn, Medicine Woman* collection.

All at once everything fell into place. Liana was on her way to meet Ogden, who was most certainly *not* dead, whatever Seamus thought. They had been in it together from the first. This entire "haunting" was nothing but a scheme to defraud Aunt H. of whatever remained of her money. As well as her sanity.

Without further hesitation, I turned to follow Liana into the rose garden.

Though she didn't have much of a head start, it still took me a couple of minutes to locate her in the riot of dead brambles, overgrown roses, and tall stone urns. I heard her crashing around and moaning before I saw her; clearly, she didn't think she was being followed.

As Liana's whimpers grew louder, I slowed my steps. I thought I saw the shimmer of her nightdress a few yards ahead, but I lost sight of it again in a pocket of mist that came down as effectively as a curtain.

When I came out on the other side, there was no sign of Liana.

Not only had I lost sight of her, I could no longer hear her.

I swore softly and stood motionless, listening to the croaking of the frogs that now ruled the stagnant fish ponds. My eyes strained the tumbling, twirling mist.

Where the hell had she gone? *Had* she finally noticed me trailing her?

There.

What was that? The snap of twigs? A pebble skittering across the walk? Something—someone—was moving slowly along the path.

To my relief, I spotted Liana still weaving and wavering as she made her way toward…a light. Yes, a blurry circle of illumination shone through the branches several yards ahead. What was that? The beam of a flashlight? Was Ogden coming to meet her? I stared, stared…

It seemed large for a flashlight beam.

My mouth was suddenly dry, my heart thudding in my ears as I tried to decide what to do if it was indeed Ogden. Should I confront him or follow him? Definitely, I should try to film them with my phone. And if I could record their conversation, all the better.

But as I watched, the light seemed to shrink, retreating into the trees, moving farther from the house—and Liana.

A strange feeling came over me.

That flitting, nebulous glow was not a flashlight beam. I had seen that weird light before. It was the same uncanny, fuzzy iridescence I'd witnessed at the first séance. Hell, I'd chased that light down the stairs only a few nights ago.

I watched Liana's shadowy figure stumbling along, arm outstretched.

Had I got it wrong? Was Liana pursuing the light?

I started forward, feeling the chill of the damp stone beneath my slippers. Previously I'd been angry and self-righteous, determined to catch Liana and Ogden red-handed, but now I felt…afraid.

I wasn't sure why, but my sense that something ominous was about to happen grew steadily as I made my way across the slippery, uncertain terrain.

When I reached the end of the garden, there was no sign of the spectral light—or Liana.

I listened.

In the distance I could hear a car engine, and farther away a dog barking. Nothing else.

Where had she gone? Assuming she had not collapsed and was lying unconscious in the grass, there were only two possibilities. She could cross the long, empty meadow to the

Carter School House—the property now owned by Rational Christians United—or she could go down into the maze.

I really hoped Liana was making for the old schoolhouse. But the meadow, though full of mist and shadows, was not so misty or shadowy that I could have mistaken Liana wafting across the grass and wild flowers in her flowing nightie for a tumbleweed or fence post.

That left the maze.

No one in their right mind would venture down into the maze at this time of night, but there was no guarantee Liana was in her right mind.

I turned and retraced my steps until I reached a place where I could safely climb down the rank, weedy slope.

Even as a kid, the maze held zero charm for me. Sure, it was mysterious and secret—largely forgotten—or at least ignored—by the adults in my life. It was also dark, damp, and damned eerie. As much as I'd enjoyed exploring Green Lanterns, the maze had not been one of the places I'd hung out.

I half ran, half slid the last few feet, landing safely, if muddied, at the bottom of the slope. I listened for a moment, my eyes probing the flickering shadows and trailing mist.

Even with half the trails swallowed by hedges and strangled by tree roots, I had a bewildering choice of possible pathways. I knew from unhappy experience some of those avenues wound in circles, some zigzagged in diamond patterns, and others looped endlessly around themselves. Aside from scaling the hillside, there were only two ways out: one path led back to the rose garden above, one led to the old swimming pool.

If I hadn't been uneasy before, the memory of the swimming pool took care of that. Aunt H. had mentioned the pool being drained earlier in the summer because of cracks in the plaster. As far as I knew, it hadn't been repaired, refilled—or properly fenced off.

Not good. An empty swimming pool with a concrete floor? Not good at all.

The more I considered the possibility of Liana blindly racing around in the dark, chasing the bouncing ephemeral ball, the more alarmed I became.

Because as much as I did not trust Liana, as much as I wanted to believe she was playing along with some scheme of Ogden's, her grief seemed genuine. Granted, she was an actress, but if she was faking her despair, she was one of the best actresses I'd ever seen—and I'd seen plenty of great performances by now.

I started in the general direction of the pool, pushing my way through what felt like a long, endless tunnel of cobwebs and vines and dead branches. Sharp, twiggy stems snatched at my robe and scratched my face and hands. At this rate, I'd be lucky not to end the night with an eye poked out.

I crossed an overgrown path, shoved my way through another thicket, and felt the scrape of stone beneath my soaked slippers. I turned my phone flashlight downward. There, beneath the dead leaves and dirt, was the path to the swimming pool.

At least I was headed in the right direction.

I followed the uneven walk for a few more yards, and then, as suddenly as the curtain rising on a performance, the mist cleared and I reached an iron gate in the middle of a wall of relatively tidy hedge. The gate was open, hinges creaking mournfully in the morning breeze. I went through and found myself on the long grassy lawn separating the maze entrance from the swimming pool.

By then it was dawn, and in the red-gray light, I could make out a faraway figure in white walking along the edge of the pool.

What the hell was she doing? Where did she think she was going?

I kicked off my slippers, shrugged out of my dressing gown, and took off running across the grass. My heart was in my throat, my stomach in knots. Every moment I expected to see Liana tumble off the coping and plunge the thirteen feet to the bottom of the cement floor.

"Liana!" I shouted.

The white figure never turned, never hesitated. She continued her wobbling progress down the length of the pool—moving toward the ladder of the high diving board.

This can't be happening. Except it was. I saved my breath for the last sprint across the cement deck.

She was halfway up the ladder when I reached her. I sprang up the rungs and grabbed her ankle. A little too enthusiastically as it turned out because she nearly toppled off.

Clutching the railings, she shrieked, "*Whaa—?!* What's happening? Let me go! What are you doing?"

"What are *you* doing?" I shouted back. "Are you out of your mind?"

Liana stopped kicking at me and cried in a feeble voice, "*Artie?*"

"Yes, it's Artie. What the hell are you doing up there?"

She didn't answer, bending over the ladder. Her shoulders shook. She began to sob in harsh gulps.

"Liana?"

No reply. Only those terrible, tearing sobs.

"Liana, get down here, or I'll pull you down," I warned. I still had her ankle in a death grip, and I wasn't kidding. I'd cheerfully help her break an arm or a leg before I'd watch her kill herself.

She wailed, "Why did you have to come? Why couldn't you leave me alone?"

"Why couldn't I…"

"*I want to be with Ogden!*"

"You're not going to be with Ogden!"

She screamed and gave a ferocious kick at my head with her free leg.

I couldn't block her and still hang on to her, so the kick connected. For a split second I saw stars, and she was free— and using that freedom to scramble up another rung.

I shook the stars out of my eyes and lunged after her, grabbing a fistful of her filmy nightdress and yanking her back. The nightgown ripped. Liana screeched, lost her hold, and came tumbling off the ladder. We both landed on the cement deck.

It hurt, no question, and it hurt Liana more than me because her screams changed noticeably in tone and tenor.

"*My arm!*" she cried, writhing around on the deck. In the pallid light she looked like an agonized cloud. "You broke my arm!"

"It's better than you breaking your neck." I bent over her. "Here, let me see."

"Don't touch me! You bastard, Artie. You had no right to stop me. Ogden *wants* me. He *needs* me. He sent the light for me…"

Better he had sent the men in the white coats, but whatever. I let her rant and rave while I tried to check her over. She was holding her right arm to her chest, but otherwise seemed sound enough, given the energetic slapping and flailing going on.

"Can you stand, Liana?"

"Leave me alone. I'm going to tell Halcyone to send you away."

Yeah? Likewise. But I didn't say it. I was sorry she was injured, but I'd have been a lot sorrier if she'd jumped off the diving board.

"Can you walk, or should I carry you?"

"Go to hell!"

I wasn't sure I could lug her all the way back to the house. She wasn't a big woman, but I wasn't exactly in training. On the other hand, I didn't dare leave her, in case she decided to finish the job. I could use my cell to call emergency services, but the last thing we needed was to give the local gossip mill more fodder. They'd have a field day with this story. Somehow we had to keep this hushed up.

"Liana, you can walk or I can carry you, but I'm not leaving you here. Which is it going to be?"

She sat up and said, "Don't. Touch. Me," in classic actressy accents.

I made an as-you-wish gesture and stepped back. But of course she couldn't get to her feet without the use of both arms. After a couple of pained tries, she glared at me, held out her good hand, and I helped her stand.

We had to take the long way back, and it was not pleasant. Even knowing what I did about Liana—or rather, Lacey—I didn't enjoy hearing her anguished gulps and whimpers as we dragged our way up the drive to the house.

Midway there she faltered, and I caught her right before she swooned. I hauled her the rest of the way, carried her in through the kitchen and up to her bedroom. I deposited her on the bed, where she lay limp and waxen-faced, and hurried downstairs to phone Dr. Tighe.

By then the sun was up, but when I reached the ground floor, I found the kitchen was still cold and empty, the shades over the double sink drawn. The coffee machine was off.

I'd been trying to come up with a suitable story for Betty and Tarrant, but it seemed to be unnecessary, though usually by this hour Betty would be fussing over the stove and Tarrant would be sitting in his shirtsleeves, listening to local radio and making revolting sucking sounds as he dunked his doughnut into his steaming cup of coffee.

Was Betty ill again? Was Tarrant officially on strike? I filled the coffee machine with water and measured out the grounds. After the night I'd had, I needed fortification before I tried to explain to Dr. Tighe why Liana needed to be locked up where she couldn't harm herself or my aunt STAT.

I was closing the refrigerator, carton of cream in hand, when my gaze fell on something pink. I went rigid with shock. There on the floor, protruding from behind the long wooden farm table, was a foot. A woman's foot encased in a worn, rose-colored slipper.

"Betty?" I could hear the alarm in my voice.

She's fainted, I tried to reassure myself. That was why the kitchen was still dark.

Dark and unnaturally quiet.

I set down the cream and walked over to where she lay. I stared down.

Betty had not fainted. Even without feeling for her pulse, I knew she was dead. She sprawled utterly, unnervingly motionless in her faded, flowered bathrobe. The eyes in her gray face bulged up at me with horror.

CHAPTER EIGHTEEN

I jumped as the coffee machine made a sound like a death rattle and squirted dark liquid into the glass pot.

Betty dead. Despite the evidence of my eyes, it seemed unbelievable. Betty was practically an institution. She was part of Green Lanterns. Part of my childhood—though she wasn't really that old. I hadn't thought people died of high blood pressure these days. She took medication, after all.

Where the hell was Tarrant?

Did he know? He *had* to know. Father and daughter always rose at the same hour.

On autopilot, I turned and crossed to the door leading to the Tarrants' living quarters. The door was closed. I knocked, and when there was no answer, I opened it and went inside.

There was no sign of Tarrant. I checked the bedrooms. Tarrant's room did not appear to have been slept in. Betty's room was a different story. The bedside lamp was on. The bed was unmade, the sheets and blankets rumpled.

Perhaps sometime toward morning, Betty, alone and feeling unwell, had gone into the kitchen for a glass of water and suffered some kind of seizure. But then what? What had happened to Tarrant that he still wasn't back from his nighttime prowling?

Or had Tarrant returned, found Betty dead, and…what? Panicked and fled? No way. Why the hell would he? He would have phoned for help, right? Even if he had panicked—and I'd never seen Tarrant panic; I'd seen him angry, offended, outraged, but not panicked—but even if he *had* panicked, he wouldn't have left her lying there, surely?

Or maybe he had phoned for help and was outside waiting for emergency services to arrive? I returned to the kitchen, went to the window, and looked out at the wide spread of driveway. Two small brown birds rose from the ivy, skimmed the asphalt surface, then fluttered upward toward the trees and out of view. A pale sun was soaking up the last remnants of overcast. It was going to be another lovely day.

Not for Betty. God. Poor Betty.

Impatiently, I shrugged the maudlin thought aside. Anyway, that scenario didn't make any more sense than the previous. Liana and I had been walking up the driveway less than fifteen minutes ago. We'd have seen Tarrant.

But there was no sign of him anywhere.

The whole situation was crazy.

I glanced back at where Betty lay. The sight of her sad pink slipper made my stomach curdle. How long had she been like that?

I made myself walk back to the table, kneel, and touch her hand. She was cold. Cold like I'd never felt another human. And that terrible expression…

I rose, went back into the Tarrants' rooms, took an afghan from the sofa, and carried it to the kitchen to cover Betty. Then I ran upstairs to Aunt H.'s room and tapped softly on the door.

She murmured inquiry, and I opened the door, peering through the gloom until I spotted her sitting up in bed. "Artie? What is it, dear?"

"It's bad news, Aunt H. I'm sorry."

"What bad news? What's happened?" She was fully awake now, her voice sharp as she reached for the bathrobe lying across the foot of the bed.

"It's Betty—Ulyanna, I mean. I'm afraid she's…dead."

"*Dead?*"

"Yes."

Aunt H. sank back on the bed. "But she can't be. How? What happened?"

"I don't know. She must have had a stroke or a heart attack or something. I found her when I—" I broke off, suddenly remembering Liana and the events of the night before. I'd completely forgotten I was supposed to be summoning the doctor.

"When you what?" Aunt H. asked, staring at me.

"It's a long story. In other news, I think Liana's had some kind of breakdown."

"Over Ulyanna?"

"No. No, I'll explain later. The thing is, can you sit with her while I phone the doctor and look for Tarrant?"

Aunt H. was looking more bewildered by the minute. "Has something happened to Tarrant?"

"I don't know. He doesn't seem to be around anywhere. I don't know if he found Ulyanna and went for help or—"

"Went for help? Why wouldn't he call 911? I don't understand."

"I don't understand either," I admitted. "Maybe he panicked."

"*Tarrant?* Panic?"

"I know it doesn't seem likely. None of it seems likely, frankly." With increasing desperation, I said, "Look, me old darling, could you please, *please* go sit with Liana so she doesn't chuck herself out a window or something? As soon as I know anything, I'll report back."

Without another word, my aunt rose from the bed, slipped on her robe, and firmly tied the sash. "Go," she told me. "Leave Liana to me. And never mind about phoning the doctor. I'll take care of it. The thing for you to do is find Tarrant. This news is liable to break him."

I was thinking about my aunt's words as I returned downstairs and found the kitchen still deserted—barring the blanketed form behind the wooden table.

Maybe Betty's death *had* broken Tarrant. Maybe it had been the final straw.

I went out through the kitchen door—keeping an eye out for Tarrant—and jogged across the sun-dappled grass to the garage. I slipped in the side door, flipped on the light, and counted cars in the gloomy illumination. The green station wagon was not there.

Did that mean that Tarrant *had* gone for help?

Leaving Betty behind?

No. That made no sense.

But this made no sense either. Why would Tarrant flee Green Lanterns without a word—in what was technically my aunt's station wagon.

I headed upstairs to knock on Seamus's door. By the time I reached the landing, I could smell the coffee brewing, and my stomach knotted unhappily as I remembered Betty and my earlier attempt at scoring caffeine.

Seamus opened the door almost immediately. He was wearing jeans and holding an electric razor, which he switched off at the sight of me. His brown hair was damp and scented of Herbal Essences; his smile was lopsided.

"Didn't anyone ever tell you it's bad manners to leave without a word in the middle of the night?"

"Uh, no, as a matter of fact. Anyway, it was dawn. Or nearly. But I apologize. I'd like to do it again. Not the leaving in the middle of the night part. The earlier stuff. Meantime, something's come up—and I don't mean that in a playful, flirtatious way."

His brows drew together. "Are you okay?"

"So far, but our numbers are dwindling fast. Betty—Ulyanna, that is—is dead, Tarrant is missing, and Liana tried to kill herself last night, supposedly on orders from Ogden."

"You—" His jaw dropped, his eyes widened, and for a gratifying instant he seemed speechless. "Are you— This is for real?"

"Only too real. I just checked downstairs, and the station wagon is gone. Do you have any idea when Tarrant left?"

"I'm not even sure when *you* left. I was out."

I nodded automatically. He *had* been out, which, considering the days he was putting in trying to whip the garden into shape and the nights he spent watching the house and searching the grounds, was probably not surprising.

"I think I might have heard Tarrant leaving while I was wandering through the maze trying to find Liana."

"Wandering through the…" I saw him make the conscious and determined decision to let that pass. He said instead, "Have you phoned the police?"

"No. Aunt H. is phoning Dr. Tighe."

Seamus frowned. "You can't keep this hushed up, Artemus. If Tarrant killed Betty—"

It was my turn to gape. "If Tarrant killed— What are you talking about? Tarrant never killed Betty. I didn't say Betty was murdered. I think she just had a heart attack. She looked…"

I started to say she looked natural enough, but remembered her expression—I doubted I'd ever manage to forget it. Her features had been frozen in horror.

"I'd better take a look," Seamus said grimly.

I felt a wave of relief. *Yes.* Great idea. This was Seamus's area of expertise, after all. And the truth was, it hadn't even occurred to me that Betty's death might have been a violent one. Maybe Tarrant *had* lost his mind and struck her. Stranger things had happened at Green Lanterns.

"Pour yourself some coffee, and I'll finish dressing." Seamus stepped aside.

I went into the kitchen and found a clean mug in the cupboard. Seamus had closed the bedroom door behind him, but after a minute or two, I heard his voice. He was on the phone. I sipped my coffee, eyeing the broken lamp in the trash bin—the bent linen shade sat on the linoleum counter—and tried to hear Seamus's half of the conversation.

I couldn't make out the words, but his tone sounded official.

A short time later he opened the bedroom door. He wore his usual jeans and a blue Reading Diver T-shirt. He also wore an air of authority he hadn't displayed before. Or at least not so obviously.

"Who did you call?" I asked.

He hesitated. "My boss at SFPD."

"I see."

His eyes met mine steadily. "Instinct tells me things are going to happen very quickly now."

"Which means what?"

"I meant what I said last night. If I'm able to return the money Foxworth stole, there's a very good chance I can keep your aunt out of trouble. Assuming she's willing to cooperate."

I said slowly, "You think Tarrant found the money and is on the run?"

"I think there's a very good chance that's what we're looking at."

I smiled sourly. "And you think he killed Betty?"

"Clearly you don't." His smile was wry. "Okay. Maybe she did die a natural death. Maybe they argued and she had a heart attack. We won't know until we hear from the coroner. Meantime, I think we should go take a look."

I put my coffee cup in the sink. Said with a briskness I didn't feel, "Let's do it."

When we reached the house, Dr. Tighe's car was already parked in the driveway. We went into the kitchen and found him kneeling beside Betty's body. Seamus offered his ID, and Dr. Tighe said, "You're full of surprises."

Seamus shrugged.

"All right, Sergeant Cassidy. I've already sent for the coroner's van. There are no signs of violence. It looks to me like a massive cerebral hemorrhage. Ulyanna was always a little too lackadaisical about taking her medication. I warned her about it more than once."

"Time of death?" Seamus asked.

Dr. Tighe grimaced. "You know better than to ask. If I had to guess, I'd say somewhere around three, four in the morning."

Seamus glanced at me. I knew what he was thinking. Betty had died right about the time we had headed over to his place. God. Hopefully, it wasn't hearing us fumbling our way outside that had triggered her fatal attack.

"Where's Tarrant?" Dr. Tighe asked suddenly, glancing around the gloomy kitchen as if only then noticing we were alone. "He's going to take this very badly."

"We don't know," I said. "I thought maybe he'd gone for help, but that doesn't seem to be the case."

"Gone for help? Why wouldn't he just use the phone?"

Seamus shot me a warning look.

"No idea," I replied. "If you're done down here, will you come upstairs and examine Liana? I think she may have broken her arm. Although frankly, that's the least of it."

"So Hallie mentioned. What exactly went on here last night?" He snapped shut his leather bag and looked from me to Seamus. He did not appear to be in any hurry to get upstairs.

Now that I thought about it, Dr. Tighe was one of the only doctors I knew who still carried an old-fashioned doctor's bag. But then he was one of the only doctors I knew who still made house calls. Granted, these days his bag held his iPad and a host of other gadgets as well as some of the more traditional tools of the trade.

I offered my version of events to Dr. Tighe and Seamus—leaving out my reason for being outside the house before dawn. Seamus already knew my reason.

"Let me make sure I understand you. Liana *told* you Ogden instructed her to kill herself?" Dr. Tighe questioned.

I tried to recall Liana's exact words. "She said he had sent the light for her."

"The *light*?" Seamus and Dr. Tighe repeated in unison—and with the same inflection.

I started to answer, then rethought. I had to make a choice, and considering everything, I decided Liana was expendable. "Yes," I said. "She kept babbling about seeing a light. I think she believed she was pursuing that light through the garden and to the pool."

"And she believed the light was Ogden?" Dr. Tighe asked.

"That's how it sounded to me."

"I see." He was frowning. "Maybe her case is more serious than I realized."

I wasn't lying when I said, "I think so. I believe she'd have thrown herself off the diving board if I hadn't been there."

He said a little wearily, "Very well. I'll have a look at her."

When Dr. Tighe left the kitchen, Seamus asked, "Was there a light?"

"Yes."

Seamus continued to study me. "Could it have been a flashlight?"

"I thought so at first, but it didn't look exactly like a flashlight beam. It was larger than that."

"It could have been a high-powered flashlight."

"Maybe."

"No?"

I said reluctantly, "I think it was too high in the air for a flashlight beam. And the way it moved was odd. It sort of floated and drifted and bounced its way through the trees."

"What do you think it was?" Seamus sounded curious rather than skeptical, which was a relief to my, frankly, over-strained nerves.

I shrugged. "I don't know. The light didn't leave the maze, though."

"Which means…what?"

"No idea." I glanced down once more at Betty's shrouded form. "Do you mind if we get out of here?"

His face changed. "Yeah, of course. I'm sorry, Artemus. I realize this has to be upsetting for you." To my surprise, Seamus wrapped his arms around me. "I know you were fond of her."

Greg had not been much for hugging, so for a second I just stood there straight and awkward, but then I realized I *was* upset. I *had* been fond of Betty. And it felt very nice to be hugged by Seamus.

I hugged him back. Hard. "Thanks. She was kind to me when I was a kid." I turned my face to his, offering a twisted smile. "She was always hopeful I'd outgrow this being-gay thing."

Seamus snorted. "God, I hope not." And he kissed me.

It was a quick kiss. This wasn't the time or place for romance, but it was wonderfully comforting.

We went outside to find the coroner's van had arrived. Seamus directed the attendants to the kitchen door, and we walked a little way down the drive. The sun was shining cheer-fully. The air smelled fresh and sweet. If felt like any ordinary summer day—which made the events of the night and morning seem all the weirder.

"Maybe Tarrant got into an accident?" I suggested after a moment or two.

"Anything's possible, I guess." Seamus sounded unconvinced. He gave me a sideways look. "You know, Tarrant's disappearance means I'm going to have to interview your aunt as soon as possible."

I sighed. "I know. I'd like to be there when you do."

He shook his head. "I can't do that. I'm already hanging out a mile."

"Then her lawyer should be there."

"No. That's not a good idea."

Up until then I'd been feeling close to Seamus, but all that vanished. "I'm not going to allow you to interrogate her like she's a common criminal—"

"Artemus—" Seamus stopped walking, catching me by the arm so that I had to stop too. "You've— I'm asking you to trust me. I'm not out to trick or trap your aunt. I'd think you would know that by now, but since you don't…okay." He expelled a long breath, as if he had to gather himself. "If she's truly innocent of all wrongdoing, she's got nothing to fear. If she *is* involved…I'll do my best to help her navigate the legal waters. In which case, we might want to keep a few things off the record. Do you get what I'm saying? I have a vested interest in things working out for her."

He gazed with unmistakable meaning into my eyes, and I felt my face warm.

Seamus didn't wait for my answer. "So there's that. But I'm also an officer of the law, and I have a responsibility and a duty to fulfill the trust placed in me. I'm walking a very fine line here. Please don't put me in a worse position than I'm already in."

I'd been with Greg nearly four years, and I don't think in all that time I'd ever seen him that honest, that open. Seamus had a mix of strength and vulnerability like few men I'd known—myself included.

He waited for my answer, his face solemn as life or death.

That kind of honesty demanded reciprocity, however awkward and unfamiliar. I said, "I haven't known you that long, so this isn't easy for me."

"I know."

Probably not. Then again, maybe he did.

"My instinct is to trust you, but my instinct has been wrong before. If it was just me... But Aunt H. has been there for me my whole life. She's my entire family. I don't have anybody else."

Seamus didn't say a word, just continued to gaze at me with those grave, searching blue eyes, and I could read the message there as clearly as if he'd said it aloud.

Once again I felt my face heat—so strange because I've never been given to blushing—and I said gruffly, "But you don't really know me. Memorizing a dossier isn't the same as trying to live with someone who squeezes the toothpaste from the middle of the tube, eats the last of the ice cream without telling you, or borrows your favorite shirt and never gives it back."

Seamus looked alarmed. "You always eat the last of the ice cream?"

"No. Greg did. You know what I'm saying."

"I do know what you're saying," he replied, smiling but serious once more. "And I'm looking forward to getting to really know *you*. The you that forgets birthdays and anniversaries—"

"I'm good at birthdays and anniversaries."

"—the you that fudges his tax returns—"

"Nope. Never."

"—the you that squeezes the toothpaste from the middle of the tube—"

"Okay. Yes. Guilty as charged."

"And I hope you feel the same. But even if you don't, I'm going to try to help your aunt out of this. Although that's partly up to her. Fair enough?"

Sometimes there are no guarantees. No safety nets. Sometimes you just have to take a chance.

I nodded. "Fair enough."

CHAPTER NINETEEN

I could tell by Dr. Tighe's face that the news was not good.

"What's the verdict?" I asked when he came downstairs after nearly an hour spent examining Liana. I'd been hovering outside the dining room, waiting for him while Seamus used the phone in Ogden's study to contact local hospitals and the police station.

"The good news is her arm isn't broken. Her shoulder is dislocated."

"What's the bad news?"

"She says the reason she was running through the garden last night is you frightened her."

"*What?*"

He nodded grimly. "She said her room was hot and stuffy, so she stepped outside for some fresh air. You came rushing out of the dark, and being topped to the gills with cold medication, she became frightened and disoriented and ran into the garden."

"That's… That's absurd."

"It sounds absurd to me," Dr. Tighe agreed. "But it's going to be hard to disprove it. She's perfectly lucid. In fact, she's more perked up and energetic than she has been in months.

Most of that temper is aimed at you, but it's still a change for the better."

"She didn't say anything about the glowing light or Ogden telling her he needed her with him?"

"Nope. She says that sounds like something you made up to cover for having nearly knocked her off the diving board and causing her to injure her shoulder."

I floundered. "Something I… Of all the… How the hell does she explain climbing up the diving board in the first place?"

"Panic and cold meds."

I gave a laugh of disbelief.

Dr. Tighe was sympathetic but regretful. "I did what I could to suggest she might like to get away from Green Lanterns for a while, but she's not having any of it."

"I'm telling you, she would have killed herself last night if I hadn't been there. I don't care how good an actress she is, she's a danger to herself and others. Especially my aunt."

"Well, Hallie's no fool," Dr. Tighe said in bracing tones. "She listened to everything I had to say and everything Liana had to say. Forewarned is forearmed."

I said grimly, "Yeah, but she doesn't know who and what she's dealing with."

Dr. Tighe studied me curiously. "Who and what is she dealing with?"

I remembered Seamus's words of warning and shook my head. I said instead, "Could we bring in a private nurse? Someone who could keep an eye on her without seeming to keep an eye on her?"

"I thought of that too. She shot the idea down."

"So there's nothing you can do?"

Dr. Tighe grimaced. "Well, I've given her some pretty strong pain medication for the shoulder. That ought to keep her quiet for a few days."

"Thanks," I said glumly. "Let's hope she bothers to take it." And let's hope she didn't spike Aunt H.'s tea with those pain pills. I put nothing past her at this point.

"Any news of Tarrant?" Dr. Tighe interrupted my scowling reflection.

"Nothing so far. Seamus—er, Cassidy—is phoning around the local hospitals in case he had an accident."

"Good. Cassidy seems like a capable fellow."

"Yes." And why I felt like *I'd* received the compliment, I had no idea. And less idea why the doctor was giving me that particular look of approval.

"Odd about Tarrant," Dr. Tighe said as I escorted him to the front door. "Very odd."

Odd didn't begin to cover it, but I agreed, promised to phone immediately if Liana's condition deteriorated (one could always hope), and saw Dr. Tighe off. I went to find Seamus.

He must have finished his phone calls because he was sitting at Ogden's desk, gazing thoughtfully at the bookshelves. His eyes lit when he saw me.

I felt myself brighten in answer. It was a long time since I'd felt like this about anyone—or anyone had felt like that about me. It was nice.

"Any news?" I asked.

"Hm? No. Nothing. No accidents reported involving a green 1990s Chevy Caprice wagon. No patients matching Tarrant's description admitted to any hospitals." He absently rubbed the underside of his chin. "Do you know if the blueprints for this house still exist?"

"I don't know. You're still thinking there might be a hidden room somewhere?"

"I guess it's moot if Tarrant found the money and is on the run."

"True." I sighed. "I just saw the doctor off."

"With Liana in tow?"

"Hardly." I recounted Liana's version of events as recounted by Dr. Tighe.

At the end of my recital, Seamus looked thoughtful. "Is there any chance Liana might have deliberately lured you out to the garden?"

"Why would she?"

"You're your aunt's sole beneficiary. Correct?"

"Well, yes. There are probably a couple of bequeathals to the Tarrants—" I remembered there was only one Tarrant now and fell silent.

"But the bulk of her estate goes to you?" Seamus prompted.

"Right. Yes. Maybe something of sentimental value will be earmarked for Liana. Anyway, according to you, Aunt H. is broke."

"Her liquid assets are gone. She still has this house and everything in it. The land alone has to be worth several million dollars."

"True."

"What's the likelihood that, with you out of the way, your aunt might change her will in favor of Liana?"

"Not strong." I said it with confidence, but on reflection, I wasn't all that sure. Aunt H. did consider Liana family. That would probably change once Seamus had his little chat with her, but as of this moment, it was feasible that if I ceased to exist, Aunt H. might leave Green Lanterns to Liana. There was literally no one else left. And with no money or family of her own, Liana would probably strike Aunt H. as a worthy candidate. After all, she'd been supporting her sister-in-law for half a decade already.

Seamus said, "There's no reason to believe Liana—or rather, Lacey—is someone with a strong moral compass. In fact, for all we know, she may have pushed Foxworth into embezzling from his companies. The assumption has always been that she went along with Foxworth's schemes, but maybe she was the mastermind all along."

I tried to reconcile that theory with what I knew of Liana. Even the Liana I'd known pre-Ogden's demise didn't strike me as a convincing Lady Macbeth. And post-Ogden, she was pretty much a basket case.

Then again, Liana was in actuality Lacey the actress, willing to run off with her embezzler pornographer boyfriend and able to successfully pretend to be his sister for years while living under the roof of his new wife.

I said, "Maybe. But last night she couldn't have known at what point I'd be walking up from the carriage house—or that I'd chase after her."

"I know."

"Besides, I would swear she planned on throwing herself off that diving board."

"I wasn't there, so I can't argue. But I think you should be extra vigilant from now on."

If I were you, I would leave Green Lanterns at once…

I recalled Roma Loveridge's warning, and shivered as though an invisible hand ran an icy fingertip down my spine.

I opened my mouth, but my aunt spoke from the doorway behind me.

"Artie—" She paused at what was clearly my visible jump of guilt. "I'm sor—oh. And Mr. Cassidy. I didn't realize…"

She was puzzled, and I didn't blame her.

"Hey, Auntie H.!" I sounded as nervous as I had when I was ten years old and she'd caught me in this very room, flipping through Edwin's full-color anatomy books. "How's Liana?"

Aunt H. sighed and pushed her hair wearily back from her forehead. "She's sleeping, thank heavens. She was in such pain, but the pills Dr. Tighe gave her put her right under."

She looked like she could have used one of those magic pills herself. Wan with fatigue and stress. Her eyes were dark, her mouth colorless. She had changed into slacks, and despite the heat of the day, a pullover sweater.

"Good," I said vaguely. "That's good." I could feel Seamus's gaze. I knew what he wanted. I also knew that once he spoke to her, everything was going to change. Maybe some of the change would ultimately be for the better. Maybe not. It was the *maybe not* I feared.

It wasn't that I believed for one instant that Aunt H. had known anything about Ogden's criminal past—let alone been complicit in it—but she was going to be stricken by what Seamus was about to tell her. And thanks to Liana, she was not in the best head space to start with. That was the only bright spot in all this. Surely after Aunt H. heard what Seamus had to say, she would send Liana and her pals in the spirit world packing.

"Has something happened?" Aunt H. inquired, looking uncertainly from me to Seamus.

"Yes, I'm afraid so," I said.

Her face clouded over. "Is it to do with Tarrant? I've been very worried about him. This isn't like him. He would never knowingly have left Ulyanna."

"Tarrant? No. It's nothing to do with Tarrant." I threw Seamus a pleading look, though I wasn't sure what I was pleading for. *Go easy on her? Break it gently? Can we do this later?* In any case, he wasn't looking at me. He was sizing Aunt H. up with a cool, appraising stare I didn't like.

I said, "Aunt H., it turns out Mr. Cassidy is a police officer. He wants to ask you a few questions."

"A police officer?" Aunt H. looked blank. Then her expression changed to one of genuine terror. She recovered at once, but I couldn't unsee that expression. Surprise, yes. Confusion, yes. Either of those emotions would be expected. But terror? Why should she look terrified at the idea of talking to the police?

"Questions about what?" Aunt H. asked.

Seamus said quietly, "Artemus."

I glared at him but said to her, "Look, darling, believe it or not, he's on our side. Just hear what he has to say. Meanwhile, I'm going to make some phone calls and see if I can track down Tarrant."

Aunt H. looked even more confused, but she met Seamus's gaze, and her chin rose. "Of course," she said. "Ask whatever you like, Mr. Cassidy. Or should I address you by some other rank?"

"Cassidy is fine," Seamus said. "Would it be all right if we sat over here by the windows, Mrs. Bancroft-Hyde?"

His tone was courteous, respectful, and I relaxed a little. This was going to happen whether I liked it or not.

Aunt H. threw me a strange look before answering coolly, "As you like."

Seamus didn't look at me. All his focus was on my aunt now.

He had asked me to trust him, so I would try. At least until he gave me a reason not to.

It was almost unnerving to walk into the kitchen and find everything returned to normal.

By "normal," I mean Betty's body had been whisked away and all emergency vehicles and personnel had departed. What was not normal was to find the room cold and empty and silent.

I'd reassured Aunt H. that I would resume the hunt to locate Tarrant, but standing there staring at the blinking coffee machine and the unlit stove, I knew we had more pressing problems. As in who was going to do the cooking and cleaning and laundry and grocery shopping around here now? As heartless as that no doubt sounded, the question had to be considered.

Sure, in the short term I could take over the cooking and washing up. But that was a temporary measure at best. What about the long term? What about next week when my vacation ended and I had to fly back to New York? Assuming things had calmed down enough that I could leave.

Things had been bad enough when it had been up to poor Betty and Tarrant to try to keep Green Lanterns running.

With all that had happened, would it even be possible to hire replacements?

I considered this grimly—and then realized I was taking it for granted Tarrant was gone for good.

Maybe Seamus was wrong about Tarrant being on the run. Even if Tarrant had found whatever was left of Ogden's embezzled loot, I still found it hard to believe he would have left Betty ill or dying. I sure as hell didn't believe he'd killed her. Besides, Dr. Tighe had said all indications were that Betty had died a natural death.

What, then?

Had Tarrant found Betty dead and suffered some kind of psychotic break?

Wasn't that as likely as any other scenario?

What *were* the other scenarios? So much had happened over the past twenty-four hours, I was starting to lose track.

What were the facts?

The simplest and most straightforward fact was that Betty had died, apparently of natural causes, at some time during the night.

I winced, remembering the ghastly expression on her face. Had she looked like that because she knew she was dying? Or had she seen something that terrified her into having a stroke or a fatal heart attack?

Like what?

Like her father sneaking off into the night with Ogden's ill-gotten gains? Like Liana wafting around like Vampira? Like Ogden's ghost? Like Ogden himself—not dead and still very much alive?

Was that so far-fetched an idea? Seamus thought so. But what was the alternative? That Ogden's disgruntled spirit had returned and was haunting Green Lanterns?

I will never rest until you have paid for what you did.

There was more going on here than Tarrant or Liana or maybe someone else searching for some missing embezzled funds—and whatever it was, it had started with Ogden's death.

I thought of Aunt Halcyone's cryptic comments about responsibility and guilt. The fear in her eyes when she'd learned Seamus was a cop.

As much as I didn't want to believe it, even I had to admit Ogden's death looked less and less like an accident and more like murder.

CHAPTER TWENTY

Someone rapped sharply on the glass panes of the kitchen door, jolting me out of my bleak thoughts.

I went to the door and found Cyril on the kitchen stoop. His hair stood up in wet spikes, and his shirt was on inside out.

"Hey, I just heard on my police scanner," he said. "Poor old Betty! I keep remembering those butterscotch cheesecake bars she used to bake for us when we were rehearsing *Almost, Maine*. You're the one who found her?"

"Yeah, it was pretty aw—" I broke off. "Oh, for Christ's sake. You're here as a *reporter*?"

"Of course." Cyril seemed surprised at my glower. "That's what I do. That's my job."

"There's no story here. She died a natural death."

His jaw dropped. "Boy, did you turn into a snob, Bancroft. Housekeeper or not, she still gets her 836 characters of obituary."

"That's not what I mean, and you know it."

Cyril cocked an eyebrow. "Do I?"

I muttered under my breath and pushed the door wide. "Whatever. Come in. I actually do have some questions for you."

"Yeah?" Cyril followed me inside. He looked around the kitchen, his face losing some of its usual good cheer. "Damn. You can really feel the change already."

"I know. Although, to be honest, it's been like that since I arrived last week. Green Lanterns is a different place since Ogden died." Ironic, given that Ogden had hardly been the source of all the light and warmth I had previously associated with Green Lanterns. I added, "That's off the record, by the way."

Cyril gave me a chiding look. "You know, I came as much to see you again before you go back to New York as I did to report on Betty."

I made a face, acknowledging the likelihood of that. "Anyway. There isn't much to tell you. According to Dr. Tighe, she died of a stroke sometime early this morning."

Cyril nodded. "I heard. No autopsy required. When will the funeral be?"

"I don't know. I don't know how we can plan her funeral without talking to Tarrant."

"You found her in the kitchen?"

I nodded at the floor behind the table.

He said in the tone of one giving his opening sentence a test run, "She died with her boots on. I guess that's the way she'd have wanted it."

Was it? Had Betty really not had other dreams or desires than to spend her life cooking and cleaning for other people?

"Her slippers, if you want to get technical."

Cyril grunted. "Where do you think Tarrant is?"

I gave him a considering look.

Cyril said, "He's got a girlfriend. She hasn't heard from him since the day before yesterday."

"Tarrant has a *girlfriend*?"

Cyril chuckled. "He sure does. Betty introduced them. They went to the same church."

I still couldn't get over the idea that Tarrant had had a girlfriend.

"It's weird his taking off like that." Cyril was following his own line of thought. "Maybe he just couldn't handle Betty dying so suddenly? They say no matter how old you are, losing a kid is the worst thing that can happen to you."

"Maybe. He loved her. In his own unique way."

"Was there anything odd in his behavior during the past week?"

I laughed. "Was there anything not odd in his behavior *ever*?"

"Good point. He was always kind of eccentric. And he got worse once you left. Of course, he wasn't the only one."

At my look, he shrugged. "You said yourself things have been…different for a while now."

I couldn't argue with that.

Cyril asked a few more general questions about how long Betty had been employed, whether I knew if she had other family members. It was sort of depressing to realize that I'd known Betty my entire life, but really knew very little about her personal life.

"Hey, I wanted to ask you. What was the thing with the balloons?" I interrupted, suddenly recalling that flash of… whatever it had been the night before. Epiphany? Insight? Free association?

"What are you talking about?"

"The silver balloons that were released a couple of days ago. I only heard half the story on the radio. Something about a memorial service?"

"Oh. Hart Lenton. Right. He disappeared a couple of years ago on his way home from work."

"He *disappeared*? Russian Bay has an open missing-person's case?"

"What? No. Lenton wasn't from Russian Bay. He was from Jenner."

"That's less than an hour away."

"So?"

"Who was he? What did he do?" I demanded.

"He wasn't anyone. I mean, he was an ordinary guy, by all accounts. Loving husband, devoted dad, good neighbor."

The doubt in the back of my mind was so nebulous, I wasn't even sure of what I was suspicious. "Was he a PI, by any chance? An insurance investigator? Anything to do with law enforcement?"

"No. Nothing like that. No ties to law enforcement. No criminal ties either. He was a contractor. Small-business owner. Nothing that would involve kickbacks or bribes."

"What happened to him?"

"No one knows. That's the reason for the balloon release every year around this time. The family wants to boost the case's media profile. It's what people do in these cases."

"How long did you say this guy has been missing? Over a year?"

"Two years at least."

"Two years." My excitement faded. Two years was too long, right? Too long for what I was thinking—not that I had really formulated my thoughts, beyond the realization that if Ogden was still alive, he'd have had to find a substitute corpse for himself.

According to Seamus, that possibility had already been explored and dismissed. Nobody—no body—alive or dead was missing or unaccounted for in Russian Bay.

Besides, if Ogden was still alive, what was Aunt H. so afraid of?

I had just said goodbye to Cyril and opened the refrigerator to consider our options when Seamus entered the kitchen.

His expression was grim, and I braced for battle. Clearly, we were going to be on opposite sides.

"Well?" I said by way of greeting.

His eyes flickered, not missing the lack of welcome in my tone. "We need to talk."

"Where's Aunt H.?"

"Upstairs, checking on the Labanca woman."

I had to remind myself that Liana was actually Lacey Labanca. "So talk," I said. "It's not like we're not all in the loop now."

"Actually, we're not all in the loop. I've asked your aunt to keep what I told her about Labanca to herself for now. At least until she's off those pain pills the doctor gave her. I don't want anyone arguing that I coerced her into a confession while she wasn't in her right mind."

"I see."

Seamus sighed. "I'm not the bad guy here, Artemus. This isn't my fault. And if it wasn't me, it would be someone else. Someone who wouldn't give a damn about you *or* her."

That was true. I was not being fair to him. But I loved my aunt. I owed her everything. She had been a girl in her twenties when she assumed my guardianship. Her own parents had died only eighteen months previously—to be followed by the loss of her beloved brother. But she had made sure I felt safe and loved from the day I arrived. I was going to do whatever I had to, to protect her.

"What did she tell you?" I asked.

"Nothing." Seamus's mouth was a straight, unsmiling line. "Not a damn thing. Which is not going to help her. Which is not going to allow me to help her."

"Does it not occur to you that maybe she doesn't know anything?"

He shook his head. "No. She knows something. That's obvious. It's even obvious to you, or you wouldn't be glaring at me the way you are."

I tried to tone the glare down to a more moderate SPF 15. "What did you say to her?"

"I told her exactly what I told you last night. She claimed she was hearing it all for the first time. That she knew nothing about Ogden's former identity or his previous life. But I don't think any of it came as news to her."

"She's good at hiding her feelings."

"Even so."

"You're never going to convince me that she killed Ogden for that money."

I couldn't quite read Seamus's expression. I was surprised when he said, "No, I have to agree with you. I don't think she gives a damn about the money."

"But you still think she knows where it is?"

He hesitated.

"Let me talk to her."

"I wouldn't try to stop you even if I could. I'm hoping you'll talk some sense into her."

"Even if I can't, what you really care about is recovering the loot, correct? And at this point it looks like Tarrant found the money and fled with it."

Seamus said reluctantly, "Maybe. We don't know that for a fact."

"But there are strong indicators."

"Again, maybe."

"Okay, but even if Tarrant didn't find the money—even if he left for some other unknown reason—the main thing that matters to you is being able to hand back whatever is left of the money Ogden embezzled. So before you make your mind up, before you talk to anyone, before you do *anything*, give me a chance to find that money."

Seamus looked pained. "I wish it was that simple."

"It can be that simple."

"Artemus—"

"You said last night you didn't believe Aunt H. knew anything about Ogden's past when she married him. Whatever ultimately happened, she got drawn into it through no fault of her own."

Seamus frowned as though staring into some bleak and unpromising distance. "I'll do what I can. I already promised you that. But how much I'm able to cover for her depends on what the Labanca woman has to say when she's finally awake. And what version of events Tarrant gives when we track him down."

Before I could answer, Seamus's cell phone rang. He glanced at the number, then automatically glanced at me. His expression gave nothing away. "I've got to take this."

I nodded. I didn't think it was a good sign that he didn't want to speak in front of me.

Seamus went out the kitchen door, and I went back to studying the contents of the fridge, though nothing I saw on the shelves registered on my consciousness.

I could only think of one reason Aunt H. would decline to trust Seamus, and that was because her secret was something she knew no one in law enforcement could overlook. Something like homicide.

By now I'd had time to reflect—resulting in new ulcer-inducing worries. If Aunt H. *had* killed Ogden—Foxworth—it had been premeditated. And that was going to be a much bigger deal to try to make disappear, recovered funds or no recovered funds. True, Seamus had said he didn't plan to poke his nose into Ogden's demise, but his comments about Liana and Tarrant were a reminder that he might not have a choice in the matter.

I needed to talk to Aunt H. I needed her to be honest with me, however painful that conversation was for either or both of us. And I needed that to happen as soon as possible.

I closed the fridge.

Before I could head upstairs, the back door opened and Seamus reappeared. His eyes were shining, though his expression was somber.

"Russian Bay PD found Tarrant's car."

"His car? Not Tarrant?"

"Just the car so far."

"Where was it?"

"Bay View Street."

"Bay View Street? That's weird." Hard to imagine what might draw Tarrant to that part of town. The Pioneer Market had been closed for years. There was a dog park, a Salvation Army store, and the boarded-up former headquarters of Rational Christians United.

"I've got to go," Seamus told me. "This could be the break I've been waiting for."

"Sure."

"Talk to your aunt, Artemus. We're running out of time. Try to convince her that the best way out of this mess is to tell me what she knows."

"Yes," I said. "I'll try."

He stepped back, started to pull the door shut, but then opened it again and crossed the kitchen to me. His hand locked on my shoulder, and he drew me in and kissed me—and then kissed me again.

His eyes were soft and strangely dark as he held my gaze. He said softly, "You can trust me. I swear it."

Before I could answer, Seamus was gone. The kitchen door banged shut behind him.

CHAPTER TWENTY-ONE

I had to knock several times—and with increasing force—before my aunt opened the door to Liana's sitting room.

Aunt H. gazed out at me but said nothing. It was very weird. Like looking at a stranger.

"Can I speak to you?" I whispered.

She hesitated, glancing over her shoulder at the darkened room beyond.

"Look, darling, we're going to have this out," I said. "So you may as well come quietly."

Aunt H. murmured her exasperation and slipped out into the hall, closing the door soundlessly behind her. "We'll have to talk here. I don't dare leave her for long," she said.

I nodded, keeping my voice down. "That's one of the first things I wanted to talk to you about. We need to get a nurse to watch over her. Even if she really was who you thought she was all these years, you can't be responsible for her. She's crazy."

"Artie—"

"No. I'm serious. You didn't see her last night chasing imaginary butterflies through the maze at midnight. If I hadn't been there, she'd be lying at the bottom of that swimming pool right now. She's a danger to herself *and* you. And me, for that matter. To everyone in this house."

"Artie. Dear. I'm perfectly capable—"

"You don't know what you're dealing with," I interrupted.

Her mouth curved without humor. She said dryly, "I'm beginning to get the picture."

I winced. "I'm sorry. Sorry you had to find out like that. You didn't know, did you? Not until Seamus told you."

"I didn't know the whole story, no. I did realize a long time ago that Ogden—Oscar—wasn't who I imagined when we married. By that, I don't mean I guessed he was using a false identity. *That* never occurred to me." She shook her head as though even now she had trouble believing she had been so blind.

"Then you didn't know about Liana either? You didn't suspect?"

I'd never heard that edge to my aunt's laugh before. "No. As a matter of fact, this is something of a relief. I'd suspected something far worse."

"Yikes," I said as her meaning sank in.

Aunt H. said, "It was hard to miss the fact that Liana—Lacey's—feelings were not exactly…sisterly."

"Why didn't you ever say anything to me?"

Her look was a mix of affection and impatience. "It wasn't something to trouble you with. You had your own life."

I thought of her annual spring visits to New York. Each year she'd seemed a little more tired, a little more worn down, but I'd never guessed the reason. Even disliking Ogden as I did, I hadn't attributed the change in her to him. Partly because Aunt H. had never spoken a disparaging word about her new husband. Discretion, circumspection, pride—sure, there was a time and a place for all that, but there was also a time and a place for being honest and admitting you needed help.

"Do you have any idea where that money is?" I asked.

"There's no money." She said it with absolute certainty.

"Seamus seems pretty confident—"

"Yes," Aunt H. said crisply. "Cassidy is a very confident young man. He's used to being right. But he's not right about this. By the end, Ogden and I argued constantly about money. He bitterly resented being financially dependent. After he spent everything I could give him, he borrowed from our friends. It was…embarrassing. To say the least."

"Why in God's name didn't you divorce the bastard?"

She gave another of those odd, edged laughs. "I was going to."

I stared at her in surprise. "Wait. You *were*?"

"Yes." Her smile twisted at my expression. "I'm not *that* big a fool, Artie."

"I should hope not. Did he know?"

"Yes."

I considered. Didn't this change everything? "Is that why you believe his—his—" Even now I felt ridiculous saying it aloud.

Aunt H. said calmly, "His spirit has returned? Yes."

"And that's what you meant when you said Ogden might believe he had cause for grievance?"

She hesitated. "Yes," she said without any of her previous conviction.

Hmm. *Warm, warmer…cold!* Somehow my line of questioning had gone off the rails.

I persisted. "Did you tell him the afternoon of the accident that you wanted a divorce?"

She seemed to be picking her way through her answer. "I had informed him previously. We did argue about it again that afternoon."

"And that's why you feel responsible? Because Ogden would have been distracted while he was driving? The weather was bad…"

"He was a horrible driver," Aunt H. said almost absently.

"He was," I agreed. "Which is why you shouldn't feel guilty about the accident."

She said nothing.

I studied her face. "Right?"

She seemed to think it over before finally saying, "It doesn't matter what I think, my dear. Ogden's spirit believes he has been wronged."

I groaned. "Aunt H. you can't *really* believe—"

She said with asperity, "Then how do you explain the things that have happened here? You've searched for a so-called rational solution, and you haven't been able to find one."

I remembered the weird floating light in the garden the night before. I said nothing.

Aunt H. said, "The fact that Ogden was an embezzler and an adulterer doesn't change anything. His spirit has returned to Green Lanterns. Regardless of who and what he was in life, in death he's seeking reparation."

"Well, go fucking fish!" I called to the ceiling.

"*Artemus!*"

"I mean it. He made your life hell when he was alive, and I can't stand the fact that you're giving him permission to continue on in the afterlife."

She looked alarmed. Did she think Ogden was listening to us even now? "You don't know what you're saying."

"I know exactly what I'm saying. First of all, I don't believe Ogden has returned from the dead. I'm not even convinced he *is* dead. Yes, I know I can't explain away the lights and the spooky laughter and the footsteps and all the other apparent manifestations. I'm guessing Roma is in on it, whatever the plan is. Maybe Ogden is having an affair with her too—"

"Stop it at once!" Aunt H. snapped, and I guess old habits die hard, because right on cue, I shut up. I watched her struggle to control her voice and face. "Artemus, dearest, I know this has been a strain on your nerves as much as anyone's. I blame myself. It was very wrong of me, cowardly of me, to drag you into this. I meant what I said before. I want you to leave Green Lanterns."

"Not a chance."

She hung on to her patience. "Nothing you can do is going to stop whatever is going to happen—be it in this world or the next."

"You're going to have to throw me out of the house, then, because I'm not leaving."

Again, I had the odd impression I was looking at a stranger, but she regained control. Mostly. She couldn't quite hide her ire. Her eyes sparked with unfamiliar temper. "This is a ridiculous conversation. Of course I'm not going to have you thrown from the house. I'm asking you to respect my wishes and leave."

"I can't do that."

Even as I said it, though, I felt a pang for my own home and my own life in New York. How the hell long *was* I going to be trapped in the alternate universe of Green Lanterns?

Her chest rose and fell, and then she said, "We'll continue this conversation later. I'm not comfortable leaving Liana for too long."

"I'm not clear why she's even still here now that you know what you know about her."

Aunt H. opened her mouth, thought better of it, and repeated more ominously, "We'll continue this conversation later."

She opened the door to Liana's rooms and vanished inside.

The day passed.

That about summed it up.

There was no word from Seamus, but Police Chief Kingsland showed up around three o'clock, asking to speak to Aunt Halcyone. I was afraid he was there to arrest her—at the very least interrogate her—but it turned out Aunt H. had summoned him. My next fear was that Aunt H. was going to confess to him.

They retreated to the music room, where they spoke behind closed doors for about forty-five nail-biting minutes. Then the door opened, and Aunt H., looking eerily serene, returned upstairs to resume her vigil over Liana. Chief Kingsland joined me in the kitchen, where I was making lasagna.

"Your aunt wants you to go back to New York," Kingsland informed me.

He was a bit older than Aunt H. Tall, lean, and sort of handsome in a rawboned way. Like Aunt H., he had aged a lot over the past year. There was more gray in his red hair and unfamiliar lines around his dark eyes. I knew they had grown up together and were still very good friends. I vaguely remembered some rumor about Kingsland's wife being committed to a mental hospital a few years earlier, although I had my doubts about that. I knew from personal experience it was not easy to have people permanently locked up, even when they posed a danger to themselves.

I set the cheese grater and remaining nub of mozzarella aside. "And you're going to forcibly evict me if I won't go?"

Kingsland grinned. "Nope. I'm on your side. I don't know what the hell is going on around here, but I don't like it. I think you should stay put for now."

"You don't believe in ghosts?" I asked.

"No. I don't." He handed me a business card. "This is my cell phone and pager number. Don't hesitate to use it."

"Thanks." I tucked the card in my shirt pocket. "Any word on Tarrant?"

"As far as I know, they haven't found him yet." He nodded politely. "I'll see myself out."

A few hours spent scouring the Internet confirmed that Seamus was correct. No one, alive or dead, had gone missing in Russian Bay—or even Sonoma County—around the time of Ogden's death.

As stumbling blocks went, it was kind of an insurmountable one.

There had definitely been a body in Ogden's car. Burned to a crisp, yes, but not to the extent where it couldn't be recognized as human.

Worse, though there was no hard evidence, according to one newspaper report, there were indications—the position of the body and lack of skid marks on the road—that Ogden had been unconscious, maybe even already dead, when his BMW went off the road.

The good news was there was no sign the car had been tampered with. The bad news was there appeared to be at least a possibility that an accelerant had been used to magnify that DNA-destroying fire.

It was worrying, no question. The lack of skid marks and the position of the body could be explained by Ogden having suffered some kind of fatal stroke or seizure in the seconds before the accident. The accelerant used was gasoline, which would have been present at the scene anyway. There was no prosecution-worthy proof of foul play, and it seemed that the police—Chief Kingsland—had never even entertained the idea of investigating the accident as a homicide. All the same, I now understood where the rumors about Aunt Halcyone knocking off Ogden had started.

The fact that she had no motive for murdering her husband didn't seem to have discouraged the gossips. It comforted me, though. I could not think of any reason Aunt H. would have to resort to killing Ogden. He couldn't stop her from divorcing him, and what other motive could there be?

I wasn't sure why she was so willing to assume the guilt for his death, but that was between her and her conscience.

An online search of Roma Loveridge was equally unrewarding. I tried searching for complaints, claims of fraud—I even checked her out on the Better Business Bureau website. There was nothing. Roma seemed to be exactly what she presented herself as: the last of a long line of respected (all things being relative) spiritualists.

Finally, I amused myself searching for Seamus Cassidy. Despite the 614,000 results that turned up within .43 seconds, I couldn't find anything about *my*—er, using the term "my" loosely—Seamus. That wasn't a bad thing. I was a big fan of keeping one's private life…private.

We all had our secrets.

CHAPTER TWENTY-TWO

Seamus returned by dinnertime.

"No sign of Tarrant," he told me as I pulled the bubbling lasagna from the oven. He sniffed appreciatively over my shoulder. "Is that lasagna? It smells fantastic."

"Yeah, it's one of my specialt—"

I broke off as he gave me a quick peck on the mouth. I laughed. I wasn't used to playful—these were not playful circumstances—but I liked his good humor and his easy affection.

"*And* he can cook," Seamus informed the ether.

"Enough to survive. Anyway, Tarrant. Where would he go? *Why* would he go?" I elbowed the oven door closed, transferred the casserole dish to the counter, opened the lower oven door, and pulled out the toasted garlic bread.

"My theory is he caught the nine a.m. bus across the street from the church headquarters. Which means he could be in San Francisco by now. We've got an APB out on him, but locating him could take time."

I shook my head. "I don't know."

"What don't you know?"

"I'm having trouble buying the idea of Tarrant on the run with Ogden's ill-gotten gains."

"He's been searching for something these past weeks. If it wasn't the money, what was it? And why did he take off without a word?"

"Oh, I believe he somehow found out about the money and was hunting for it. I don't think he found it."

"Why's that?"

"First, because I spoke with Aunt H., and she swears there was no money."

Seamus opened his mouth to object, but I kept talking. "Hear me out. Aunt H. says she and Ogden fought constantly about money, that he was bitter at being dependent on her, and that he had started borrowing from their friends and neighbors."

Seamus spread his hands like I had just handed over a basketful of nothing.

"But the main thing is Betty. It's too much of a coincidence that Betty would die the same morning Tarrant goes missing."

"It's not a coincidence at all. I'm guessing Ulyanna's attack was brought on by something Tarrant said or did this morning. They probably argued. And when Tarrant saw what had happened, he snapped."

It sort of made sense, yet I just couldn't quite believe this scenario of Seamus's. It was also hard to believe that Betty had died only that day.

I said, "Betty's expression. Did you notice it?"

"Yes." Seamus looked ill at ease, remembering. "That doesn't mean anything, though. Even when people die a natural death, they don't always look like they do when they're prepared for a viewing."

I was quickly losing my appetite for lasagna—or anything else. "She looked scared to death."

"I know. Where are you going with this?"

"What if what Betty saw was Tarrant being murdered?"

"*Whoa.* That's quite a leap."

"Yes, but it's not impossible."

"No, but it's pretty unlikely. What are you basing that theory on? Who's your suspect? What's the motive?"

"Maybe Liana and Roma Loveridge working together."

"Seriously?"

I shrugged. "No. Well, I don't know. I just—I'm hoping you'll keep an open mind because, while I know I'm biased, I really don't believe my aunt knows anything about that money. And without the money, she had no motive for getting rid of Ogden. Oscar. Whoever."

Once again Seamus opened his mouth, and once again I cut him off. "She'd have divorced him. There's no reason she couldn't have divorced him." I closed my mind to my own suspicions—and the memory of Aunt H.'s guilty demeanor.

Seamus looked unconvinced. "The thing you learn in police work is 99 percent of the time, the most obvious solution is the correct solution."

"But there's always that one percent."

"True. Anyway, let's table the discussion for now. Neither of us got much sleep last night, and I don't know about you, but I can't think straight when I'm starving."

I assented. "Dinner's ready when you are."

Aunt H. joined us for dinner after heating up canned soup for Liana and taking it upstairs on a tray.

"How's she doing?" Seamus inquired, and I knew he was wondering how long until he could question Liana.

Aunt H. said, "Still very groggy. She's agreed to have someone from the RCU come and stay tonight."

"Thank God for small mercies," I said. "At least you'll be able to get some sleep tonight."

Aunt H. said nothing.

"RCU?" Seamus asked.

"Rational Christians United," I said. "Our new neighbors."

"Oh, the cult."

Aunt H. began to splutter. "I think *cult* is perhaps an exaggeration. The church seems to do a lot of good work locally."

"I notice you're not a member," I said. "I still have trouble believing Liana is."

"She joined shortly after Ogden's death. She found it very difficult to come to terms with losing him. She's been less involved lately."

"So many séances, so little time," I said.

"Whatever gets you through the night," Seamus said.

Aunt H. studied him curiously and then glanced at me. Meeting my eyes, she smiled faintly, ruefully.

"I thought the RCU had died out years ago. What brought them back?" I asked.

"The economy. And Reverend Ormston."

"I don't remember Reverend Ormston."

"Is that the guy on the fliers?" Seamus asked. "The one who looks like Biker Jesus?"

That started Aunt H. spluttering again. "I don't know much about him," she said finally.

"The Bancrofts have always identified as Episcopalian," I told Seamus. "Carpenter Jesus is as blue collar as we get."

"Ah."

Aunt H. rolled her eyes at this sacrilege. "I believe he was a friend of Reverend Hornsby. He moved from San Francisco about six years ago. By that time the church was in decline."

"Village scandal," I informed Seamus. "The very married Reverend Hornsby was caught fooling around with his organist."

Aunt H. shook her head at me. More in sorrow than in anger, as Horatio said to Hamlet—although in Aunt H.'s case it was more in resignation. "Ormston took over from Hornsby, with Hornsby's blessing, and from everything I've heard, completely revitalized the church. I think the RCU is only second in size—and influence—to St. Teresa's. Even Tarrant started attending services." Aunt H. sighed. "I suppose I should consult with the reverend regarding Ulyanna's funeral arrangements. I keep hoping we're going to hear from Tarrant."

Seamus and I exchanged looks but said nothing.

The doorbell rang as we were finishing up dinner.

Sister Regina was small, slim, and dark-haired. She looked about seventeen. A serious, solemn seventeen, but still. A kid. Then again, all she had to do was not fall asleep during the night, so after a brief interview, Aunt H. bade us good night and escorted the teen angel of mercy upstairs.

Seamus and I gathered up the dinner dishes and carried them into the kitchen.

I set my load in the sink and said, "I think these can wait until tomorrow. I'm calling it a day."

Seamus hesitated. Said tentatively, "Do you want company tonight?"

It was my turn to hesitate, to be tentative. "I do, but I really am beat."

"Right. Of course." He looked flatteringly disappointed.

I was unexpectedly disappointed too. I did not want to say good night to Seamus—and that had nothing to do with not wanting to face those cold, dark rooms upstairs alone.

I said slowly, "If you don't mind sleeping together when it really *is* just sleeping…"

He brightened, grinned, said immediately, "I don't mind. Sleeping is one of my favorite things."

"Tell me the story of your life," I said.

It was about an hour after Seamus and I had retreated upstairs. We'd taken turns splashing around in the bathroom and were now settled in each other's arms in the boat of a bed I'd used to lie awake in, dreaming of a guy like Seamus wandering into my life.

Instead, Greg had wandered in, and I'd gone with that.

At the time, I'd believed that being with the wrong guy was preferable to being alone.

Now I knew better.

Seamus grinned. "Am I auditioning?"

I quirked an eyebrow. "Are you?"

He made a sound of amusement, tipping his head as though to study me better in the lamplight.

"Not a lot to tell. I'm a born and bred New Yorker—sorry, I lied; you guessed right that day in the garage. Age thirty-three, Protestant, O-positive blood type, unmarried, no kids, registered Independent, annual income just under $100K."

"The ideal man," I said lightly. "Is that what you always wanted to be? A cop?"

"I wanted to be a playwright."

"You're kidding."

"I wish I was." He laughed without self-consciousness. "No. I've got a box full of terrible scripts to prove it."

I found this charming, which had to be proof I was seriously falling for Seamus Cassidy.

"How did you end up on the force?"

"Och, I come from a long line of Irish cops," he said with a not-too-shabby Irish accent. "Anyway, no regrets. I like it. I'm good at it."

"Your interest isn't solely financial crimes, is it? Don't you have a background in cults and mind control?"

"Cults? *Me?* No."

"Oh. I saw some textbooks on the shelf in your living room that made me think you had an interest in that kind of thing."

"No. Those books were there when I arrived. They're not mine. Except the cooking with booze book. That's mine all right."

I laughed.

He said, "What about you?"

"Did I grow up wanting to be a theater critic? Uh, no. I don't think anyone grows up dreaming of being a theater critic."

"What did you want to be?"

I made a face. "I wanted to act, dahling, of course."

"What happened?"

"Those who can, do. Those who can't, critique."

"You're a very good critic. I love reading your columns."

I laughed. "Thank you."

"No, but I'm serious. I like the way you think."

I laughed again, self-consciously. "Okay. Tell me three surprising things about yourself."

"Now I feel like I really *am* auditioning."

"They don't have to be big things."

He looked ceilingward, thinking. "Hmm. Well… I'm the oldest of triplets."

"Triplets!"

"Yep. I'm allergic to honey."

"How can that be?"

He held up three fingers. "And I have a cat named Milo."

"I like cats. How old is Milo? What kind of cat is he?"

"Three. He's a cool cat."

I snickered.

Seamus said, "He's not like a show cat or anything. I don't know what breed he is. I found him as a kitten. Or he found me."

If this kept up, I was going to fall in love with Seamus in short order. "How is it you're not already in a relationship with somebody?" I asked suspiciously.

He made a thoughtful *mmm* sound.

I raised my head. "Or are you?"

He scowled. "Hell, no. I wouldn't be lying here in bed with you if I was in a relationship."

I relaxed against him again. "Good."

He reached up to stroke my hair. It felt nice. His touch was sure and gentle. I thought how different it would be to be in a relationship with someone like him. Someone with a sense of humor. Someone who was sure of himself. Not arrogant, just…a guy who knew who he was and where he was going. Someone to whom gentleness came naturally, instinctively.

"Can I ask you something, Artemus?" he asked softly.

I closed my eyes. "How did I end up with a cheating asshole like Greg?"

"No. Who was Anthony Clarke?"

I was still for a moment. I opened my eyes to scrutinize his face. "Where did you hear that name?"

"His name came up in conjunction with yours a couple of times."

I made a sound of disgust. "I bet. And people complain about unemployment when the local gossip mill is still operational?" Not that I was surprised. There had been plenty of talk at the time—and Tarrant and Betty had both been present at the first séance when Tony had supposedly appeared.

Seamus said calmly. "Gossip is a useful resource in my line of work." He stroked my hair again, and I knew he was trying to communicate silently that this was not something meant to threaten or hurt.

"Tony was a friend." I considered Seamus for a moment. Considered how open and honest he had been. Not with everything, but his interest—feelings—for me. I amended, "My first boyfriend. We were sixteen." Sixteen. A different planet in a different solar system.

"What happened?"

"I'm sure you've heard. He killed himself."

"I did hear that. I'm sorry."

I sighed, and even I could hear what a long, weary sound it was. "It was a long time ago."

It was. And yet it still hurt if I opened my heart to it—something I had become practiced at avoiding.

I said, "He was great. I…liked him. A lot. Everybody did. He was smart, funny, talented—*there* was someone who could actually act." I sighed again. The memory of Tony was always going to be a weight on my chest. I said, "He was also bipolar, which none of us—his friends—knew."

Seamus gave a quiet *ah*.

I was surprised by how much I wanted him to understand, to not blame me. But it was still hard to get the words out. "We hadn't been seeing each other long. It was all still really new. We had an argument. It was something stupid. Trivial. So trivial, I honest to God am not sure to this day if I really do know what the argument was really about. At the time, I didn't think a lot about it. It was just…a disagreement." I cleared my throat. "I told him to go to hell."

Seamus made a pained sound as though he was watching it unfold with me.

After a moment, I said, "He thought we were breaking up. He thought it was over. He drove out to Timber Landing and jumped off the cliff."

"Jesus Christ."

"Yeah."

"I'm so sorry," he said again.

My eyes stung. It was silly. But there had not been a lot of sympathy for me back then.

"Thank you. It took me a long time to realize that it wasn't my fault. That it wasn't really about me. I did love him—was falling in love with him, anyway—but that's not always enough."

Intellectually, I really did understand and believe that, but I can't deny that hearing Seamus's instant, heated, "Of course not. Of course you weren't to blame. You were a kid. You weren't equipped to deal with that," felt like balm on an open wound.

"Yes. We were both kids, and it wasn't anyone's fault. It was a tragedy." I added, "And a really bad introduction to romance and relationships."

Seamus started to respond but stopped at the sound of a floorboard creaking outside the bedroom door. We both sat up, listening. The floorboard squeaked again. I scrambled off one side of the bed. Seamus rolled in the other direction, diving for his clothes and pulling out a large and serviceable semiautomatic pistol out of the neat pile of jeans, T-shirt, socks, and briefs.

At my look, he whispered, "Not usually in the bedroom, no."

I yanked open the door.

A lamp sat on a long table midway down the corridor. The muted light cast sharp shadows across the ceiling and walls—and revealed that the hall stood empty. All was quiet.

Seamus appeared at my shoulder, tense and alert.

A light shone from beneath Aunt H.'s door. A paler band glowed beneath Liana's.

We waited. Nothing happened.

"What do you think?" he whispered.

I thought our nerves were wearing thin. I thought a night-light made all the difference in the world.

I said, "Bathroom run? A craving for hot milk that won't be denied?"

We continued to stand motionless, not speaking, just listening.

Wood creaked near the head of the staircase, but the landing was empty.

It was an old building. Its bones ached and groaned at night. All the same…

I whispered, "I'm looking for those blueprints tomorrow."

Seamus nodded.

CHAPTER TWENTY-THREE

Three things happened the following day.

The Sonoma County Sheriff's Office crime lab reported finding blood in Tarrant's—well, legally, Aunt H.'s—station wagon.

Seamus was abruptly summoned to San Francisco by his superiors.

Aunt H. informed me over scrambled eggs and English muffins that Liana wanted Roma to conduct a séance that night.

"I hope you told her no," I said to Aunt H. "I hope Roma had the sense to tell her no."

"There's no reason for you to attend," Aunt H. said. "In fact, I'd prefer you didn't."

"There's no reason for any of us to attend."

"Artemus…"

"In what universe would this be a good idea?" I demanded.

"You profess not to believe, so how can it hurt?" Aunt H. retorted, unexpectedly—and unfairly—turning my own words against me.

"Let's start with the fact that two nights ago Liana was galloping through the meadows and woodlands, insisting Ogden wanted her to join him in the Hereafter. What's to stop her from deciding Ogden—Oscar—might require additional company, since he's been none too subtle in hinting *you're* his first choice of people he wants to spend here to eternity with."

"There's no running away from this."

"Of course there is! I mean, running away from what? I don't understand."

"The only chance of helping Ogden understand—"

"Darling, there was *blood* in Tarrant's station wagon," I cut in. "Do you not see the ramifications of that?"

"I don't believe for one minute Tarrant killed himself."

"Me neither!"

"Nor do I believe supernatural forces did away with him."

"Total agreement. I would love to know what you *do* believe?"

Aunt H. eyed me without favor.

"I'm waiting," I said.

Aunt H. said, "I believe that your mind is closed. I believe that the only way to deal with this situation is to confront it head on—with an open mind, yes, but also an open heart. Whatever remains of Ogden, whether we call it a spirit or a psychic echo—"

"Or a total and complete sham," I couldn't help saying.

Aunt H. gave me a level look. "—is angry, bitter, believes itself wronged. The only way to resolve that situation is to try to communicate with him—it. Roma has proven herself the best conduit for that."

I said, "Will you not even consider that this is all one big elaborate con?"

To my astonishment, Aunt H. said cryptically, "Suppose it is? The path is still the same, isn't it?"

And to that, I really didn't have an answer.

Following our unsettling breakfast, I phoned Police Chief Kingsland and informed him of the evening's scheduled festivities. I wasn't sure what he could do about it, but I thought having a cop on call would not be a bad idea. I had to leave a message because he was in a meeting. I also had to leave a message on Seamus's cell.

"We're going to have another séance tonight," I said. "I hope you'll be back in time to hold my hand." I was trying to project a bit of sangfroid, but I couldn't help adding, "I have a bad feeling about this."

After that, I wasn't quite sure what to do. What *could* I do?

I'd promised Seamus to try and get my hands on the original blueprints for Green Lanterns, so I asked Aunt H. about them.

She said she had no idea where they were. She had not seen them in years. She said they might be anywhere.

It was only sheer dumb luck that made me ask one more question.

"When was the last time you saw them?"

Aunt H. looked vague. "I believe it was just before my last trip to New York." Her expression changed. She said slowly, "Yes. That's right. Ogden—Oscar—was asking for them."

I stared at her. It seemed too much to hope for. "Why?" I asked. "Why did he want them?"

"I-I'm not sure. He had an idea that it would make sense to knock the wall down between the music room and his study."

"No, it wouldn't."

She ignored that. "It didn't come to anything. Obviously."

"And that's the last time you saw the blueprints to the house?"

"Yes."

I left another message for Seamus after that conversation—from the front lawn, where I was sure I couldn't be overheard.

"You're right. Somewhere in this house, there's a secret passage. Og—Oscar was asking for blueprints right before the last trip my aunt made to New York. She stayed with me two weeks. The timeframe would be tight, but when money is no object, you can make things happen. Call me back when you can." I cleared my throat, said awkwardly, "I miss you."

That bit of information—that one little piece of the puzzle—changed everything.

I sat down on a sunny stone bench in the garden Seamus had hacked and chopped into submission and spent the next ten minutes using my phone to scour the Internet for everything I could find on Hart Lenton.

There wasn't an enormous amount of information on Lenton previous to his becoming a missing person. Cyril had been right. Lenton seemed to be a very ordinary guy. In fact, the kind of guy one might think—if one was a sociopath—could safely drop out of the world without leaving much of a hole.

But that's where one would be wrong—because Lenton had been loved.

His parents loved him, his siblings loved him, his wife and three little daughters loved him. Even his in-laws loved him. And his neighbors. And his employees. And his minister. And the kids he coached in Little League. And his lodge brothers at the Loyal Order of Moose club.

Maybe Lenton had gone quietly into that good night—maybe not—but the people he left behind had not stopped yelling about it since.

I stared blankly into the green tangle of trees and vines beyond the paths that Seamus had cleared, trying to make sense of all these scattered nuggets of information.

Six months before his death, Ogden had been looking at blueprints of Green Lanterns.

Five months before Ogden's death, Hart Lenton—a local contractor specializing in the restoration of historic buildings—had disappeared after meeting with an unknown client.

There were obvious problems with the theory taking shape in my mind. To start with, if Ogden had murdered Lenton, his decision to disappear had not been spur-of-the-moment, had not had to do with the police closing in on him, had not had to do with Aunt H. asking for a divorce. He had been planning whatever it was he was planning for some time.

Secondly, where would Ogden have stored Lenton's body for five months?

And finally, what had—what *was* he planning?

It had to be more than faking his death, didn't it? Why go to those lengths—why commit murder—when he could simply disappear and start over again?

The only way it made sense was if he did not want to start over, if he had something to gain by *not* disappearing.

But being declared dead was pretty much the same thing, so…

No, I was missing something.

I couldn't see how Ogden being presumed dead got him anywhere. He could not inherit, should something happen to Aunt H. Wouldn't anyway. I was next in line.

I frowned, thinking that over, remembering Seamus's suggestion that Liana might have deliberately lured me out to the garden.

The first problem with that theory was that Liana couldn't have had any idea I would be in lure-able range that night. The second problem was Liana was pretty unreliable these days. Would someone as calculating as Ogden would have to be, choose Liana as his accomplice? Unlikely.

But he might use her as his dupe. Oh, hell yeah. *That* made sense. Liana, floating around in her grief-stricken fog, was about as suggestible an accessory before, during, and after the fact as one could hope to find. Then it simply became a question of logistics. How to best communicate Ogden's wishes to Liana?

Answer? Through séances conducted by Roma Loveridge.

Which meant Roma *was* in on the whole charade. She had to be.

It still didn't really solve the question of what Ogden hoped to get out of faking his death. Even if there was some convoluted scheme to get me out of the way or convince Aunt H. to change her will in favor of Liana…then what?

It wasn't like Ogden could return from the grave and cash in. In addition to getting both me and Aunt H. out of the way, he'd have to figure out some means of getting Liana to hand over her inheritance to him. Granted, Liana could be in on the whole scheme. But no. I really didn't think that was the case. I really did think Liana believed Ogden was dead. I believed she was going mad with grief.

Maybe the plan was Liana, in turn, would leave everything to Roma.

And then Liana too would be gotten out of the way?

That was a lot of getting people out of the way. Three potential victims and counting—and that wasn't even including Hart Lenton.

According to Seamus, Ogden had no history of violence.

Plus, none of this solved the problem of Ogden being inconveniently and officially dead—and therefore unable to openly take advantage of his ill-gotten gains.

No. For any of this to make sense, there had to be a way for Ogden to return to life.

Which would require a miracle.

A miracle.

I sat up straight. "Oh, my God…"

I had it. Just like that, I had the answer.

Now the problem was how to prove it.

CHAPTER TWENTY-FOUR

"I thought you'd decided to spend the evening out."

Aunt Halcyone greeted me with less than her usual warmth when I arrived back at Green Lanterns slightly before eight.

A summer storm had rolled in during the afternoon, and the cool, wet scent of outside wafting through the large central hall seemed to collide with the stuffy, dusty warmth of the house, creating its own mini weather front.

Tension crackled in the air.

I leaned in to kiss Aunt H.'s Chanel-scented cheek. "I never said that, darling. Of course I'm going to be here to welcome Ogden home."

The grandfather clock on the landing melodiously chimed the hour.

She frowned and touched my shoulder. "Artemus, you're soaked to the skin. What on earth? Where have you been all day?"

"For the last three hours I've been dealing with a flat tire. There's no spare in the Bel Air." And before that I'd been speaking with Cee Cee Lenton in her cubbyhole of an office at Building Heritage, LLC.

I was now sure of my facts—and scared to death. Not so much for myself—although I suspected no one in this house was safe—but for Aunt H.

"Oh no!" Aunt H. exclaimed. "In this rain?"

"Is Seamus back?" I asked. He'd left a message while I'd been speaking with Mrs. Lenton, letting me know he would be late returning to Green Lanterns—and, as if I wasn't worried enough, warning me that the police were currently operating on the assumption that Tarrant was dead. He didn't specify whether the authorities suspected suicide or murder, but I knew Tarrant had not taken his own life.

Murder, then.

Another murder.

I'd tried phoning Seamus back, but he hadn't picked up, so I'd been reduced to leaving what were probably increasingly incoherent voice mails.

"Not that I'm aware of." Aunt H. made a sound of exasperation. "The phone is dead, and the electricity keeps going out."

"The phone is *dead*?"

Aunt H. shrugged. "I don't suppose it matters. We don't get many calls these days. And you have your cell phone."

Which needed charging immediately if it was going to be our only line of communication.

"Is she here?" Liana's anxious voice floated from the doorway leading into the dining room. "Has Roma arrived?" Liana was dressed in a flowing black caftan. She wore a white turban pinned in place with an oversize onyx, her injured arm rested in a black silk sling, and her face was made up.

She looked eerily like the Liana of old—which I did not find reassuring.

"Not yet," Aunt H. told her.

Liana spotted me, and her face tightened. "Artie! You shouldn't be here. I thought he was dining with friends, Halcyone. You know how disruptive he is to the vibrations."

"There's gratitude," I said.

Aunt H. gave me a reproving look, which I interpreted to mean we were still in coddling-Liana mode. Aunt H. had not yet informed her that she knew who she really was.

Liana said, "The cards have warned—"

The doorbell rang, and we all jumped.

"Oh, thank heavens," Liana gasped, relaxing. "Roma."

"You'd better change out of those wet things," Aunt H. said, moving past me to open the door.

She was right. I did not want to risk being locked out of the séance room. While I had no idea of what might happen during that night's session, I felt increasingly, uneasily certain something alarming was afoot.

I sprinted upstairs, plugged my phone into the charger, and hastily changed into dry jeans and a warmer shirt. All the while, my thoughts raced ahead. Whatever had happened to Tarrant and Betty could not have been part of any master plan, which meant that whatever that plan was, the timetable had to be accelerated.

The room smelled faintly, comfortingly of Seamus's aftershave. The rain beat against the windows and drizzled down the glass in long silvery trails. I didn't bother to turn on a lamp, and as I moved around the bed and chairs, I caught motion behind me in the oval mirror over the bureau.

I froze, not sure if what I saw was a trick of the light or if there really was substance to that shadowy motion. I turned slowly. A fist-sized ball of mist seemed to float in front of the fireplace. For one heart-stopping second it seemed as though that pale, glimmering fog started to unfurl, grow.

It looked real. No question it looked real. The room even felt suddenly colder.

"I don't know how you're doing this, but save it for the show," I said over the pounding of my heart.

The ball of mist evaporated as suddenly and completely as a popped balloon.

I stared in astonishment at the empty air. *Had* it been a trick of the hazy light? Were my nerves getting the better of me?

No time to worry about it now. I grabbed my phone, hoping those few minutes of charging had given me vital percentage points of juice, and ran downstairs.

They had already gathered at the table when I entered the dining room. Sister Regina stood beside the light switch, looking wide-eyed and worried.

"Don't hesitate to break glass in case of fire," I told her.

Her eyes grew larger still. "Wha-what?"

"Halcyone, can't you do something?" Liana complained. "He's going to make a mockery of this."

She was seated to the left of Roma. Aunt H. sat on the right. Roma, who was in the process of draping her black mantilla over her pale hair, glanced at me without welcome.

"I'll be good," I said to Aunt H.

"Artie—"

"I'm staying."

"My dearest boy, you don't belong here."

I laughed, though I was not finding any of this funny, and took the empty chair at the foot of the table. I stretched my hands out to Aunt H. and Liana.

"Oh, Artie," Aunt H. murmured. She looked both sad and resigned as she took my hand. Her own was ice-cold.

Liana made a sound of impatience and also linked hands. In contrast, her skin felt hot, almost feverish.

"Shall we begin?" Roma inquired.

"You may turn the lights off and leave the room, Sister Regina," Aunt H. said.

Sister Regina looked only too happy to comply. She flicked the switch, the room plunged into darkness, and the double doors opened and swiftly closed. The key scraped in the lock.

"Close your eyes and empty your mind of all negative thoughts," Roma spoke in that soothing singsong. "Be at peace. We are safe here."

Liana made a small, anxious sound. Her hand was trembling in mine.

No one else spoke. The sound of rain against the windows was loudest, but I could hear Roma's slow, deliberate inhalations and exhalations.

Long minutes passed. Somewhere in the Twilight Zone a phone was ringing unanswered. Last time, the spirits had been faster to pick up.

I scanned the room, eyes probing the deep shadows. Nothing stirred. The walls remained reassuringly solid.

Somewhere overhead I could hear a shutter banging. Tarrant's handiwork coming undone.

I hoped Chief Kingsland got my message. I hoped Seamus was on his way. Not that I had any clear idea of what either of them could do at this point.

Roma moaned something unintelligible. Her body jerked. Her breaths grew rough and unsteady.

"He's coming," Liana whispered. "I can feel it!"

My scalp crawled with tension, the very hair on my arms standing on end. I squeezed Aunt H.'s hand in reassurance, and she squeezed back.

Roma's head fell back, her body arched, and she began to mumble her version of ancient Egyptian.

The spate of gibberish broke off, and Roma said in normal tones, "Are you there, Lord Rekhmire?"

Silence.

"Is there another spirit with you?"

Liana made an anxious sound.

There seemed to be a pause before Roma murmured, "Spirit, have you a message for one of those in attendance?"

Silence.

Silence.

Had the operator dropped the call?

Roma shivered suddenly. She sounded almost alert as she said, "I don't understand…"

This time there was something…uncanny in the pause that followed.

Liana said, "Where is Ogden? What is Ogden saying? *Tell us!*"

"I… I…"

We all watched in silence as Roma began to shake.

"So…much…anger…"

"So…much…hate…"

So…much…bad…acting. Although, in fairness, given the way my heart was jumping around my chest, the performance was not without its strengths.

Aunt H. whispered, "What does he want?"

"Despair…"

"Oh, Ogden. *Ogden*," wailed Liana.

"Darkness…"

"Why did he kill Tarrant?"

The voice was hard and flat as a slap across the face, surprising everyone into silence.

Although the most surprising thing was that it was *my* voice.

The room fell utterly silent.

Then Roma let out a long sigh and slumped forward onto the table as though someone had let the air out of a rubber doll.

"You've killed her!" screeched Liana, snatching her hand from mine. "I knew it was a mistake to let you take part—"

"*Look*," Aunt H. interrupted in a strange voice.

I could see the outline of her profile in the gloom. She was staring at me. No. She was staring *behind* me.

Liana screamed.

I think I stopped breathing. Even without looking, I could feel that terrible cold. A chill like no other. It took every ounce of will power I had to turn in my chair—and what I saw had me on my feet in an instant.

The cloud of milky-white substance we had witnessed before was swirling less than a foot from me.

We all watched, wordless, stricken, as the glowing mist seemed to roil in the air, unfolding like smoke through water, spreading, stretching…taking form.

"Ogden," Liana whispered.

Phosphorescent, fuzzy…but yes, the shining vapor seemed to be taking the form of a man.

First the torso, then the arms and legs, and finally the head.

I stared and stared as the features began to resolve themselves. A craggy jaw, blunt nose, and piercing eyes that seemed to bore right into me.

What the hell?

I knew that face all right. I'd spent nearly an hour that afternoon staring at a photograph of it. Him.

"That's not Ogden," I said.

CHAPTER TWENTY-FIVE

"**O**h my God," Aunt H. said softly. "Artie's right."

Liana gave a little scream of protest, and rose. "It is Ogden. It has to be him." She took a step toward the misty outline but faltered. "It *has* to be," she repeated, but I could hear the doubt in her voice.

"It's Hart Lenton," I said.

The wavering white shadow seemed to deepen, solidify— and then fade again. As though there was a short in the wiring.

"Roma!" Liana cried. "Roma, tell them!"

Roma still slumped, unmoving, over the table.

As we watched, Lenton's features blurred, his form soft- ened, melting away into shapeless, shimmering light.

"He can't speak without the conduit of Roma," Aunt H. said wonderingly.

Lenton's form suddenly vanished like a pinched-out candle.

Liana sagged back into her chair. "I don't understand. Who is Hart Lenton? Why has he appeared to us? What can this mean?"

I said, "Hart Lenton was a contractor who specialized in renovating historic homes. Ogden hired him to restore the entrances to the Prohibition-era passageways this house is riddled with."

Aunt H. and Liana said in unison, "*What?*"

"I don't think it was originally part of Ogden's plan to murder Lenton—"

"Artie, what are you saying?" Aunt H. demanded.

"I'm saying Ogden murdered Hart Lenton and faked his own supposedly fatal accident."

"But…that's not possible."

"Ogden needed a body, and they were roughly the same height and build—plus it was a way of making sure Lenton could never testify about the work he did, in case news of the haunting of Green Lanterns ever reached him."

"You're *crazy*!" Liana cried. She reached over to jog Roma's shoulder. "Roma, wake up! You've got to stop this. Artie's saying terrible things about Ogden."

Roma began to breathe heavily, stertorously.

I have to confess my love of theater got the better of me just then because I couldn't help pronouncing, "It isn't Ogden haunting Green Lanterns. It's the spirit of Hart Lenton."

The jarring burst of laughter that followed my dramatic announcement had us all looking wildly around the room. Where was that coming from?

"Now *there* you're wrong," a voice said from the corner. "And you were doing so well too!"

I knew that voice. Recognized those amused, lightly mocking tones. But the figure that detached itself from the darkness and moved toward the table was not familiar. Even in the dim light, I could see long, unruly hair and a full beard. Biker Jesus himself.

"*Oh my God…*" Aunt H. breathed.

"Oscar? *Oscar?*" Liana leaned forward, her voice wobbling with emotion. "Is it you? Is it really you?"

"Yes, my darling. It is I."

Aunt H. said very faintly, "This can't be." I hoped she wasn't going to swoon. Not that she was the swooning kind, but having your dead husband return from the grave would test anyone's limits. It was kind of testing mine.

"But why?" Liana protested. "Why would you pretend? Why would you let me think you were dead? Why wouldn't you tell me?"

"I couldn't, my dearest. I'll explain it all later. First we have to—"

I said, "You should know that I've already shared all this with Chief Kingsland and Sergeant Cassidy."

"Sergeant—? Oh, our undercover gardener?" Ogden laughed. "Shared what? Suspecting is not proving."

"Why?" Aunt H. demanded. Her voice was steady now, fierce. "Why did you do it? How *could* you? Why didn't you just *leave*?"

"Would you like to do the honors?" Ogden seemed to be asking me.

"I would, but I don't understand why you killed Tarrant or how you killed Betty."

"Who the hell is Betty?"

"Ulyanna."

He sounded almost indignant. "I didn't touch her. She walked into the kitchen as I was slipping out through the door behind the china cabinet. I didn't say a word to her. She keeled over."

"You *killed* Tarrant?" Aunt H. said in horror-stricken tones.

"It's not something I planned. The old fool figured it out somehow and thought we were going to be partners."

It wasn't that hard to guess how Tarrant might have figured it out. All he'd need was a glimpse of Reverend Ormston skulking around Green Lanterns in the dead of night, and he'd be bound to start connecting the dots. Especially as he was a member of the church and could study Ormston on a fairly regular basis.

"I still don't understand," Aunt H. said. "What was the *point*? What was the *purpose*? What can you possibly get out of this when everyone believes you're *dead*?"

Ogden heaved a heavy sigh, as though the effort of being patient with slower intellects was wearing him down. "Turn on the light, Artemus," he instructed, adding, "And don't do anything stupid like try to open the door. I'd prefer not to shoot the girl. She's a sweet child."

I walked over to the wall switch and flicked it on. The chandelier blazed into sparkling crystal prisms of light. It threw the tableau before me into sharp relief.

Roma was slowly coming back to life. She straightened groggily, resting her face in her hands. Aunt H. and Liana sat staring as though mesmerized by the man before them. The man holding a gun. A gun currently pointed at me.

It looked like a stage prop, but I knew it wasn't.

"*Reverend Ormston?*" Liana said. "But…"

Aunt H. burst out, "I knew you were selfish. I didn't realize how cruel you were. How long did you plan this?"

Ogden did not seem offended. He tipped his head as though considering. "About three years of planning. One year of execution. Don't look like that, my dear. I assure you, I had every intention of settling down here permanently as Ogden Hyde. Or, let's be honest, as Ogden Bancroft. But the opportunity to take over the church was quite literally a godsend. I could hardly ignore it."

"Is that what happened to the money you stole?" I asked. "You used it to take over the church?"

Ogden made a sound of contempt. "Are you serious? Most of that money was used to create the identity of Ogden Hyde. Plastic surgery is expensive. Starting a publishing company is expensive. Courting women like Halcyone Bancroft is expensive."

"The property next door to Green Lanterns was purchased by the RCU for over a million dollars," I said.

"And property is expensive," Ogden agreed. "It's also the best investment there is."

Which was why he couldn't leave bad enough alone, why he hadn't been satisfied with setting up an identity and a new life, why he had set his sights once more on Green Lanterns. This time minus the encumbrance of Halcyone Bancroft.

I said to Aunt H., "The idea was you would change your will in favor of Liana, and then Liana would donate everything to the church. Correct?"

"Correct," Ogden said. "That was—and is—the plan."

"What's...going on?" Roma asked. She blinked owlishly at Ogden, who ignored her.

"But why all the rest of it? Why pretend you had returned from the dead?" Aunt H. questioned.

"*What?*" That woke Roma up.

"Because Liana and the church would immediately come under suspicion. I needed people to start wondering if there was a good reason for you to take your life. People love ghost stories, so what better way to establish your guilt than to have my ghost accuse you of murder?"

"It's not possible that you could deceive me," Roma said. "There *is* a spirit here. I've made contact with it. Several times."

"You were the easiest of all to fool." Ogden smiled. With all that wild hair and the beard, he looked more like a pirate than his old self.

Roma said haughtily, "The only fool present is *you.*"

Had she even noticed he was holding a gun on us?

My cell phone rang.

Ogden jerked I realized he was more on edge than he seemed. Not a bad actor, Ogden. In fact, a very good actor.

"Don't answer that," he warned.

"I'm pretty sure it's for you," I said. "I've recorded as much of this as I could on Cassidy's voice mail. He's my only contact set up for Emergency Bypass."

Ogden's face changed. He raised the pistol. Liana screamed. Aunt H. stood in front of him.

"No!" I cried. "There's no point. It's over."

And it was. All at once, the hall outside seemed full of voices and footsteps. Heavy blows rained down on the double doors of the dining room. The doors rattled in the frame.

A deep voice boomed, "This is Police Chief Kingsland. In the name of the law, open this door!"

I had no idea cops actually said "in the name of the law." Or maybe that was just Kingsland. He was pretty old school.

Instead of shooting, Ogden grabbed Aunt H., holding her in front of him as the double doors burst open. Kingsland and the mob of uniformed officers behind him halted in the doorway, weapons drawn.

Suddenly the room smelled of gun oil, leather, and rain. Alien. Dangerous. I felt sick with the knowledge that the scales could tip the wrong way. The moment stretched and stretched, seeming to balance on a razor's edge.

"Don't be stupid, Foxworth," Kingsland said. "You've got one chance of walking out of here alive."

"I'm so sorry, Kenneth," Aunt H. burst out. "I thought it was you. I thought you sabotaged his car." She looked and sounded way too calm for someone with a gun pointed at her head, and I knew she believed she was going to die.

"It's all right, Hallie," Kingsland said gruffly. "I'm happy to kill him for you now."

Nobody's gun so much as wavered, but I could see the officers' eyes sort of flickering and looking sideways.

Ogden laughed. He sounded a little hysterical. "I thought so. That's *exactly* what I thought. And under my own roof!"

Someone answered him, but I don't know who and I didn't hear what they said. A panel in the wall behind Ogden slid soundlessly open. Seamus stepped out, his weapon trained on Ogden's back. He began to move cautiously toward Ogden and Aunt H.

My heart stood still. If a floorboard squeaked—and the floorboards in this old house *always* squeaked—Ogden would swing around and shoot Seamus. I could think of nothing to do to help. The two people I cared about most in the world might die in the next instant—while I had to stand helplessly by, watching. Even if every cop present shot Ogden, it didn't mean he wouldn't have time to squeeze the trigger.

Seamus's face was white and set. Wet hair was plastered against his forehead, and his jacket was dripping. Each drop seemed to hit the floor like a cannonball, but I don't think Ogden heard anything. I think it was the alert stillness of the men watching Seamus from the doorway that warned him just as Seamus got within arm's length.

Ogden cast a quick, alarmed look over his shoulder, saw Seamus, and hurled Aunt H. into him. Aunt H. stumbled, Seamus hauled her behind him, and Ogden dived for the door in the wall. The panel slid shut with a snap.

The cops rushed into the room.

"Jesus Christ, I don't believe it," Kingsland roared. "*Get* that sonofabitch."

I reached Seamus, who grabbed my shoulder. "You okay?"

"Yes. Fine. Are you *crazy*? You could have been sh—"

He was already gone, running out into the hall, which was crowded with still more uniformed officers spreading out through the rooms and thundering up the staircase.

"Where does that passageway end?" Kingsland shouted.

Aunt H. was shaking her head. "I didn't know there *was* a passageway."

"I want every room in this house searched top to bottom—and get them out of here!"

"There's got to be an entrance in the study," I called.

"Check the study," Kingsland ordered as a group of sheriff deputies—was every law-enforcement agency in the county here?—hustled us all out of the dining room and into the central hall.

"I don't understand," Roma was protesting all the way down the length of the hall. "You don't understand. You don't realize what you're dealing with."

Liana—Lacey—was sobbing and calling for Ogden.

I put my arm around Aunt H.'s shoulders. "It's all right now, darling," I told her, and she patted my hand as though she was reassuring me.

"Oh, Artie. Sending for you was the best decision I've made in five years." Though she was shivering, there was color in her cheeks and light in her eyes. She almost looked like the old Aunt H.

I was beyond relief on multiple fronts. "So that was the big secret? You thought Chief Kingsland arranged an accident for Ogden? And you felt you were to blame?"

She nodded. Tears glistened in her eyes. Not for Ogden or herself. Tears for Chief Kingsland. How the hell had I missed *that* development? But then, I hadn't been there for that development—just the years of loyal friendship that preceded it.

"Kenneth was up for reappointment, and Ogden threatened to send a letter to the city council telling them that we had…were…"

"Ogden tried to blackmail the chief of police?"

"He was completely unbalanced by the end."

"You think?"

She opened her mouth to remonstrate, but there was a blood-curdling scream from overhead.

"Holy shit!" someone yelled. "*Look out!*"

A body came hurtling down from the third story, crashing against the white banisters and just missing the eight-arm macaroni bead crystal chandelier before smashing facedown on the gold-and-black Aubusson carpet.

The giant gilt-framed portrait of my aunt gazed quizzically down on all that remained of the late and mostly unlamented Oscar Foxworth.

EPILOGUE

"**W**hat I want to know is how the hell did you find the opening to that secret passage in time?" I asked Seamus.

It was three o'clock in the morning, and we were spooned together in bed in the chauffeur's quarters. We were not trying to sleep, though. Both of us were too wound up. Every light in the place was on.

The main house too was still ablaze, but it was empty—of anyone living, at least. Crime-scene tape roped off the drive, and sheriff deputies were posted at each entrance. Liana—I still had trouble thinking of her as Lacey—had been hospitalized for shock, Roma had, presumably, gone home to consult her Ouija board, and Aunt H. had left with Chief Kingsland.

Seamus kissed my shoulder. "I didn't. I was waiting for Foxworth to arrive. I just followed him in."

"You were here at the house the whole time?"

"No. After your message about interviewing Lenton's wife, I busted my butt to get back here. When I saw him sneak across the drive and cut the phone lines, I knew you were right. Whatever was going to happen would happen tonight."

I shivered, and his arms tightened. "Warm enough?"

I nodded. Had to clear my throat. "What you did tonight. That was…"

"A little theatrical?" he finished wryly.

I shook my head. "Brave. The bravest thing I've ever seen. Thank you."

He grunted.

"And please don't ever do it again."

"*Me*? My heart stopped when I heard you ask him why he'd killed Tarrant."

I admitted, "I got a little carried away in the heat of the moment."

My head bounced on his shoulder as he chuckled. "Anyway. All part of the job." He added with elaborate casualness, "Although, for the record, there's not a lot of death and danger in the Financial Crimes Unit. In case that's a concern."

I was following my own thoughts. "You didn't think my suspicions of Reverend Ormston were a little far-fetched?"

"Yeah, I sort of did. I mean, at one point in this scheme he would have had to be appearing as both Reverend Harry Ormston and Ogden Hyde. Even if he was mostly interacting within two largely different social circles, it was still a huge risk."

"One thing he never lacked was confidence."

"That's the truth."

I wanted to thank him again. I wanted to ask him what his plans were and whether he would be returning to New York soon. Or at all.

I opened my mouth, and he said, "I also thought it wasn't a coincidence Tarrant's car had been left near the RCU's old headquarters. Plus, I always thought that beard looked fake."

No question of whose beard he was referring to. "It wasn't fake, though. He did grow his hair and beard out."

"All the same, something about him always struck me as phony."

"Well, yeah."

The rain thundering down on the roof filled in the silence between us.

After a time, I asked, "Where do you think Tarrant's body is? In one of the passageways?"

"I doubt it. There are practical reasons not to try to store a body in a house. Even a house the size of Green Lanterns. He must have dumped it into the bay when he dropped the car off."

I mused that over, shook my head. "I don't think so."

"No?"

I recalled the glowing light that had drawn Liana into the maze. "My best guess is it's somewhere in the maze. In a shallow grave. I bet that's where he kept Lenton's body too. That would explain why there was barely any body left, let alone any DNA."

"God," Seamus muttered.

We didn't speak after that, but the silence felt safe, comfortable. "Should we try to sleep?" Seamus whispered.

I nodded, although I was a little afraid of what my dreams would be like. He let go of me, sat up, turned off the lamp, and burrowed back down beside me in the blankets.

"I should turn off that living-room light," he muttered. "But I don't think I have the energy to walk that far."

We breathed in soft unison, his breath warm against my ear.

"When are you going back to New York?" he asked abruptly, sounding unexpectedly wide-awake.

I opened my eyes, gazed at the oblong of light from the living room stretching across the carpet. "As soon as things have settled down here. You?"

I held my breath, waiting for his reply.

"There are some loose ends to tie up, but probably next week."

My heart lightened. I nodded.

He began tentatively, "Do you think you'd want to…"

"Yes," I said without hesitation.

"Really?"

"Yes. Of course yes."

"That's great! What a relief," Seamus said, and it sounded heartfelt.

I laughed and craned my head to kiss him. "Is it? What did you imagine was happening here?"

"Well, I wasn't sure. I was worried maybe this was just kind of a holiday romance for you."

"You have a peculiar idea of going on holiday. We'll have to work on that." I was still smiling, and I could feel the line of his cheek crease in response.

"Suits me."

I closed my eyes again, willed myself to sleep. But I kept thinking about what I had seen in my bedroom that evening—and then later during the séance.

I thought from the even tenor of his breathing, Seamus had drifted off, but he said softly, his thoughts seemingly running along the same lines as mine, "If Foxworth was telling the truth…if it wasn't him…what was it?"

I didn't answer.

"You don't think—?"

"I don't know."

"That deputy sure as hell saw something on the third floor. There was no open window for the fog to get in. But somehow Foxworth, who's been skulking around in the dark up there for the last year, got so disoriented and panicked, he fell over the banister?"

I will never rest until you have paid for what you did…

"I don't think we're ever going to know. And maybe there are some things it's better not to question."

"Maybe," Seamus said. He yawned so widely, I heard his jaw crack. "But whoever said that didn't have to fill out a police report."

A few minutes later he was snoring quietly, musically into my ear.

I wished I could turn down the burner on my thoughts. Maybe Hart Lenton's ghost *had* played a role. Maybe Roma *was* really psychic—if a bit hit and miss. Did that mean Tony's spirit truly *had* appeared during the first séance?

He says you must not blame yourself. There was nothing you could have done.

I was surprised at much I longed for that to be true. It would be nice to believe…

I sighed. The band of light from the living room fell squarely across my face. I should just make the effort to get up and turn it off.

I grabbed the blankets, started to pull them back, and the living-room lamp flicked off. I sank back against Seamus and gazed out the rain-streaked window. I could see the pale, smiling face of the moon gazing in at us.

ACKNOWLEDGEMENTS

Heartfelt thanks to Keren Reed and Kevin Burton Smith.

ABOUT THE AUTHOR

Author of over sixty titles of classic Male/Male fiction featuring twisty mystery, kickass adventure, and unapologetic man-on-man romance, **JOSH LANYON**'s work has been translated into eleven languages. Her FBI thriller *Fair Game* was the first Male/Male title to be published by Harlequin Mondadori, then the largest romance publisher in Italy. *Stranger on the Shore* (Harper Collins Italia) was the first M/M title to be published in print. In 2016 *Fatal Shadows* placed #5 in Japan's annual Boy Love novel list (the first and only title by a foreign author to place on the list). The Adrien English series was awarded the All Time Favorite Couple by the Goodreads M/M Romance Group.

She is an Eppie Award winner, a four-time Lambda Literary Award finalist (twice for Gay Mystery), an Edgar nominee and the first ever recipient of the Goodreads All Time Favorite M/M Author award.

Josh is married and lives in Southern California.

Find other Josh Lanyon titles at www.joshlanyon.com, and follow her on Twitter, Facebook, Goodreads, Instagram and Tumblr.

For extras and exclusives, join Josh on Patreon.

ALSO BY JOSH LANYON

NOVELS

The ADRIEN ENGLISH Mysteries
Fatal Shadows • *A Dangerous Thing* • *The Hell You Say*
Death of a Pirate King • *The Dark Tide*
Stranger Things Have Happened
So This is Christmas

The HOLMES & MORIARITY Mysteries
Somebody Killed His Editor • *All She Wrote*
The Boy with the Painful Tattoo • *In Other Words...Murder*

The ALL'S FAIR Series
Fair Game • *Fair Play* • *Fair Chance*

The ART OF MURDER Series
The Mermaid Murders •*The Monet Murders*
The Magician Murders

OTHER NOVELS

The Ghost Wore Yellow Socks
Mexican Heat (with Laura Baumbach)
Strange Fortune • *Come Unto These Yellow Sands*
Stranger on the Shore •*Winter Kill*
Jefferson Blythe, Esquire • *Murder in Pastel*
The Curse of the Blue Scarab
Murder Takes the High Road

NOVELLAS

The DANGEROUS GROUND Series

Dangerous Ground • Old Poison • Blood Heat

Dead Run • Kick Start

The I SPY Series

I Spy Something Bloody • I Spy Something Wicked

I Spy Something Christmas

The IN A DARK WOOD Series

In a Dark Wood • The Parting Glass

The DARK HORSE Series

The Dark Horse • The White Knight

The DOYLE & SPAIN Series

Snowball in Hell

The HAUNTED HEART Series

Haunted Heart Winter

The XOXO FILES Series

Mummie Dearest

OTHER NOVELLAS

Cards on the Table • The Dark Farewell

The Darkling Thrush • The Dickens with Love • Don't Look Back

A Ghost of a Chance • Lovers and Other Strangers

Out of the Blue • A Vintage Affair

This Rough Magic • Lone Star (in Men Under the Mistletoe)

Green Glass Beads (in Irregulars)

Blood Red Butterfly • Everything I Know

Baby, It's Cold • A Case of Christmas

Murder Between the Pages

SHORT STORIES

A Limited Engagement • The French Have a Word for It

In Sunshine or In Shadow • Until We Meet Once More

Icecapade (in His for the Holidays) • Perfect Day • Heart Trouble

In Plain Sight • Wedding Favors • Wizard's Moon

Fade to Black • Night Watch • Plenty of Fish

The Boy Next Door • Halloween is Murder

COLLECTIONS

Short Stories (Vol. 1) • Sweet Spot (the Petit Morts)

Merry Christmas, Darling (Holiday Codas)

Christmas Waltz (Holiday Codas 2)

I Spy...Three Novellas • Point Blank (Five Dangerous Ground Novellas)

Dark Horse, White Knight (Two Novellas)